W9-BRN-063

Dear Reader,

Within these pages you will find three uplifting stories of courage. The stories, written by some of Harlequin's most beloved authors, are fiction, but the women who inspired them are real. They are women who have dedicated their lives to helping others and all are recipients of a Harlequin More Than Words award.

Through the Harlequin More Than Words program, established in 2004, Harlequin awards ordinary women for their extraordinary commitment to community and makes a $10,000 donation to the woman's chosen charity. In addition, some of Harlequin's most acclaimed authors donate their time and energy to writing novellas inspired by the lives and work of our award recipients. The collected stories are published, with proceeds returning to the Harlequin More Than Words program.

Together with Susan Wiggs, Sharon Sala and Emilie Richards, I invite you to meet the Harlequin More Than Words award recipients highlighted in these pages. We hope their stories will encourage you to get involved in charitable activities in your community, or perhaps even with the charities you read about here. Together we can make a difference.

To learn more about the Harlequin More Than Words program or to nominate a woman you know for the Harlequin More Than Words award, please visit www.HarlequinMoreThanWords.com.

Sincerely,

Donna Hayes
Publisher and CEO
Harlequin Enterprises Ltd.

# More Than Words

## STORIES OF COURAGE

## SUSAN WIGGS
## SHARON SALA
## EMILIE RICHARDS

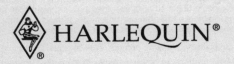

# HARLEQUIN®

TORONTO • NEW YORK • LONDON
AMSTERDAM • PARIS • SYDNEY • HAMBURG
STOCKHOLM • ATHENS • TOKYO • MILAN • MADRID
PRAGUE • WARSAW • BUDAPEST • AUCKLAND

ISBN-13: 978-0-373-83623-9
ISBN-10:   0-373-83623-6

MORE THAN WORDS: STORIES OF COURAGE

# CONTENTS

# SEANA O'NEILL
## ᖰ Cottage Dreams ᖰ

C ancer. It fractures the lives of families, can bring financial hardship, interrupts work schedules and taxes families emotionally.

Seana O'Neill knows from personal experience these intimate details of loss and distress after watching her mother and two uncles battle cancer. So, as she sat on her Haliburton, Ontario, cottage deck in 2002 an idea came to Seana that would not only change her life, but give hope and healing to hundreds of people living with the disease.

"It's not fair to just have this place sitting empty when it could be filled with people," she remembers saying of her cottage at the time.

It was Labor Day weekend and Seana was at a crossroads in her own life, not sure if she wanted to go back to her film career in Toronto. In the end, lifelong cottager Seana decided she would like to share her cottage with those who would not otherwise have the opportunity to get away. She was inspired to invite cancer survivors to her cottage when she wasn't there—and thought other cottagers might do the same.

She was right. The response to the idea was immediate and sparked the creation of Cottage Dreams. The registered charity connects cancer survivors and their families with donated cottages to help bring families back together, to recover, reconnect and rebuild their lives—all in a soothing natural setting.

In only one short year, Cottage Dreams went from idea to reality and placed its first six families. Today the cottage-lending program has grown to include hundreds of cottages across Ontario and has made hundreds of placements.

"When you start something you really believe in, you do it because something is burning inside you," she says today. "I thought, 'I can't ignore this.'"

*Nothing else like it*

Though the health care system provides patients with the support they need while in treatment, it stops when they finally walk out the doctor's door. Cancer survivors have to find a way to rebuild their lives. But it's not an easy task. A cancer diagnosis often brings financial hardship for patients and their families. Not able to work for lengthy periods, patients often find that a time away to heal and reflect is unaffordable.

This is when Seana and Cottage Dreams take over. The organization provides, at no cost, an opportunity to move on to emotional, spiritual and physical recovery. Whisked away to a natural setting, families are removed from the doctor appointments, hospital visits and other harsh and exhausting realities of their illness.

In other words, to speed healing there's nothing like listening to the gentle lap of the lake as your kids watch for falling stars.

*Making a difference*

Of course, Cottage Dreams is all about making wishes come true. And to hear the families tell it, Seana and her team do that and much more.

"Cottage Dreams has been a sense of new beginning for my family and me. After treatment was the perfect time to spend some quality time together and reconnect as a family," says one happy cottage visitor.

But the visitors are far from the only people to benefit from the program. Cottage owners who donate their properties also report positive benefits.

"To sum up my experience with Cottage Dreams—it made me feel good," says a donor.

Cottage Dreams makes Seana feel pretty good these days, too, although starting the project meant long hours, and trying to convince a few naysayers.

At the beginning, many of the people she spoke to asked

Seana how Cottage Dreams would handle insurance, whether tax receipts would be issued and how Seana would choose the lucky families to stay at the cottages. But Seana wasn't worried. She soon talked to an insurance company, a cottage-rental agency and a lawyer. The rental agency and insurance company got on board almost right away and found innovative ways to ensure Cottage Dreams would be successful. Her lawyer, however, wasn't convinced.

"The lawyer said, 'It's going to cost you ten grand and I can't guarantee you anything. It probably won't fly,'" she says, pausing for a moment before continuing. "So I got another lawyer."

Her new lawyer sat on Seana's board as chairman for three years.

*Changing and growing*

Seana's passion and commitment galvanize people. From the grassroots support of local families in cottage communities to major corporations, government and cancer research organizations, she's brought people closer. She says she's still amazed she was able to pull it together, but at the same time she had faith in her abilities to get the job done.

"I knew from the beginning that coordinating would be my strength. Also being a Virgo helps," she quips. "My mother would attest to that."

But running Cottage Dreams has meant changing and growing the organization so it reaches and helps as many people as possible. In the beginning, Cottage Dreams accepted only those in the recovery stage—within nine months of the treatment's completion.

After talking to other people who could use a week's respite, however, Cottage Dreams has extended its focus to include people in the middle of treatment and, in one case, a father of three young children who had an inoperable brain tumor. The doctors said if the man were placed within three months, he would still be well enough to enjoy himself.

"So we rush. Those people go to the top of the pile," Seana says.

Ask Seana what she's most amazed by, however, and she says she's been inspired by the inherent goodness in the people Cottage Dreams touches. One woman, a single mother undergoing chemotherapy, once told Seana to go ahead and give her space to someone else. "I'm sure there are more deserving people out there than me," the woman e-mailed Seana.

These are the lives Cottage Dreams strives to reach—not just in Ontario, but across Canada. Plans to expand nationwide by 2010 are under way.

"We're getting more families through the program, so we're getting more feedback. It really shows us we're making a difference," Seana says.

And Cottage Dreams is offering hope and respite, one cottage at a time.

For more information visit www.cottagedreams.org or write to Cottage Dreams, 33A Pine Avenue, P.O. Box 1300, Haliburton, Ontario K0M 1S0.

# SUSAN WIGGS

## ⊸ HOMECOMING SEASON ⊱

## ❧—SUSAN WIGGS—❧

Susan Wiggs's life is all about family, friends…and fiction. She lives at the water's edge on an island in Puget Sound, and she really does commute to her writers' group with her friend Sheila in a seventeen-foot motorboat.

According to *Publishers Weekly*, Wiggs writes a "refreshingly honest romance," and the *Salem Statesman Journal* says that she is "one of our best observers of stories of the heart [and who] knows how to capture emotion on virtually every page of every book." Booklist characterizes her books as "real and true and unforgettable."

She is the proud recipient of three RITA® Awards and four starred reviews from Publishers Weekly for her books. Her novels have been translated into more than a dozen languages and have made national bestseller lists, including the

*USA TODAY* and *New York Times* lists. She's been featured in the national media and is a popular teacher at writers' workshops and conferences worldwide.

The author is a former teacher, a Harvard graduate, an avid hiker, a boater out of necessity, an amateur photographer, a good skier and terrible golfer, yet her favorite form of exercise is curling up with a good book. Readers can write to her at P.O. Box 4469, Rollingbay, WA 98061 or visit her on the Web at www.susanwiggs.com.

To my beautiful friend, Shannon, a survivor

## ✥—ACKNOWLEDGMENTS—✥

The author wishes to acknowledge the following individuals for their input and inspiration—the amazing Seana O'Neill and all the Cottage Dreams host families and guests, especially Phil Barley, Patty Varvouletos and Marie Stothart. Thanks to Marsha Zinberg of Harlequin for thinking of me.

# CHAPTER ONE

**M**iranda Sweeney's white paper gown rustled as she shifted her weight on the exam table and pulled the edges together to cover herself. "Just like that, it's over?"

Dr. Turabian closed the metal-covered chart with a decisive snap. "Well," he said, "if you want to call twenty-five rounds of radiation, nine months of chemo and two surgeries 'just like that.'" He took off his glasses and slid them into the pocket of his lab coat. "I couldn't be happier with your tests. Everything's where we'd hoped and planned for it to be, right on schedule. Other than taking your immunotoxin every day, there's nothing more you have to do."

Miranda blinked, overwhelmed by the news. "I'm...I don't know what to say." Was there a rule of etiquette in this situation? Thank you, Doctor? I love you?

"You don't have to say anything. I think you'll find getting better is a lot easier than being sick." He grinned. "Go. Grow your hair. Come back in three months and tell me you feel like a million bucks."

He left her alone, the heavy door of the exam room closing with a sigh. Miranda went through the motions of getting dressed, all the while mulling over her conversation with the doctor.

You're done.

*I'm done.*

Stick a fork in her, she's done.

After a year of this, Miranda didn't believe you could ever really be *done* with cancer. It could be done with you, though, as you lay on the medical examiner's table like a waxy victim in a crime show.

Snap out of it, she told herself. For once, the doctor's advice didn't make her skin crawl—no precautions about nausea meds and gels and post-op limitations. Nothing like that. His advice was so simple it was scary. Get dressed and get on with your life.

She tore off the crinkly paper smock and wadded it up, crunching it into a small, tight ball between the palms of her hands and then making a rim shot to the wastebasket. Take *that*.

As she reached up to pull her bra off a hook, a familiar, unpleasant twinge shot up her right arm. The post-op sensations never seemed to end, although her doctor and surgeon assured her the tingling and numbness would eventually go away.

Which was—as of a few minutes ago—over.

She told herself she ought to be laughing aloud, singing "I Will Survive" at the top of her lungs, dancing down the corridors of the clinic and kissing everyone she passed. Unfortunately, that was the last thing she felt like doing. Maybe the news hadn't quite sunk in, because at the moment, she simply felt hollow and exhausted, like a shipwreck victim who'd had to swim ashore. She was alive, but the fight for survival had taken everything from her. It had changed her from the inside out, and this new woman, this gritty survivor, didn't quite know what to make of herself.

She turned to face the mirror, studying a body that didn't feel like her own anymore. A year ago, she'd been a reasonably attractive thirty-eight-year-old, comfortable in her size-10 body and—all right, she might as well admit it—downright vain about her long, auburn hair. During the months of treatment, however, she had learned to avoid mirrors. Despite the earnest reassurances of her friends, family, treatment team and support group, she never did learn to love what she saw there.

Some would say she'd lost her right breast and all her hair, but Miranda considered the term *lost* to be a misnomer. She knew exactly where her hair had gone—all over the bed pillows, down the drain of the shower, in the teeth of her comb, all over the car and the sofa. Shedding hair had followed in her wake wherever she went. Her husband, Jacob, had actually woken up one day with strands of her wavy auburn hair in his mouth. Over the course of a few days, her scalp had started to tingle. Then it stung and all her hair had come out and it wasn't lost at all. It had simply become detached from her. She collected it in a Nordstrom's bag and put it in the trash.

As for the other thing she'd "lost"—her breast—well, she knew darn well where that had gone, too. During the surgery, the tissue had been ever so carefully bagged and tagged and sent to the hospital pathology lab for analysis. Her diagnosis was made by someone she'd never met, someone she would never know. Someone who had typed her fate onto a neat form: infiltrating ductal carcinoma, stage one, tumor size 1.5 cm, nodes 15 negative.

She was considered lucky because she was a candidate for TRAM flap breast reconstruction, which took place immediately following her mastectomy. A separate surgical team came in and created a new breast, using tissue from her stomach. She'd struggled to be matter-of-fact about her reconstructed breast, figuring that if she didn't make a big deal of it, then it wouldn't be a big deal. Even though her counselor and support group encouraged her to acknowledge that an important, defining part of her was gone, that her body was permanently altered, she had resisted. She claimed she hadn't been that enamored of her breasts in the first place. They simply...were there. Size 34B. And after surgery, they still were, only the right one had been created with body fat from her stomach, something she didn't exactly mind losing. And the tattooed-on nipple was something of a novelty. How many women could boast about that?

Miranda knew she should be weeping with relief and gratitude just about now, but she still didn't like looking at herself in the mirror. The reconstructed breast seemed slightly off-kilter, and although the skin tone and temperature were exactly the same as her other breast, she couldn't feel a thing there. Nothing, nada. And her belly button was pulled a bit to one side.

According to the members of her support group, she was supposed to look in the mirror and see a survivor. A phenomenal woman whose beauty shone from within. A woman who was glad to be alive.

Miranda leaned forward, looked carefully. Where was that woman?

Still in hiding, she thought. Her gorgeous self didn't want to come out to play.

After an agony of baldness, she was getting her hair back. Her brows and eyelashes. Unfortunately, the fledgling fuzz of hair on her head was just plain weird. She had a terrible feeling that it was coming in whitish gray. But it was her real actual hair, growing in strangely soft and baby fine, as though she had just hatched from an egg. Her skin was sallow, and new lines fanned outward from the corners of her eyes. The whites of her eyes were yellow. She still hid beneath hats, scarves and wigs. She didn't like looking like a cancer patient even though that was exactly what she was. Correction, she told herself. Cancer survivor, no longer a patient.

She turned away, grabbed her bra and finished dressing, pulling on her khaki twill pants and a front-button shirt. She disliked the twinges she felt whenever she pulled a shirt over her head. It was as though her body kept wanting to remind her that she'd been nipped, tucked and rearranged, and there wasn't a darn thing she could do about it. She slung her butter-yellow sweater around her shoulders and loosely tied it by the sleeves, knowing the morning chill would be gone by now. With a deliberate tug, she put on her hat. Today's accessory was a sun hat made of cotton duck, which she'd chosen for comfort rather than style.

She finished putting herself together—handbag, cell phone, keys—and walked through the now-familiar putty-colored hallway of the clinic. There was soothing Native American–style artwork on the walls and soothing New Age music drifting from speakers in the ceiling. As usual, everyone here was busy, hurrying somewhere with a chart or heading into one of the exam rooms. And as usual, everyone she passed offered a distracted but sincere smile of encouragement.

The waiting room was a different story. There, patients seemed almost furtive as they studied magazines or checked the inboxes of their BlackBerries. It was almost as if they didn't want to make eye contact for fear of seeing something they shouldn't—hope or despair or some combination of both—in the eyes of another patient.

Miranda realized none of the people in the waiting room could know she was leaving the place for good. She wouldn't be back for three whole months, and then only for a checkup. Still, she felt an odd flicker of survivor guilt as she passed through the room, past the burbling tabletop fountain, the aspidistra plant that had doubled in size since she'd been coming here, the magazine rack, for the last time.

She stepped out into the dazzling sunshine of an Indian summer afternoon. For a moment it was so bright Miranda felt disoriented, as if she had lost her bearings. Then she blinked, dug out her sunglasses and put them on. The world came into view. Seattle in September was a place of matchless beauty, a time of warm, golden days, incredibly clear skies and crisp nights that held the snap of autumn in the air. Today had been graced with the kind of weather that made normally industrious people sit out on the patios of urban cafés, sipping granitas and tilting their faces up to the sun.

From the hospital on First Hill—also known as Pill Hill, thanks to the abundance of hospitals and medical centers in the area—she could look toward the waterfront and see the bustle of downtown, with its disorganized tangle of freeways and the distinctive spike of the Space Needle rising above Elliott Bay. Farther in the distance lay Seattle's signature defining view— deep blue Puget Sound lined by evergreen-clad islands and inlets, the horizon edged by mountains that appeared to be topped with blue-white whipped cream. It didn't matter whether you'd been born here—as Miranda had—or if you were a newcomer, Puget Sound dazzled the eye every time you looked at it.

A car horn blasted, causing her to jump back onto the curb. Whoops. She'd been so busy admiring the scenery that she hadn't been paying attention to the signals. She dutifully waited for the little green pedestrian man to tell her when it was safe to move forward. It would be incredibly ironic to survive cancer, only to get squashed by a bakery truck.

She hiked half a block to the bus stop and checked the schedule. The ride that would take her home to Queen Anne, the area where she lived, wouldn't be here for another thirty minutes.

She sat down on a bench and dialed Jacob on her cell phone.

"Hey, gorgeous," her husband said by way of greeting.

"I bet you say that to all the girls."

"Only when I hear your special ring, babe."

"You're using your driving voice," she remarked.

"What's that?"

She smiled a little. "Your driving voice. I can always tell when you're on the road."

He laughed. "What's up?"

"I just came from Dr. Turabian's."

"Are you all right?" This, of course, was his knee-jerk reaction these days. Jacob found the whole cancer business terrifying, and to be fair, most guys his age didn't expect to find themselves helping a young wife through a life-threatening disease. Jacob even seemed afraid of her, scarcely daring to touch her, as if he feared she might break. At first, he had accompanied Miranda to all her appointments—the tests and treatments, the follow-up visits. He was wonderful, trying to mask his near panic, yet Miranda found his efforts so painful to watch that it actually added to her stress. In time, she found it simpler to go on her own or with one of her girlfriends. At first Jacob had fought her—*I'm coming with you, and you can't stop me*—but eventually, he accepted her wishes with a sort of shamefaced relief.

"It was my last visit," she reminded him. "And it went just as we'd hoped. All the counts and markers checked out the way Dr. Turabian wanted them to." She took a deep breath. The air was so sharp and clean, it hurt her lungs. "I'm done."

"What do you mean, done?"

"Like, *done* done." She laughed briefly, and her own laughter sounded strange, like the rusty hinge to a door that rarely opened. "He doesn't want to see me again for three months. And it's unexpectedly weird. I don't know what to do with myself. It's as if I've forgotten what I used to do before I had cancer."

"Well." Jacob sounded as though he was at a loss, too. Afraid to say the wrong thing. "How do you feel?"

She knew what he was really asking: "When can you start back to work?" Her sabbatical from her job had definitely taken a toll on the family finances. Though she felt a pinch of annoyance, she didn't blame him. Throughout this whole ordeal, he had kept the family afloat, juggling work and extra household responsibilities so she could focus on getting on with her treatment, which touched off an exhaustion so crippling she couldn't work. His job, in beverage sales to large grocery chains, kept him constantly on the road. He earned a commission only, no base salary, so every sale mattered. And Lord knew, the bank account needed all the help it could get. They had budgeted for their house on the assumption that they'd be a two-income family.

"I feel all right, I think." Actually she felt as if she had run a marathon and crossed the finish line with no one around to see her do it. The world looked the same. Traffic still flowed up and down the hills, boats and barges still steamed back and forth across the Sound, and pedestrians still strolled past, oblivious to the fact that she'd just completed cancer treatment and had lived to tell the tale.

"Good," said Jacob. "I'm glad."

She watched a pigeon stroll along the sidewalk, poking its beak at crumbs. "Me, too. I'd better let you go. See you tonight?"

"I'll try not to be too late. Love you, babe."

"Love you." She put away her phone and pondered their habit of declaring their love, something they now did without thinking. When she'd first been diagnosed, telling her husband and kids "I love you" every time she parted from them or hung up the phone had seemed mandatory. Facing her own mortality made her painfully cognizant of the fact that every "goodbye" could be the last. Even though her prognosis had been good, she'd been careful to make certain everyone in her family heard her say "I love you" every day. As time went on, however, repetition and habit sucked the meaning from the phrase. Nowadays, signing off with "love you" was not that much different from "see you later."

Rifling through her wallet for her bus pass, she found a note she'd written to herself on a slip of paper. In her support group, other members were big on telling you to write down affirmations and positive thoughts, and keep them tucked in your pockets, your purse, wherever you might come across them. Miranda recognized her handwriting on the note, but she had absolutely no recollection of writing it. The note said, "You can't have today back. So make sure you spend it in the best possible way."

A wise sentiment, to be sure, but it didn't really illuminate what the "best possible way" meant. Did it mean surrounding herself with friends and family? Helping a stranger? Creating an original work of art? She should have been more specific. She folded the note and put it back in her wallet.

The landscaping by the bus stop was uninspired—laurel hedges, asters and mums. The plantings were hardy and dependable, if a bit boring. Miranda adored gardening, but she had become a bit of a snob about it. One of the things she'd promised herself during the treatment was that she was going to get back into gardening.

In the blue distance, the white-and-green ferryboats of Puget Sound glided back and forth between the islands to the west. A tourist was parasailing over Elliott Bay and Miranda felt a smile unfurl on her lips. What a beautiful thing to do, floating high above the blue water, the rainbow-colored chute blooming like a flower in the cloudless sky. From this distance, the tether that bound the rig to the speedboat was invisible, so it really did look as if the person was flying free.

Miranda had never been parasailing. Maybe she should try it one day. She glanced at her watch, and then at the bus schedule. Maybe she should try it now.

Oh, come on, she told herself. You'll miss your bus.

There's always another bus. You can't have today back, a wise woman had once written.

Miranda got up, hoisted the strap of her bag onto her shoulder and started walking. It was an easy walk since it was all downhill. She must have been going at a perfect pace because every single pedestrian light turned green as she approached it. She got the feeling the whole of downtown was urging her on.

As she crossed to the waterfront by way of a pedestrian overpass, she walked through the usual gauntlet of panhandlers. And like the other pedestrians, she averted her gaze, though even without looking, she could picture them perfectly—drowsy castoffs layered in old clothes, all their possessions in a shopping cart or knapsack. Most had battered cups out for change, some with crudely lettered signs that read, Spare Change or simply God Bless.

Miranda kept her eyes trained straight ahead. If you pretend not to see them, they're not really there. She couldn't do it, though, and she experienced the guilt anyone would feel for these people. She reminded herself that there were shelters where panhandlers could go for help, and all they had to do was show up. And of course, everyone knew you shouldn't give them money. They'd only spend it on beer.

Then it struck her. So what if they spent their meager donations on beer? Maybe that was all that stood between them and the urge to walk off the end of a pier and sink to the bottom of the Sound.

She slowed her pace and took out her wallet. There were five panhandlers stationed apart at regular intervals, like sentries sitting guard duty. She didn't have a lot of cash on her but she gave everything away, every cent, trying to divide it evenly among them. A couple of them whispered a thank-you, while the others merely nodded as though too weary to speak. Miranda didn't care. She wasn't doing this for the thanks.

When her wallet was empty of cash, she stuck it in her back pocket and continued to the waterfront. Down on Alaska Way, a busy street that hugged the shoreline and bristled with piers, she encountered another panhandler, this one a woman sitting on an apple crate and holding a sign marked Homeless. Need Help.

Miranda hesitated, then made eye contact with the woman. "I gave all my money to the people up on the Marion Street bridge," she confessed.

"That's okay. You have a good day, now."

Miranda plucked the butter-yellow sweater from her shoulders. "Can you use this?" It was a designer piece from Nordstrom's, made of fine-gauge Sea Isle cotton. The sweater had been a gift from her mother-in-law, who believed that no problem was so huge it couldn't be solved by a great sweater from Nordstrom's.

"Sure, honey, if you don't mind giving it up."

"I don't mind." She handed over the sweater.

"Oh, that's soft. Thank you." The woman's callused hand trembled as she smoothed it over the fabric.

"You're welcome." On impulse, Miranda opened her handbag. She took out the personal items—her cell phone, her keys and a bottle of pills and stuck them in her pockets. What remained were the usual purse things—a pack of Kleenex, a comb and a lipstick, a calculator, a tiny flashlight.

"This might come in handy, too," she said.

This offer made the woman frown. "That's a nice bag," she said, but her voice was dubious.

She had good taste. It was another gift from Miranda's mother-in-law, a Dooney & Burke that had probably retailed for a few hundred dollars.

"I've got another at home."

"You're not from the mission, are you?" the panhandler asked. "I already tried the mission, and it don't work for me."

"I'm not from the mission. Just someone…passing by."

The woman still eyed her skeptically.

Miranda heard the blast of a ferry horn, the cry of a seagull. A breeze tickled across the back of her neck and gently wafted beneath the brim of her sun hat. Out of habit, her hand went up to keep it from blowing away. But then, instead of clamping down on the hat, she took hold of the brim.

Deep breath, she told herself, and then she swept the hat off her head. She was naked to the world now. Everyone who looked at her would know she was a cancer patient. Even after all this time, she felt self-conscious. She wanted to proclaim to anyone who would listen that she was more than a patient. She was a wife, a mother, a coworker, a friend. But when all your hair fell out and your fingernails crumbled and you lost your eyelashes, that was all people saw. A cancer patient.

Survivor, she corrected herself, handing over her hat. Cancer survivor, as of today.

The woman took it, then offered Miranda a brief smile and said, "You have a nice day now."

As Miranda walked away, she felt strangely light, unfettered, as though she were floating already. She hoped like heck the parasailing company took credit cards.

They did, of course. Everybody did. The panhandlers probably did.

Miranda had just given away all her money, but she didn't stop there. Feeling reckless, she paid for a spin over Elliott Bay. The guy helping her into the harness gave her hasty instructions. "There's not much to it. Just relax and let the wind do all the work. You don't even need to change out of your street clothes. You won't get wet, guaranteed."

The old Miranda, the Miranda who had never looked her own mortality square in the eye, would have been terrified. Now, though, she was matter-of-fact about danger and risk. She wondered if the harness would bother her bad arm, but decided she didn't care. She had borne worse than that lately.

"Sounds good to me." She bit her lip as he passed the straps under her breasts. Would he know that one of them was reconstructed? And why the heck should that matter? Don't be silly, she told herself.

He and his partner motored out into the bay, their little speedboat dwarfed by ferries and cargo barges. Following instructions, Miranda positioned herself on the platform and waited as the chute billowed with the wind and speed. Then they let her go off the back of the boat. For a second, she dipped downward, her bare feet skimming the water. She took in a sharp breath, bracing herself for the bone-chilling cold of Puget Sound. Then the wind scooped up the chute and she went drifting high and fast, like a giant kite on a string.

After her first gasp of wonder, Miranda remained absolutely quiet, just hanging there. She had learned how to be still and stoic during her cancer treatment. She had remained absolutely still while radiologists and oncologists had examined her. Still while the surgeons studied her and made lines on her with a Sharpie marker. Still while she lay on the table of the linear accelerator while a deadly beam of light was aimed at her. Still while the machine burned its invisible rays at her, making her skin blister and crack.

She was good at holding still. And now so ready to leave that behind and let the wind sweep her away.

She saw what the seabirds saw—the dark, mysterious under-water formations, pods of sea lions sunning themselves on navigation buoys, the container ships and sailboats, the blaze of sunlight on the water. She felt the cool rush of wind through her hair—what there was of her hair. The breeze ruffled it like feathers.

She laughed aloud and wished Jacob and the kids could see her now, a human kite tail soaring above the city, with its high-rises and skeletal orange cranes in the shipyards, incongruously set against the backdrop of Mount Rainier in all its glory. Maybe she would buy the ten-dollar photo the guys in the boat had taken of her soaring, because how often did you get a picture of yourself airborne? Yet there was something depressing in the thought of bringing a picture home to Jacob and the kids. She'd done this cool thing alone. She couldn't remember the last time they had done anything as a family.

She gave the parasailing crew a thumbs-up as they expertly reeled her in to the deck of the boat and motored over to the dock. Once on dry land, one of the guys printed up a photo from his digital camera and handed it to her. She reached into her back pocket for her wallet.

"It's on me," he said.

She put her wallet away. "Thank you."

People were extra nice to cancer patients, she had discovered. They looked at the hair loss, the broken nails, the sallow skin and the swollen bodies, and they got scared. *There but for the grace of God go I.* Being nice to victims was a form of self-inoculation, perhaps. She used to think that way herself before she became a member of the cancer club. By now, she had learned to accept kindnesses big and small, from friends and strangers.

Miranda thanked the man again. She would keep the picture as something to take out and study at the odd moment—a shot of herself soaring high and free, alone against the clear blue sky.

She needed to find an ATM. She walked up the hill from the waterfront and took the concrete Harbor Steps, and from there, headed toward Pike Place Market. She made slow progress on the stairs, which was yet another frustration of this disease. Only a year ago, she had been a busy, energetic woman with every-thing going for her—two great kids, a caring husband, a solid— if boring—job, a spring in her step. She used to pride herself on her ability to cram so much into a single day. In under an hour, she could go from company meeting room to soccer field to fixing dinner without missing a beat.

Now she got winded on a stupid flight of stairs.

That, she decided, was going to end right now.

She squared her shoulders and lifted her chin. This was a big day. She needed to make a big deal of it.

At Pike Place Market, teeming with shoppers, tourists, chefs, performers and deliverymen, she bought the makings of a feast—fresh local asparagus and morel mushrooms, yellow potatoes and wild white salmon fresh off the boat, according to the chatty fishmonger in his slick yellow apron. Spot prawns for the appetizer.

She pictured herself sitting down to a beautifully set table with her family. They had cause to celebrate. This was a red-letter day.

As she exited the market with her parcels, she paused at a row of wholesale flower stalls. Big pails of galvanized steel displayed stalks of dahlias, bells of Ireland, roses in every conceivable shade. Each burst of color was like a small celebration.

Miranda's heart expanded, and she inhaled the green fragrance of the plants. Flowers had long been a passion of hers. She was expert at growing and also arranging flowers. That hobby, like the rest of her life, had fallen by the wayside during her illness. Until she glimpsed the flower stall, she hadn't realized how much she missed it.

She asked the flower seller for a variety—gerbera daisies and rover mums, fragrant yarrow, purple statice, solidaster, hypericum berries and seeded eucalyptus. This, she decided, would be her victory bouquet—a colorful, elegant affirmation that she had survived her treatment and was ready to move on with her life.

On the way to the bus stop, she juggled her parcels and dialed Jacob's number again.

"I went parasailing."

"What?"

He had the driving voice again. Traffic sounds indicated that this was probably not the best time to explain. "I'm making a special dinner tonight," she told him.

"I was going to offer to take you out," he said.

"Thanks, but I was feeling creative, and this probably works out better for the kids, anyway. Andrew has soccer practice until four-thirty, and Valerie goes to work at the theater at eight. So...six-thirty?"

He hesitated. She heard a world of doubt in that hesitation. It was getting so that she could read his silences with more accuracy than she could his words.

"You're going to be late," she said.

"I can move some things——"

"Good idea." Normally, she tried to be accommodating of the demands of his job, but today she wanted him with her. "Call me later and let me know what time works for you."

"I won't be late," he promised.

"Just call me. Bye."

Her husband, she reminded herself, was a wonderful man. He had proven himself over and over again the past year. One of the greatest sacrifices he had made was to increase his work hours when she took her leave of absence from Urban Ice, which supplied bulk ice to commercial operations. Some weeks Jacob put in eighty hours, never complaining, simply doing what had to be done. Despite their health plan, only so many of her medical procedures were covered by insurance, like the mastectomy, but not the reconstruction, which she thought was a cruel irony. Within just hours of diagnosis, they had reached their deductible. Still, health insurance didn't cover the mortgage; that was what her salary was for. Nor did it cover groceries or utilities or taxes, or school clothes for the kids. And it sure didn't cover parasailing or the twenty dollars' worth of flowers she'd just bought.

# CHAPTER
## ⟡ TWO ⟡

Miranda got off the bus at the corner and walked halfway down the block to her house. It was a neighborhood she loved, a place rich with history and an eclectic mix of residents. Queen Anne crowned the highest hill in Seattle and commanded the best views of the city and the Sound. There were modern condo complexes interspersed with historic mansions built by timber and railroad barons long ago. The Sweeneys' street had a cozy, colorful feel to it. Arts and Crafts—era bungalows were brightened by gardens that bloomed on the smallest patches of earth, rockeries and concrete stairs leading up to friendly-looking front porches.

She and Jacob had loved their house the first time they'd

seen it six years before. There was even room for both a garden and greenhouse in the back, something she had always dreamed of. She cringed, thinking of her garden now. It had been among the first things to fall by the wayside when she was diagnosed.

She was looking forward to returning to a normal life, getting her house in order, her garden planted, her finances under control. This house was at the absolute top end of what they could afford, and when she'd taken leave from work, she'd told Jacob they should sell the place and live somewhere cheaper. He wouldn't hear of it. She suspected that in his mind, giving up the house was an admission that she wouldn't get better, that she wouldn't be going back to work. There was no way he would concede that.

She'd been grateful for his stubborn insistence on keeping the house she loved, but beginning next year, their mortgage rate would adjust, and the payments were going to balloon. She shuddered, thinking about the size of the check they'd have to write each month.

Not today, she cautioned herself. Today she was not going to worry. As she let herself in, she looked around the house and for some reason saw it with new eyes. Nothing had changed, yet she felt like a stranger here. The silence was marred only by the rhythmic ticking of the hall clock: 4:00 p.m. She had plenty of time to get dinner on the table.

She had learned to keep things simple this past year. When she bothered to fix dinner at all—which was rare—she tended to avoid complicated dishes.

"What did I used to do with myself?" she asked aloud.

Then she grabbed the flowers she'd bought, found a few vases and bowls and grabbed her stem snippers and went to work. She'd almost forgotten how soothing and satisfying it was to arrange flowers, something she'd learned from her grandmother.

In her support group, everyone stressed how important it was to keep doing the things you enjoyed throughout treatment. For Miranda, the problem was that she had a hard time enjoying anything when she was curled into a ball of nausea from chemo, or jumping out of her skin from the discomfort of radiation burns. Some days, it was all she could do to make it from one side of a single moment to the other.

It's over, she reminded herself. You're done.

"Mom?"

Miranda nearly dropped the bowl she was carrying. "Andrew. I didn't hear you come in."

Her eleven-year-old son slung his backpack onto the bench at the back door. "I tried to be quiet."

"You're good at it. A regular superspy."

He sat down and unlaced his soccer cleats. She watched him, experiencing a moment of both helpless love and keen regret. Not so very long ago, he used to come slamming into the house, announcing loudly, "I'm home. And I'm starved."

One of the drugs she'd been given caused headaches and made her hypersensitive to loud noises, and she had to ask him to tiptoe and whisper. It seemed as if the entire family had been tiptoeing and whispering for a year.

"How are you, buddy?" she asked him, using a step stool to take down a salad bowl. Another limitation—postsurgery, she couldn't lift her arm higher than her shoulder. That was months ago, but there was still discomfort. She'd learned to use a stool, ask for help or skip the chore altogether.

"Okay." He set aside his grass-caked cleats and sent her a quick smile as he stood up.

Her heart constricted with love. How tall he'd grown in the past year. How handsome. When she studied his face, she could still see her little boy there. His skin was baby soft, with a dusting of freckles saddling his nose. There was just a hint of roundness in his cheeks but that would be gone soon, as he continued to grow, his face to elongate with maturity.

Come back, she wanted to say to that little boy. I'm not ready to let you go. She hated that she'd missed out on so much while she was sick. She hated missing soccer games and school meetings, just going to the park or weekend rounds of miniature golf or paintball drills.

She wiped her hands on a tea towel and went around the counter, pulling him into a hug. He felt stiff and hesitant in her arms, this boy who used to hurl himself at her in an abandoned tangle of affection. They had taken his mother away one day, and the woman who returned was a bald, puffy-faced stranger with drains sprouting from her chest. She was tender and sore and fragile as an old woman, reeking of Radiacare gel, and for a very long time, that was the end of bear hugs.

She kissed the top of his head. He smelled…golden. Like

Indian-summer sunshine, fresh-cut grass and the curiously innocent scent of boyish sweat. "You'll be taller than me soon," she remarked, letting him go. "Next week, probably."

"Uh-huh." He went to the sink for a glass of water.

She saw him looking around the kitchen, everywhere except at her. This was another habit that had developed, and not just in Andrew. Both of her children had stopped looking at her. She didn't blame them. It was alarming to see their mother so ill. She had not been one of those movie-of-the-week cancer patients who grew more delicate and beautiful as the disease progressed. She'd simply turned blotchy and swollen, with circles under her eyes. When her hair fell out, it revealed that her scalp was weirdly ridged rather than smooth. Andrew was barely ten years old at the time of her diagnosis. Seeing her so radically altered had frightened him, and he had learned to avert his eyes.

"We're having dinner together tonight," she said. "All four of us."

"Okay," he said.

"I have good news."

That perked him up. He was apparently so used to bad news that this came as a surprise. His sister, Valerie, had quit asking altogether. "Today, Dr. Turabian told me I'm done. No more treatments."

"Hey, that's good, Mom. You're cured."

She smiled at him. The word *cured* was a dicey term. Her doctors and treatment team tended to say "cancer free" or to cite counts and markers and measures in the lab reports. She wasn't going to split hairs with Andrew, though.

"So guess what I did today," she said.

"What?"

"I went parasailing over Elliott Bay."

Finally he looked at her. Really looked. And his expression seemed to ask if she'd lost her mind. "Uh-uh."

"Uh-huh. It was awesome. You should have seen me. It was like being the tail of a kite." She took out the digital print and showed him.

"Jeez, that's you?" he said, studying the little dangling figure in the photo. "Crazy."

He didn't seem thrilled. Impressed, but not thrilled. Miranda was reminded that her son preferred things to be predictable. Traditional. It didn't matter that this was the twenty-first century. Despite all the social advances in the world, boys wanted their moms to be conventional and conservative. They wanted them in the kitchen baking cookies, wearing high heels and a ruffled apron. Where on earth did they get these ideas? she wondered. Andrew had never had a fifties-style stay-at-home mom. She didn't even own an apron. On what planet did women like that exist?

She tousled his hair. "Don't worry, I'm not losing it. After my appointment, I decided to celebrate, and I felt like doing something different."

"Okay."

He headed for the study, and she could hear the sound of the computer booting up. Andrew's new obsession was a very so-phisticated simulation game called Adventure Island. His devotion to the game had developed over the past year. Miranda didn't comprehend all the details, but as far as she could tell, the game allowed him to create his own world on the computer and populate it with people of his own imagination.

Miranda clearly saw the motivation behind the act. Andrew had fabricated a world in which he was in total control. His virtual world was an idyllic place where every boy had a pet, where dads came home from work early to play catch in the backyard and where moms didn't sleep all day or puke or cry or get rushed to the emergency room, spiking a fever. In Andrew's perfect world, the moms strapped on colorful aprons over their Barbie-doll figures, sang songs, helped with homework and baked cookies.

Dream on, kiddo, she thought as she turned on the radio to her favorite oldies station. "Ain't No Mountain High Enough" was playing and she joined in, singing loudly and tossing the salad while swaying to the beat. In the past, Andrew might have joined her. He liked oldies, too, and could carry a tune.

Unfortunately, it was too late to draw Andrew away from his virtual utopia, and Miranda felt a squeeze of regret, even as she warbled along with the radio. Prior to discovering the game, her son had spent a lot more time with her, with his friends and especially with his best friend in the world, Gretel, the family dog.

The big, affectionate Bernese mountain dog had been born

the same year as Andrew, and they'd been raised together. On Andrew's first day of kindergarten, Gretel had slunk under his bed and refused to move until he got home. When they were together, they played endlessly—chase and fetch and, Gretel's favorite, rescue. Andrew would pretend to be lost and injured, and she would drag and nudge him to safety. It was one of life's most perfect friendships—a little boy and his loyal dog.

In a twist of stunning cruelty, Gretel had died a few months ago. Of cancer.

Miranda and Jacob had tried to tell Andrew that it was just a painful coincidence, that at age ten, Gretel was old for a Berner, and that having cancer didn't mean you had to die. Andrew said he understood, but sometimes Miranda thought he only agreed with her and Jacob just to get them to stop talking about it. She had said they could get a new puppy, but that had only made Andrew furious.

"Why would I want to get another dog, just so it'll die on me?"

"Think of all the love Gretel brought into your life," Miranda had said.

"All I can think about is how much I miss her."

Miranda hadn't pressed the issue. Truth be told, she believed getting a puppy would consume more time and energy than she could afford. She told herself she'd bring it up with Andrew again once she was feeling better. Soon, she thought. Soon, they needed to have a family meeting about the issue.

Before her diagnosis, what did they used to do? It was so

hard to remember. It seemed as though that life had belonged to a different woman, a woman who had rushed in a hyped-up blur from family to work, from one overplanned, overscheduled day to the next.

Never again, Miranda thought, seasoning the salmon and popping it in the oven on a cedar roasting plank. She had lost a lot to cancer, but she'd gained at least one thing. Wisdom enough to realize that, sick or healthy, a woman needed to slow down and pay attention to the things that matter most—her family and friends. Her passions and her dreams. Provided she hadn't forgotten what those were.

An hour later, dinner was ready, but her family was not. The phone rang, and it was Jacob. "I am so sorry," he said. "I got stuck in a sales meeting with West Sound Grocery's company V.P. He kept upping his order, so I couldn't very well duck out of the meeting." Jacob could not keep the smile from his voice as he added, "I made about four times the usual commission thanks to this guy. Turns out he's a fly fisherman, too."

She couldn't remember the last time Jacob had gone fishing. "Well…congrats. Try to get home before dinner gets too cold." What else was she going to say?

She hung up feeling torn. On the one hand, he was coming home late, and she had a right to be irritated with him. On the other, he was late because he was providing for his family while Miranda dealt with being sick.

The sound of the back door slamming caught her attention. "Hello, you," she said to her daughter. "I hope you're hungry."

Valerie, who was fifteen, sullen and gorgeous, shrugged out of her black denim jacket. "Gotta go to work," she said curtly. "I promised I'd go in early tonight."

Miranda's heart sank. "How early?"

"Like, in half an hour."

"Valerie. Give your family a little time."

Her daughter's eyes, which were a lovely blue and almost totally obscured by a deep crust of coal-black makeup, flicked around the room. "I don't see any family."

"Sit down," Miranda said resolutely. "I'll get Andrew."

She found her son frozen like a statue, his rapt face bathed in the blue-gray glow of the computer screen. He appeared not to move at all except for his hand on the mouse, busily manipulating images on the screen.

"Supper, buddy," she said.

No response.

"Your sister's home, supper is on the table and it's time to eat," she said.

"'Kay." He offered a distracted grunt. "Give me a minute."

"Sorry, no can do. Put that all on standby or whatever you have to do, and go wash your hands."

"But if I stop now I'll lose this whole—"

"Andrew. If you don't stop now, I'll lose something and it won't be data."

He heaved a long-suffering sigh, saved his work and headed off to wash his hands.

Miranda manufactured a cheerful mood as she sat down to

the dinner table. "Check it out," she said. "A home-cooked meal. When was the last time we had that?"

"Thanks," Valerie said, digging in. She glanced at the clock above the stove.

"I know this past year has been rough on you guys," Miranda said. "I'm hoping we're about to hit a smooth patch, Val. The doctor gave me my walking papers today. No more treatments."

Valerie's chewing slowed. Then she swallowed and took a gulp from her water glass. "So that's good, right?"

"It's very good. I'll be taking something to prevent a recurrence of the cancer, and I have to get rechecked every three months, and then every six, and so on. Other than that, I'm a free woman."

"Well. I'm glad." Valerie resumed eating.

Miranda watched her thoughtfully. Valerie's reaction to her mother getting breast cancer had been complicated, a combination of abject horror, betrayal, rage and resentment. And finally, ambivalence. She was old enough to comprehend the stark reality of her mother's mortality, and smart enough to realize how much that put herself at risk for the same disease.

While Andrew had retreated into his virtual world, Valerie had struck out in search of a life apart from her family. Each child was looking for some kind of separation, and Miranda didn't blame them, although it hurt. Valerie found escape and diversion at the Ruby Shoebox, a vintage art-house movie theater in the funky Capital Hill district of Seattle. It was her first real job. She'd started as an usher and then advanced to cashier. Working there every Friday and Saturday night made her supremely happy.

As nearly as Miranda could tell, Valerie had found a whole new set of friends there, too—older kids who smoked cigarettes and wore berets and Doc Martens. In a matter of months, Miranda had watched her sunny, funny daughter transform into a virtual stranger. She'd turned her back on her two best friends, Megan and Lyssa, and completely ignored Pete, the boy next door, whom she'd had a crush on since sixth grade. The old Valerie was inside her somewhere, but Miranda had no idea how to bring her back. She wished she knew how to remind Valerie of the things they used to love to do together, traditions that had once been cherished but were now somehow lost in the shuffle.

For far too long, Miranda had been at a loss, too weakened by the disease to do anything about her kids. Oh, she was angry about that. She resented the disease because it had turned her into a lazy mother.

"I have something else to say," she announced, and her tone captured their attention. "We need to come together as a family. Now that my treatments are over, that's what I want to work on."

"Yeah, tell that to Dad," Valerie said.

"I intend to." Miranda turned her attention to the delicate white salmon, the fresh salad. Finally, finally, food was going to taste good to her again rather than carry that weird metallic tinge caused by her medication. "I was looking at the school calendar," she said, lightening her tone. "Homecoming is just a few weeks away."

Homecoming and all it entailed was a big deal for Valerie's school, and for the Sweeneys in particular. The game was only one component of an entire weekend of celebration, bringing in high-school alumni from all over, wearing their well-preserved letterman jackets and waving pennants proclaiming them state champions more times than any other school in Washington State. Valerie and Andrew had grown up nurtured on stories of how Jacob and Miranda had met at the high school's Homecoming dance back in 1986, when they were both seniors. And the rest, as the story went, was history.

"So I hear." Valerie stabbed at a potato with her fork. "I don't plan on going, so don't get all excited about it."

"What do you mean, you're not going? Everyone goes to Homecoming."

"Not me." She met Miranda's eyes, held her gaze an extra beat.

That was all it took to remind Miranda of last year's Homecoming disaster. As a high-school freshman, it had been Valerie's first time. She'd been soaring with excitement, having been asked by the perfect boy—Pete. She'd picked out the perfect dress and shoes, and was looking forward to the perfect evening. Then she learned Miranda's mastectomy was scheduled for the day of the dance.

Miranda had urged her to go, but Valerie had refused. "How could I?" she asked, and had spent Homecoming weekend at the hospital, sitting with her father throughout the surgery and during the terrible wait afterward. While her friends were all out celebrating, Valerie was watching her mother being transformed from her mom into some sickly stranger. Things had not gone smoothly. There were complications. And for Valerie, there was a horrible association in her mind between Homecoming and illness and worry.

All in all, it had probably been one of the worst weekends of Valerie's life. Here she was a year later, a different person, a dark rebel who rarely smiled, who was secretive and watchful, who held herself aloof from things most girls her age enjoyed—school and sports, hanging out with her friends and looking forward to things like Homecoming season.

"I hope you'll reconsider," Miranda said. "I promise you there won't be any crisis this year."

"Just not into it," Valerie said. "No big deal."

And of course, it was a huge deal, and Miranda knew it, and so did Valerie. Somewhere trapped inside the cynical stranger was a girl who wanted to be on the decorating committee, who wanted Pete to ask her to the dance. She would deny all this, but Miranda knew it was true. Sometimes she wanted to grab this pale-skinned, black-haired stranger, shake her and demand, *What have you done with my daughter?*

She suspected there were moments when Valerie wanted to do the same to her. Because Miranda—the mom she knew—had gone away, too. There were many times this past year when Miranda had looked in the mirror and seen a woman she didn't know. If she didn't recognize herself, how could her kids know her?

"Why do they call it Homecoming?" Andrew asked.

"It's tradition. A long time ago, schools wanted all their alumni to come home for a game against their biggest rival."

A car horn sounded. "That's my ride," Valerie said. "I have to go. I'll be back by eleven." She jumped up, carried her plate to the sink, grabbed her backpack. "I have my cell, I did my homework in study hall and I've got a ride home." She rattled off answers before Miranda could even ask the questions. "Don't wait up."

She was gone in a swirl of black denim and fishnet stockings, leaving a void of silence. Miranda used to be the kind of mom who was proactive, who ran her kids' lives and stayed on top of things. She was determined to regain the strength and stamina to reclaim that role. She only hoped she wasn't too late.

Jacob called again to say he was stuck in traffic on the 520 bridge, a floating bridge that spanned Lake Washington. Miranda set aside his dinner to warm later in the microwave. Andrew loaded the dishwasher without being asked. One of the few aspects of her illness that she welcomed was that her little boy had taken to doing his chores without nagging. There were moments when she almost wished he would need a little nagging, just as a reminder that he needed her.

"Thanks, good buddy," she said as he turned on the dishwasher.

"'Welcome. I'll be in the study."

That was code for, "I'll be on my computer in a virtual world where I'm in control."

The medical family therapist they had been seeing talked

with her at length about the many ways the family dynamic changed over the course of a serious illness. It was a natural process that progressed through known stages. There were things Miranda had to let go of in order to focus on getting well. Much of her hands-on mothering had to go. She had not surrendered it overnight. It had been a gradual process of renegotiation. She would not regain it overnight; she realized that. And when she finally did, she knew the whole landscape of her family would be different.

As she was straightening the kitchen, she came across a packet of information the therapist had given her. There were many components to post-treatment: support groups, Web site chat rooms and bulletin boards, opportunities to connect with women who, like Miranda, were facing the sometimes daunting chore of returning to normal life.

The hardest by far was getting to know her family again. Miranda could not imagine where to begin. With Jacob, who sought absolution by doubling his workload? With Valerie, who had morphed into an angry, distant teen? Or with Andrew, who barely had the vocabulary for expressing his deepest fears?

She turned on the radio in time to hear the final chorus of "Girls Just Wanna Have Fun," and the tune lifted her spirits, just a little. She kept telling herself she had cause to celebrate, and not to expect too much too soon.

Oh, but she did. She wanted it all. She wanted her life back. She wanted her daughter to go to Homecoming, her son to race around the block on his bike and practice armpit-farting in the bathtub. She wanted her husband to look at her with more than desperate love in his eyes; she wanted him to look at her with passion. Or, heck, she thought. Right now, she'd just settle for him getting home in time for dinner.

# CHAPTER
## ∽ THREE ∽

Jacob walked in the door at sunset, looking weary, worried and heart-stirringly handsome all at once. Miranda's husband had a wonderful face with the features of a cheerful boy who would never grow up. That was what she used to see when she looked at him. Now she saw not just a man who had indeed left every vestige of youth behind, but a man aged by worry.

At present, he had a "sorry I'm late" smile on his face and an enormous and garish bouquet of asters and mums in his arms. Bringing Miranda flowers used to be like bringing coal to Newcastle, but since she'd abandoned her garden, fresh flowers were a rarity around the house.

"Looks like somebody beat me to it," he said, eyeing the flowers she'd bought at the market.

"That would be me," she confessed. "I treated myself."

"I brought some champagne, too." Still holding the flowers, he bent and kissed her briefly. Too briefly. Just enough for her to start to savor the taste of him and the shape of his lips, just enough for her to notice, like a distant flicker of heat lightning, an echo of the passion they used to share. Like so many other things, her cancer had wreaked havoc on the intimate aspects of her marriage. She'd had a long postsurgery recovery period. In the midst of that course of the radiation treatment, she couldn't stand for clothing to touch her, let alone her husband's hands, his lips, his body. Often, even the sensation of the bedsheets rustling when he shifted at night had caused her to cry out in pain. And for several days following each round of chemo, she had been good for nothing, certainly not for reclaiming her husband.

He'd been great through it all. Better than great.

Too great.

She missed the days before the disease had struck, when he would come waltzing in from work, clasp her in his arms, plant a resounding kiss on her mouth. Or if the kids weren't around, he'd come up behind her, nuzzle her neck and whisper a wicked suggestion in her ear. It was frustrating to Miranda that she could remember those moments so vividly, but couldn't figure out how to get back to that place, how to be that sexy, carefree person again.

She warmed his dinner in the microwave and set it down

before him. They toasted each other with glasses of chilled champagne, and she savored the bubbly effervescence on her tongue. He ate with an almost comical sense of appreciation, closing his eyes and swooning until she laughed.

"So did you tell the kids?" he asked.

"I did. They seemed a bit underwhelmed. I think they might be suspicious that I'm pulling their leg. They don't really trust me to be well and stay well."

"Oh, come on. They trust you."

"They'll learn to, all over again."

He looked at her, really looked at her, for a long moment. Despite all the changes they'd gone through the past year, Jacob knew her with a depth and intimacy that ran far deeper than any illness could reach. "What's bothering you?"

She poured herself another glass of champagne. "Andrew's obsessed by that cybergame or whatever it is, and Valerie claims she's not going to the Homecoming dance."

"Sounds pretty typical to me."

"Nothing about this family is typical anymore, including us."

"Miranda—"

"I've been too exhausted to really take this up with you, but I'm getting back to normal now. And I mean it. You know I'm right."

"Every family deals with problems. We got through last year. We can get through anything." He pushed back from the table. "And that was the best meal I've had…maybe ever. I mean it."

She smiled. "Don't get too used to meals like this. I was feeling inspired and energetic, and City Fish got in a fresh catch of salmon."

"Well, thanks. It was a treat." He cleared the table, did the dishes. Like Andrew, he seemed to equate obedience with good karma. As if behaving well might help her beat the disease.

With a welling of affection and gratitude, she got up and reached to put her arms around him. He turned abruptly, inadvertently transforming the hug into a brief, awkward collision. "Sorry," he said. "I'd better get busy." He indicated his briefcase, which housed his laptop and the tyrant BlackBerry and his relay module, which gave the whole world access to him 24/7. He was able to put through orders with the touch of a button, insuring that his clients' needs were met on the instant. "I need to turn in some orders and get ready for that big regional meeting tomorrow. Um, that is, if you don't need me anymore."

*If you don't need me.* Miranda couldn't imagine not needing him, but of course, that wasn't what he meant. As far as he was concerned, he'd had dinner and cleaned up afterward, so he'd done his duty.

"It's fine," she said. Not because it was fine, but because she was in the habit of saying so.

He kissed her lightly and stepped back. "Thanks again for dinner, babe. And congrats on finishing. You are the most amazing woman on the planet."

But apparently not amazing enough to divert his attention from e-mailing an upcoming PowerPoint presentation. The thought made her feel small, resenting the job he did in order to take care of her.

She busied herself with mundane chores, delivering a stack of folded laundry to Andrew's room. There, she sat on the bed, looking around. Her son was at a crossroads between a childhood of Tonka trucks and G.I. Joes and a music-filled, phone-dominated adolescence. Apparently, computer games filled the breach.

She straightened some things in his room, and came across a stack of long-overdue library books—*The Encyclopedia of Dogs. Family Dog. How to Raise a Good Dog. The Book of Puppies.* Every single book had to do with dogs. For a boy who swore he'd never get another dog, he sure seemed interested. Then she went into the study, where as usual, he was absorbed in the computer, busily clicking and tapping as the graphics on the monitor changed and option boxes popped up.

"Hey, buddy."

"Hey, Mom."

"How about you put the game on hold for the night."

"It's not that simple. I need to find a stopping point."

"Not that again," she said in a warning voice. She knew she could make it simple by flipping a switch. That seemed petty, though, and didn't really address the issue. Besides, whether she liked it or not, the computer and games had been Andrew's constant companions when she was too sick to do the usual mom things. "Tell you what," she said, pulling a stool over to the desk. "We can find a stopping point together."

He shot her a look of suspicion.

"I mean it," she said. "I'm interested."

It was a virtual-simulation game. Though he did his best to show her the story and how it all worked, Miranda could tell there wasn't a simple explanation. Vaguely she understood there was a storyline about a family in a dangerous jungle, seeking clues to a lost treasure. Both the parents in the game had superhero qualities and each wore a special badge that had been won in some earlier ordeal. The badge, Andrew explained, gave them immortality.

"Hey," Miranda joked, "where do I sign up for a badge like that?"

"She had to kill a monster and steal a treasure from his nest."

She nodded, studying the mother on the screen, who looked like a weird cross between Angelina Jolie and Aunt Bea. The husband was the Terminator, of course, the role model of all cyberdads. The two boys in the family had special powers of their own. There was a dog, a young, eternally healthy dog.

"They should stop in the cave for the night," she said.

"Nope." He clicked the mouse, instructing them to move on. "Rabid bats."

"What about crossing the strait in that boat?"

"Too risky. Every time I get them on a boat or plane, the weather turns bad." He decided to stop the game with the characters taking shelter in a convenient tree house high above the jungle.

"I love that," she said, watching the characters settle comfortably on the branches, where they immediately fell asleep.

"I love it when you're on a trek through an uninhabited jungle and you need a place to stay and suddenly there's a perfectly good tree house right overhead."

"Very funny."

She dropped the teasing. The reason behind his obsession with the simulation game was crystal clear to her, and probably to Andrew, too. In his computer world, he was in control. No one but monsters would ever die.

That evening, Miranda spent a little time in the small backyard, inspecting the old flower beds that were normally so brilliant this time of year. Though the days of summer were growing shorter, the sunny day lingered, throwing long shadows across the patchy grass and weedy beds.

She found a pair of pruning shears that had been left out in the rain. They barely worked, but she took a few desultory snips at the leggy rosebushes. Even the hardiest plants would have to struggle to recover from a year's neglect. Some of the more fragile plants were already gone for good, having succumbed early on to the lack of attention. Maybe it was a good thing that summer was over. Before long, the garden would go dormant, and reemerge in a healthier state in the spring. Last year at this time, she had ignored the garden on purpose, terrified that, come spring, she wouldn't be around to see it bloom again. Now she was able to think of the future and actually feel a glimmer of hope.

Despite her conviction that she would get to work on her garden again, she put aside the rusty shears and went back inside.

A constant feeling of fatigue hovered around her, something she had grown used to and was looking forward to leaving behind. By nine-thirty, she was practically asleep, never having made it past the world-news pages of the daily paper.

"I'm going upstairs," she told Jacob.

"I'll wait up for Valerie."

She hesitated at the bottom of the stairs. She knew that if she asked Jacob to come upstairs with her, he would oblige. They had something to celebrate, after all. But she just felt tired, and he was absorbed in his work, frowning at the screen of his computer.

Besides, their intimacy had changed. Neither of them had wanted it to, and they'd worked hard to keep their passion alive. She had not been eager to show her reconstructed breast to Jacob, but knew that putting it off would only make a bigger deal of it. When she finally did show him, soon after her surgery, he had gamely checked it out.

Jacob had said all the right things—you're beautiful to me, you're still the sexiest woman I know, I love everything about you, most of all your courage.

She'd loved him for his sincerity, his loyalty. But at the same time, she had found herself wishing she looked the way she had when they'd married, both of them twenty-two and fresh out of college.

Miranda hovered between inviting him upstairs with her or leaving him engrossed in his work.

She decided to compromise. "Wake me up when you come to bed."

# CHAPTER
## ~~FOUR~~

The next day, she had a meeting with her boss at Urban Ice, where she had worked in the office since Andrew started school. In Seattle, providing bulk ice and cold storage for commercial operations was a little-known but essential business. With the local and Alaska fishing industries, the need for ice was never ending.

She knocked on the door of Marty's office and stepped inside. He was meeting with one of her favorite customers, Danny Arviat, a Native American from Sitka, and their running joke was that she sold ice to Eskimos.

"Hey, it's the ice queen," Danny said, standing up and shaking her hand.

"That's me." She smiled, and Marty gave her a hug. "If this isn't a good time…"

"I was just leaving," Danny said. "It's good to see you, Miranda."

"Same here."

Marty gestured to the chair across his desk. "Congratulations on your good news," he said. "We've missed you." Her boss had shown no sign of impatience when she became too sick to work and requested an open-ended sabbatical. From the start of her ordeal, he had never pressured her. One of the very few gifts of getting sick was that it allowed her to discover how much kindness there was in her life. People stepped up to help, to understand or even just to comfort her.

"I've missed you guys, too." Sort of, Miranda thought. She did enjoy her coworkers, and the company had been supportive through her illness. She was better off than many people. At least she had a job.

Still, it wasn't the sort of job she couldn't wait to get to each day. She worked there because it was safe and predictable, not because she loved it.

"You know I've always said it's not the same here without you…" Marty began.

"Uh-oh." She studied his posture, the strained set to his shoulders. "Why does that sound ominous to me?"

He took off his glasses, rubbed his temples. "Miranda, you probably remember that business has been down. Our balance sheets aren't looking too good."

"Are you saying you don't want me back?" Her stomach constricted.

"Of course we do. But…we've budgeted through to the end of the quarter, and…" He shook his head, his kindly face lined with concern. "What I'm saying is, we can't take you back until next quarter. So if something better comes along, I'll understand."

"Oh." She was surprised to feel a small wave of relief rolling through her. "I see."

"Listen, if you need—"

"I'm okay, Marty. I appreciate your honesty."

She left the downtown office feeling supremely…ambivalent. She didn't relish telling Jacob she wasn't going back to work right away. On the other hand, the prospect of extending her sabbatical didn't exactly depress her.

The good news was, she was meeting her two best friends for coffee. Sophie Bellamy, Lucy Rosetta and Miranda had been roommates as undergrads at the University of Washington and they had stayed close ever since. As she walked along First Avenue, Miranda glimpsed herself in the plate-glass windows she passed. Who was that woman? She still didn't know.

They planned to meet at the Café Lucia, an Italian-style espresso bar that belonged to Lucy. The café was tucked in a cobblestone-paved pedestrian alley near the market. On the way, she stopped at the flower stall and picked up a small bouquet to take to Lucy.

The deep aroma of imported Lavazza coffee greeted her, along with the gurgle and hiss of the espresso machine. Two of the café's six tables, with majolica-tiled tops, were occupied. Miranda went to the counter and stood before a display of sfogliatelle and biscotti.

"You look busy," she said.

"Always." Lucy Rosetta beamed as she stepped out from the work area to give Miranda a hug. "I'll fix us a coffee."

Miranda felt better just being in Lucy's presence. Lucy was an expert at priorities. When a friend dropped in, she dropped everything. She brought a tray with two cappuccinos and biscotti and they had a seat together. Lucy had declared this particular table in the café a worry-free zone. In fact, there was a small sign in the middle, next to the flower vase, with WORRY in block letters and a slash through it.

"Sophie just called," Lucy said. "She's running late."

"That's all right. Let me put these flowers in water." Miranda looked around the café. "I'll divvy them up among the tables."

"You don't have to do that," Lucy said.

"It takes thirty seconds," Miranda told her, creating a small arrangement for each table. "Look at the difference it makes."

"You're right, of course," said Lucy. "I wish I had your touch."

Sophie Bellamy joined them, rushing in with her usual burden of briefcase, purse and tote bag. There was a flurry of hugs and greetings, and Sophie requested her usual—a double espresso.

The three of them were an unlikely trio, but their differences made for a lively friendship. Lucy, the creative bohemian, held fast to her dream of running the café. Sophie had the lucrative, high-powered career. Miranda had taken the traditional route to marriage, kids and house with a white picket fence. They used to joke that if they rolled their lives into one, they'd have a woman with a perfect life, living the dream.

They'd stopped joking about that last year. The year Miranda got sick, Sophie's marriage fell apart and Lucy took out a second mortgage to keep her café afloat. Now when you put them together, they were a *Dr. Phil* show.

Miranda got up and hugged her friend. "I'm so glad you're in town."

"Not for long. I'm flying to New York in a couple of hours." Sophie's international-law firm had assigned her to a case that had her commuting to Seattle every other week. "But please," she said. "Tell me something good. I need it."

"I'm done with my treatments," Miranda announced. "The doc gave me my walking papers yesterday. I get to rejoin the human race."

Lucy's face lit up. "That's fantastic—isn't it?"

"Pretty fantastic. For the foreseeable future, I'm a free woman."

Lucy burst into tears. She buried her face in a paper napkin. "Sorry," she said.

"It's all right," Miranda assured her. "I feel too numb to cry. I might later. The crazy thing is," she confessed, "now that I don't have to fight the cancer anymore, I don't know what to do with myself."

"Anything you want," Lucy said with an airy gesture.

"I appreciate the thought, but it's not that simple. My treatment has been my life for the past year now. Now that it's over, I have no life."

"Oh, honey," said Sophie. "You're just shell-shocked, but this is wonderful. Your treatment is done. You have your life back."

"Yes and no. I can't just roll back the past year and go on as if it never happened. I've changed. My...marriage has changed. Our family has changed." There. She'd said it. She had given voice to a dark fear, which, in its own way, was more menacing than cancer.

"So change it back," Lucy said simply. "Now's your chance."

"It's not like everything was so perfect before," Miranda confided. "Jacob wasn't home enough, the kids had their ups and downs, I had the usual troubles with work."

"So now you have a chance to turn your life into something even better than you had before," Sophie pointed out.

Lucy nodded. "She's right, Miss Miranda the miracle girl. What will you do with the rest of your life?"

"This is what I love about you." Miranda took a sip of her cappuccino. "You keep things simple. You're living your dream, Lucy. When we were in college, you always said you wanted a café like the Gambrinus in Naples, and here you are."

"Bless you for saying that. I've got a ways to go before people start comparing this place to the Gambrinus."

Miranda felt better just being with her friends. She was grateful that they were here to listen and talk, even when Lucy probably had a zillion things to do in the café and Sophie had a plane to catch. Sophie was perpetually busy, always on the run.

After college, she'd gone to law school, moved to the East Coast, married, had two kids, made partner—the perfect life.

Last summer, she had divorced.

As always, Sophie was beautiful and dressed for success, but Miranda knew her friend was dealing with the pain and loneliness and upheaval of splitting up with her husband. "How are you and the kids doing?" Miranda asked. Sophie's children, Daisy and Max, were close in age to Valerie and Andrew.

"All right, I think. Daisy's busy applying to colleges this fall. Max is actually doing much better in reading. They're sad about the divorce. What kid wouldn't be?" She brightened a little. "We've got a four-day weekend together over Columbus Day. I'm taking them to this incredible place in the Catskills that belongs to my former in-laws." She sipped her cappuccino. "Sometimes I miss the Bellamys more than I miss Greg."

Miranda heard the pinch of hurt in Sophie's voice when she spoke of her ex-husband's family. Having almost no family of her own, Sophie used to be close to the Bellamys. "I'm not surprised you miss them, Soph."

"More than I ever imagined I would. And they're still so good to me." She blinked fast, close to tears.

Lucy passed her a plate of biscotti. "Aw, Sophie. There's only one thing that makes you more unhappy than being divorced from Greg, and that's being married to him."

"True," she said, visibly trying to shake off the mood. She swirled the biscotti in her cup.

"You kept your married name—Bellamy," Lucy observed.

"With a maiden name like Wiener, can you blame me? Besides, I built a successful law practice around that name and made partner. It's on the letterhead. And there's nothing wrong with the name. The problem was with my marriage."

Miranda felt as if a shadow passed over her heart.

"Sweetie, what is it?" Lucy asked.

Miranda stared at her hands in her lap. These women knew her too well. She took a deep breath and told them what had happened—or, more accurately, what hadn't happened—the previous night. "He said I was sleeping so hard, he didn't want to bother me."

Lucy regarded her thoughtfully. "So how do you feel about that?"

Miranda shook her head. "I feel like a traitor, complaining at all. I mean, Jacob's been great through all of this. But I'm ready to start feeling like a couple again, not patient and nurse."

"Although he makes a very cute male nurse," Lucy pointed out.

"You should tell him," Sophie said. "Sit him down and look him in the eye and explain what you want and need. And while you're at it, ask him what he wants and needs. His answers might surprise you."

"I like that," Lucy said. "How'd you get so smart, Sophie?"

She smiled a bit sadly. "If Greg and I had followed that advice, we might still be married. I think it's easier to be smart about other people's marriages because you don't have to actually do the work." She patted Lucy's hand. "You're the smart one, staying single."

"How come I don't feel smart, then?" Lucy gestured around the café. "I opened this place ten years ago. I know you guys think I'm living the dream, but the truth is, I'm barely staying afloat. Unfortunately, dreams don't tell you how to take care of details like making the books balance."

"Oh, Lucy." Miranda felt frustrated. Here was another thing the illness had taken from her. Forced to focus on her treatment, she'd lacked the time to be a good friend. "Isn't business picking up?"

"I need to make some changes."

"What sort of changes?"

"I'm going to have to share this retail space, lease out half the shop. The rent is killing me, so that's the solution I've come up with."

"Lease it to whom?" asked Sophie.

"Good question. I've thought of a few possibilities—a book and magazine shop would be a good fit. Cards and stationery. Yarn, maybe, or quilting." She glanced at the flowers Miranda had placed on each table. "Hey, maybe a florist."

When Miranda was young, she used to imagine she had a tuning fork inside her, one that would resonate when just the right note struck. She felt that now, a deep vibration of interest at Lucy's words. Out of habit, she dismissed the feeling. "I wish I could help."

"Oh, I'm not asking for help. What I need is a real partnership here. I'm good until the end of the year. Come January, though, something's got to give. I keep hoping the right person will just walk through that door—poof."

Miranda smiled. "So what are you thinking? A café-news-stand?"

"Those are a dime a dozen."

"A café-music store?"

"There's one less than half a block away."

"A café-legal clinic," Sophie said. "That way, I could quit this dumb job and be bohemian with you."

"Except that it's not a dumb job, it's a great one that you love," Miranda pointed out. "Don't you?"

"True," Sophie admitted. "I complain about the travel and so forth, but honestly, sometimes I think it's the one thing that has kept me from going nuts through the separation and divorce."

"My job," Miranda pointed out. "Now, *there's* something. It's the one thing I didn't miss when I was sick."

In college she had studied retail marketing, but had found her passion in a fluffy-sounding elective area—floral design. She used to picture herself amid buckets of cut flowers and greenery, surrounded by beautiful glassware and pottery, creating bouquets to brighten some woman's home, or lift her spirits when she was sad, congratulate her for a job well done, comfort her when she was sick. She would be renowned for her Homecoming corsages.

Unfortunately, self-employment was a dubious prospect, especially for someone with a mortgage and two kids, so the idea remained only a daydream, and a private one at that.

Which was why she surprised herself by saying, "I'm tempted to lease the space myself and open the flower shop I've been thinking about since college."

Sophie and Lucy looked at each other and then back at her. "It's a crazy, brilliant idea and I think you should do it," Sophie said.

"I've always said we should be partners," Lucy reminded her.

"You two." Miranda grinned, grateful to have such wonderful friends. "I'm not even sure I'll be able to get my grown-up job back." And then, without warning, she burst into tears.

To their credit, her friends sat patiently by and waited. Miranda finally pulled out a wad of Kleenex and dried her face. "God, sorry. I totally didn't see that coming."

"What's going on?" asked Lucy. "Really."

Miranda tried to pull herself together. She hoped the other customers and the girl behind the counter hadn't noticed her outburst. She told them about the meeting with Marty and her feeling that she didn't belong in her cubicle at Urban Ice anymore. "Lucy. Sophie," she asked urgently. "What if there was some cosmic reason I got cancer? That reason being I'm supposed to change my life in some way?"

"See, that's just what I was saying," Lucy said. "It's a chance to make a big change."

"It's not just the job," Miranda said. "I suppose the one thing that's not fixed is what this disease has done to my family. I feel horrible, like an ingrate, because I shouldn't be thinking about what's wrong. But there's...a sense of loss. I knew this whole experience would change me, but I saw the surgery—the loss of my breast and my hair—coming. I never predicted the loss of my family, though. I mean, we still live under the same roof, but last night it all hit home. We feel like strangers to one another. The kids have retreated, and Jacob's buried himself in work."

Sophie took her hand. "Not good," she said.

"I know. It feels like a hole in my heart."

"And I'm here to tell you, don't ignore that feeling. Because one day you might wake up and realize you've forgotten how to love that great guy you married."

Miranda's blood chilled. Though she realized Sophie was talking about her own situation, she understood the warning.

"I'm afraid," she confessed to her friends. "I've been pretending I'm not, but I am. The thing I fear most is not the disease coming back, but that I'll never be able to reclaim my family."

"Take it easy on yourself," Lucy advised her. "You built that marriage and family over sixteen years. You're not about to let it be taken away in just one."

Miranda nodded resolutely. "Easy enough to say, but you know what my family is like. We're all running in different directions. Getting us together is like herding cats. We're all on fast-forward. What I need is a Pause button."

"I think I can help with that," Sophie said. "I have an idea for you, Miranda. How about taking your family away for a little R & R?"

"I'd love to," Miranda said. "I can't remember the last time we went on vacation." She frowned, feeling a new sort of bleakness unrelated to being ill. Their lives simply weren't organized for a family vacation, even when she was well. Weekends were for catching up on the things she'd failed to finish during the week. School vacations were simply occasions when she and Jacob had to make child-care arrangements for the kids until Valerie was deemed old enough to watch her brother.

"Sometimes Jacob and I talk about piling everyone in the car and taking them to the seashore for a weekend," Miranda said. "But frankly, it's going to take a little more than a weekend. And I know what Jacob will say—we simply can't afford some big family vacation."

"I hear that," Lucy said. "I read somewhere that the average family vacation has shrunk to four days a year."

Sophie placed her briefcase on the table. "So here's my idea." She pulled some brochures from her briefcase and placed them on the tiled tabletop. "I learned about this from a client of mine. It's an organization they have in Canada, called Cottage Dreams. It was created so that cancer survivors could spend some time away with their families after treatment. It gives them a chance to recover and look to the future once again. Anyway, I wanted to tell you about it because even though we don't have anything like this in the States, I had an inspiration. I started thinking what it would be like to be a host family. And I have a proposal to make you."

Miranda glanced at the information on the table. The glossy pictures of lakeside cottages looked impossibly romantic and remote.

"Remember I mentioned that Greg's family has a summer camp in the Catskills," Sophie continued. "Camp Kioga, on Willow Lake. It's been in the Bellamy family for years, and they renovated it last summer. There's a perfect, perfect cottage that's completely empty this time of year and I've asked the Bellamys if your family could use it for a week. They didn't hesitate for an instant. They would love it if you'd come."

"Oh, good Lord, yes," Lucy added. "It's brilliant."

Sophie was never one to beat around the bush. "I think you and your family should do it as soon as possible. Greg's family was wonderful when I asked them, and they really want you to use the cottage."

"It's a great idea," Lucy said. "Miranda, you finally got off the roller coaster. Just a week at this cottage could change your whole perspective."

Miranda felt a tug of yearning, as though something inside her signaled *yes*. There were a dozen things she could say— probably should say. "It sounds like heaven," was what came out.

Sophie and Lucy beamed at each other. Miranda knew then that this was a planned ambush. Her friends had intended all along to present this idea to her. She didn't mind, though. The idea of a hideaway with her family seemed magical to her. But also…impossible.

"…to JFK, and then you rent a car from there. It's about a three-hour drive through some of the prettiest countryside you've ever seen," Sophie was saying, and Miranda realized she had drifted off to the realm of fantasy. The mention of travel arrangements brought her crashing back to the real world.

"Unfortunately that's probably going to be a deal killer," she confessed. She told herself that these were her two best friends;

she could tell them anything. But still it pained her to admit that she and Jacob weren't in such great shape financially. "Airfare for four makes it a bit too rich for my blood," she confessed.

"He*llo?*" Sophie gave a dry laugh of disbelief. "In case you haven't noticed, I've been commuting between New York and Seattle for months. I've got enough frequent-flier miles to fly a small army there and back."

"I couldn't take —"

"Maybe not," Sophie interrupted. "But I can give."

"I don't get it. Why would you do this?"

"Because you're my friend and I love you, and I know you'd do the same for me."

"But the Bellamys—they don't even know me."

"That doesn't matter," Sophie said, her expression softening. "It's…um…I suppose they realize that it's a fragile time for a family. Ours as well as yours."

Miranda nodded. What an enchanting, impossible idea. There was no way Jacob would ever go for it.

# CHAPTER
## ◦∽FIVE∽◦

A week away in the wilderness seemed like the most remote of possibilities for Miranda and her family. Yet the more she thought about her conversation with Sophie, the more she was convinced that this was what her family needed. Healing time away.

It was so very simple, yet so vital. Miranda was already aware that recovering from this devastating illness was much more than just a physical process. There were emotional and spiritual components that were just as important. She also knew that being in a natural environment, far from everyday distractions, played a crucial role in healing, too.

When she got home, she changed into dungarees and gum

boots, and headed out into the garden. There was something that happened to her out here, digging in the dirt, working with her plants. She gained a sense of her own worth, felt a connection to the earth and to nature. Just being outside, breathing the air and contemplating the gardening chores ahead felt right.

She didn't make much headway before fatigue set in, but she refused to get discouraged. She had cleaned up a patch of earth, planted some cosmos seeds that would bloom in the spring, thrown a barrowful of clippings into the compost bin. It was enough. She felt satisfied. But...lonely.

She welcomed the shush of the school-bus brakes at the corner bus stop. Valerie would be home in a few minutes. Miranda shook out her gloves and removed her boots, then went inside to fix their favorite snack—chips and salsa, and limeade to drink.

"Hey, thanks," Valerie said, putting down her backpack. "I'm starved."

They sat together at the counter, nibbling the chips. Miranda told Valerie about Sophie's offer. "So what do you think?" she asked. "Can you see our family doing something like this?"

Valerie laughed without humor. "Come on, Mom. You think the whole world is going to stop for a week while we go commune with nature?"

"Maybe we're the ones who need to stop, not the world."

"Dad'll never go for it."

"I'm asking *you*. Would you go for it?"

Valerie shrugged, putting on her I-don't-care attitude, the

one she'd worn for the past year. Then, keeping the blasé mask in place, she said, "Pete asked me to Homecoming."

A year ago, those exact words had elicited delight from both mother and daughter, because a year ago, cancer was a remote concept, not a real threat. Then came Miranda's diagnosis, a bomb dropped on the unsuspecting family. Being sick had brought all Miranda's deepest, fiercest mothering instincts to the surface. She'd wanted to protect her children at all costs. She'd even tried to reschedule her surgery so it wouldn't coincide with her daughter's first formal dance. The two surgical teams wouldn't hear of it, though, and cancer had scored its first victory against her.

Over the past year, everything they did and said to one another took on a special significance. Faced with the possibility of not seeing her children into adulthood, Miranda worked hard—too hard—to impart lessons or extract meaning from every possible situation. She caught herself working so hard at mothering that she forgot to enjoy her children.

So now, when Valerie made her casual announcement, Miranda had to tamp down the urge to jump on the opportunity, insist that her daughter go this year. She restrained herself from marching Valerie to Pete's house to accept the invitation.

One of the things she had to avoid with her kids during the year of her illness was doing all the emotional work for them. Part of growing up was figuring out how to navigate their way through life on their own. And there, beneath the surface of that excellent parenting advice, was the unspoken terror: She had better teach them independence from her now, because she could be gone this time next year.

With great care, she took a drink of her limeade and set down the glass. "Oh?" she asked. Just that. Nothing more.

"I'm going to tell him no," Valerie said.

"So you haven't given him an answer yet."

"I was just so...so shocked when he asked that I blurted out that I'd let him know. God. I should have told him no right then and there."

"But you didn't."

"I will," Valerie said softly. "I wanted to...think about it a little bit." The expression on her daughter's face said it all. She wanted to go to Homecoming, just like any girl her age.

Before bed that night, Miranda felt inexplicably nervous with Jacob. Only tonight, it wasn't about making love. It was a terrible feeling in her stomach—the sense that she had drifted so far from him that he was now a stranger. He lay in bed, the pillows propped behind him as he tallied the last of the day's sales.

"Always working," she said, leaning down to place a kiss on his head.

He offered a distracted smile. "I don't mind. You know that. How did your meeting with Marty go today?"

She took a deep breath. "He was really nice, as always. Really understanding."

"So, did the two of you..." Jacob hesitated. It broke her heart, the way he resisted pressuring her.

"Marty would be just as glad if I waited until next quarter. For budget reasons, he says." She watched his face. Impulsively, she reached out, grazed the back of her hand along his cheek. "If you think that's okay."

"Sure, honey." There was not a single beat of hesitation in his reply, and she loved him for that. Then the worry moved in like clouds across the sun. "Are you all right?"

She smiled. In the past year, she had learned that "all right" was a relative phrase. Sometimes "all right" meant her postsurgery drainage tubes were working properly. Other times it meant she had lost the last of her hair, or that the gel for her radiation burns was having a soothing effect.

Taking a deep breath, she said, "Better than all right after yesterday's visit with Dr. Turabian."

He waited. "Yes?" he prompted, somehow knowing there was more.

She got it out, all in a rush. "I want us to go away together, the four of us."

The worry darkened his face even more, but he quickly shook it off. "I guess we could drive down to the shore for a weekend—"

"That's not what I'm talking about." She told him about Sophie's idea. "The Bellamy family has made an incredibly generous offer. They've got a cabin at a place called Willow Lake—"

"Offer? God, Miranda. What are we, a charity case now?"

She ached for him. Her proud husband. Sometimes, though,

SUSAN WIGGS

his pride blinded him to the bigger picture. "That's not what this is about," she said. "It's not a handout."

"We don't even know these people—"

"We know Sophie. Jacob, there's still so much we need to do. This past year has fractured our family. It's devastated our finances and wrung out our emotions. All the pain of the surgery and treatment was nothing. I could deal with it. But I can't deal with losing my family. Sometimes I think if I hurt any more, I'll break into pieces."

He set aside his paperwork. "Honey, you're not losing us."

"But everything's changed. The kids, you and me, *us*. We need to do this," she insisted. "It hit home yesterday, when I got back from my appointment. Just because I've finished treatment doesn't mean all is well. This family's been damaged, Jacob. It's had its heart ripped out, and all four of us are suffering. We're in a post-traumatic state."

"You just finished," he pointed out. "We'll adjust, but we need time. I feel better already, knowing the worst is behind us."

"We need more than time. We're strangers, Jacob. Andrew spends all his time creating a virtual family with some computer game. Valerie is never home, and she's completely changed the kids she hangs out with. You're always working. And we—" She didn't want to go there, not right away. "I miss you, Jacob. I miss us, together. I miss the way we used to be."

"A week in somebody's lakeside cottage is not going to be a cure-all," he said.

"It's not," she agreed. "And it isn't supposed to be. What it

84

could be, I think, is a start to the healing this whole family needs. We can't go on the way we have been. We're strangers under the same roof that used to house a happy family. We need this time away—from work and school and stress. I know it's only temporary, but we'll have a chance to focus on each other, with no distractions or interruptions."

"Honey, I do see your point," he said, "but unfortunately, we can't swing it right now. The kids have school, and I've got some major surveys coming up at work—"

"Jacob, we're always going to be busy. It's the nature of our family. I accept that. What I hope you'll accept is making time for what's important to you, even if it doesn't seem like the most responsible course of action. I already talked to Andrew's teacher and Valerie's adviser. They both agreed to put the kids on independent study for the days we're away."

"When I'm not working, I'm not earning anything," he reminded her, as if she could ever forget. She could tell he was struggling to be patient.

"I'm aware of that. We'll just have to deal with it."

"Miranda, sweetheart, maybe we can plan something for the holidays or next summer." He took her by the shoulders and kissed her forehead. "Right now, we can't afford to go."

She blinked back tears. "We can't afford not to."

# CHAPTER
## ∽ SIX ∽

"**O**kay, this is not what I generally think of when someone says New York." Miranda gazed in wonder out the window of the rental car. For miles around, she could see nothing but rolling hills draped in a patchwork of glorious fall color, each gentle rise cleft by a narrow country road or rocky stream. Occasionally they passed through quaint towns with white-painted houses and picket fences, funky resale and outdoor shops, colonial-style village greens and church spires.

"Me neither," said Jacob, behind the wheel of the rented Ford Escape. "Pretty up here."

The kids were asleep in the backseat. The red-eye flight from

Seattle to JFK had made for a very short night, and the drive up into the Catskills had taken its toll on Andrew and Valerie.

Miranda reached over and patted Jacob's leg. Given his worries about their financial situation, his agreeing to take time out from work was a big step for him. He had been good-natured and positive throughout the whirlwind preparations that kicked in once they decided to go for it. Miranda knew him well, though. She knew he lay awake at night, worrying and crunching numbers in his head.

A familiar twinge of anger pinched her heart. Not at him. In the very worst moments of her illness, she certainly had been angry at Jacob. Ridiculously, insanely furious at him. How could he stand by her bed looking so young and healthy and handsome while she lay on rubber sheets, bald and gray-faced, her body misshapen by surgery and swelling, and dripping drains sprouting from her body? It wasn't fair.

Yet her anger at Jacob was always fleeting, an irrational flash of emotion. This man was the love of her life. More than once, he had broken down and vowed that he would willingly trade places with her, take her pain away if he could. And he meant it. She knew that. He made her ashamed that she got angry at him.

They drove through Kingston, designated by an historic marker as the first capital of the state of New York. They stopped to fill up the gas tank and drive past the regional hospital. Miranda had spoken at length with her doctor, and she didn't anticipate any problems, but he advised her to make sure there was a hospital nearby.

Just in case.

In contrast to the charm of the river-fed hills that surrounded the region, the hospital was sleek and modern, its glass-and-brick edifice sharp against the blue autumn sky.

"Want to stop in?" Jacob suggested. "Familiarize yourself with the place?"

"No, thanks. I've seen enough of the inside of hospitals to last a lifetime." She had a love-hate relationship with them. On the one hand, the hospital was the place that had saved her life; it was filled with caring, dedicated people. On the other, it was a repository of sickness and grief, and represented the terrible threat and stark consequences of her disease.

Valerie woke up as they drove westward along a scenic state road. She blinked at the dazzling golden autumn light. "Are we there yet?"

Miranda twisted around on the seat to look back at her. "Just about. Take a look outside. The scenery is absolutely beautiful here."

"I'm not into scenery."

Miranda ignored her daughter's sour attitude. "Check this out—a covered bridge."

"Cute."

"Wake up your brother and tell him to look at the bridge."

Valerie nudged Andrew with her foot. "Hey, geek-boy. Mom says wake up and check out the bridge."

"Back off," he groaned, wiping his face with his sleeve. Then he looked outside gamely enough. "Cool."

Jacob slowed down as they crossed the bridge. Briefly, they plunged into shadow, and the wooden bridge deck creaked beneath the tires of the car. When they emerged on the other side, they were greeted by a painted sign that said, Welcome to Avalon. Population 1347.

"Looks like a happening place," Valerie said.

"Come on, now," Jacob cajoled her. "At least try to act as if you're enjoying this."

"Oh. Okay. It's charming, like something out of a Washington Irving story. And the turning leaves are beautiful. And, gee, did you know that according to legend, Avalon is the name of the place King Arthur went to die? There. Is that cheerful enough for you?"

"Nice," Jacob murmured, gritting his teeth.

"At least we got you out of a week of school," Miranda pointed out.

"I didn't ask to get out of school," Valerie said. "And I've got that big honkin' assignment due when I get back, so it's not like I'm actually getting a break."

Valerie's teachers and adviser had been very supportive all through Miranda's illness, and this week was no exception. "You'll be back just in time for Homecoming," Mrs. Pratt had pointed out, handing Miranda the paperwork for independent study.

Valerie hadn't met her adviser's eyes. She'd simply mumbled her thanks and ducked out of the school office. This week she had just four things to do. She had to read "The Specter Bridegroom" by Washington Irving. She had to write an essay, do a math assignment and a biology project on the structure of mosses and lichens.

They made a stop at a grocery store, where they bought a week's worth of provisions, including things for the barbecue and for s'mores, since they were planning to build a campfire by the lake. Driving through the beautiful small town, they made one final stop at a family-owned place called the Sky River Bakery, where they treated themselves to jam kolaches, homemade bread and freshly squeezed cider from a local farm. With Miranda reading from the printed directions they'd been sent, they drove along the river road, resplendent now with fall color. A few miles outside town, they were plunged into wilderness along a narrow road that followed the curve of the Schuyler River.

The colors of the turning leaves ranged from pale buttery yellow to deep fiery pink, so vivid that, coupled with the blue of the sky, they hurt the eyes. Miranda found herself blinking back tears. I'm so glad I'm getting to see this, she thought.

She reached over and switched on the radio. The tail end of "I'm Gonna Be (500 Miles)" by the Proclaimers was playing and she glanced across at Jacob. She could tell by the funny little smile on his face that he remembered the song the way she did. He used to belt it out to her, complete with phony Scottish accent, in the mornings when they were younger. Much, much younger. Young enough to risk being late for work because they needed to stay in bed just a little longer.

She hadn't thought about those days in quite a while. She

hadn't thought about much of anything in quite a while. She'd been too consumed by her illness—first, learning all she could about it, then choosing a course of treatment, then following that course even if it killed her.

That was chemo, she recalled. It was designed to kill things off. In destroying the cancer cells, it tended to take other things with it—hair, eyelashes, energy, appetite. Dignity. You couldn't very well hold on to your dignity when you had nine different doctors feeling you up.

"We're supposed to be watching for a wooden sign on a tree," she said. "That's where we turn."

"Spotted it," Andrew said. Wonder of wonders, he even sounded slightly excited. "There, on the left."

The rustic sign pointed out an even narrower gravel road that led them uphill. They passed a No Trespassing—Private Property sign, and the last of civilization fell away. Here, it was hard to believe they were not all that far from town. It felt as if they were the first pioneers, blazing a trail into unknown territory.

"Looks like we've found it," Jacob announced.

Miranda sat forward, peering out the window at the rustic timber archway with Camp Kioga Established 1932 spelled out in wrought-iron twigs. Past the gateway, the camp opened up before them, a breathtaking compound with rustic buildings, broad meadows and sports courts. Cabins and bungalows bordered a placid, pristine lake—Willow Lake, glittering like a sapphire and crowned by a tiny island with a gazebo.

Jacob parked in front of the main pavilion, a huge timber structure marked by flags flying from three poles in front. There was a railed deck projecting out over Willow Lake. According to Sophie, the pavilion, with its huge dining hall, used to be the main social center back when the camp was in operation.

They got out of the car, and everyone was quiet for a few minutes, trying to take it all in. Miranda pictured the camp in its heyday, when families from the city flocked to the mountains. The air smelled impossibly sweet, of fresh wind and water and the dry, crisp aroma of turning leaves. The reflection of the colorful trees in the water gleamed. Miranda nearly flinched at all the beauty.

All but one of the buildings had been closed and shuttered for the season. Jacob pointed out a large, well-kept cottage set off by itself at the edge of the lake. There were fresh flowers on the front porch and a Welcome banner hanging under the eaves. "I guess that's where we're staying," Jacob said.

The digital photos Sophie had sent them didn't do the place justice. It was a beautiful timbered lodge, solid with the passage of years. The porch had a swing, two rocking chairs and a hanging bed suspended from chains. A pier jutted out over the lake; tied to it were a kayak and a catboat with its colorful sail furled like a barber's pole.

Inside, the cottage was intimate, with cozy reading nooks, an upstairs loft under slanting ceilings and dormer windows, a river-stone fireplace. The main bedroom featured a bed with a birch-twig headboard and a bathroom with a deep, claw-foot-tub. Everywhere, Miranda found small touches that helped her understand why it was so hard for Sophie to say goodbye to the Bellamy family—a collection of postcards dating back fifty years and more, framed photos from the era when Camp Kioga was a bungalow colony, pictures in handcrafted frames, vintage posters of the Adirondack Great Camps. Each bed was covered in a handmade quilt, and there was a cedar chest filled with colorful striped Hudson's Bay blankets.

The cottage had been readied for them with thoughtful care. Kindling and firewood were stacked by the fireplace and wood-stove. There was a crockery vase of dried flowers on the table and jars of colored leaves on the windowsills. They found a collection of art supplies and a guest book on the coffee table, opened to a blank page. On the scrubbed pine dining table, they found a handwritten note of welcome, signed by Jane and Charles Bellamy. There was also a collection of literature about the camp, an area nature guide and trail map.

"Wow," said Miranda, taking it all in. "This is paradise."

"Can I go look around outside?" Andrew asked.

"Sure. Don't get lost in the woods."

"Mo-om." Andrew ran out of the house and pounded up and down the dock, then raced into the woods behind the lodge. His small, compact body expressed exuberance with every move he made and it was a joy watching him. For the first time since this ordeal had started, Miranda looked at her son and had the sense that everything was going to be all right.

She felt both gratitude and nervousness as they brought in

their things. She was grateful for the opportunity they had been given but suddenly and unexpectedly anxious about the unbroken string of days stretching out before them.

"Well?" asked Jacob. "Is this what you had in mind?"

She smiled at him, still nervous, then looked at Valerie. "Even nicer. And you know what's crazy?"

Valerie nodded. "No TV. No phone. No computer. That's crazy."

Miranda tried to shrug off her daughter's glum sentiment. "To me, what's crazy is that I'm having trouble remembering who I used to be…what I used to be like before I got sick. I got so used to running from one appointment to the next, and waiting around for tests and monitoring myself that I lost myself. I lost who I really am. So this week, my job is to find that person again."

Valerie raised her eyebrows. "Are you sure you quit the anxiety medication, Mom?"

"Very funny." Miranda had stopped taking it, and a part of her missed the way the prescription pill softened the harsh edges of her worry. Another part of her felt triumphant. That bit by bit she was reclaiming control of her life. Relearning how to manage her emotions on her own was a huge part of that.

They spent the day settling in and exploring the camp. Miranda took pictures of everything, capturing a loon in flight, the sun filtering through the forest, her children's faces, her husband turning to grin at her while leaves fell all around him. Dinner that night was a simple affair—spaghetti, salad and bread, ice cream for dessert. Afterward, she and Jacob took their glasses of wine outside to sit on the porch and watch the sun go down across the lake. In the yard in front of the cottage, the kids played badminton, their voices echoing brightly off the water. They played until it was too dark to see the birdie and the first stars of twilight appeared. A chorus of peepers rose from the reeds down by the lakeshore.

Swaying slightly on the porch swing, Miranda felt a rare sense of contentment as she looked around at each of their faces. "Just let me savor this for a minute. I have all my favorites right here with me, right in this moment."

"Not Gretel." Andrew swatted the ground with his badminton racket.

"Nice," Valerie muttered. "Way to go, moron."

"Well, it's true," he grumbled.

"I miss Gretel, too," Miranda said, wishing the mood could have lasted a few more minutes. "Come on. We'd better go inside before the mosquitoes find us."

Jacob did a surprisingly good job making a fire in the wood-burning stove. Once that chore was over, though, everyone seemed to be at a loss.

"So what, exactly, are we supposed to do?" Valerie asked.

Andrew rummaged through his backpack. "Good question," he said.

"We sit around and talk, or draw and paint, play cards and board games, or read, or…just be together as a family," Miranda said. "Listen, this is not going to work at all if we don't make it work." She looked at Jacob for support, but he didn't seem to be listening. He was standing at the big picture window, staring out at the darkening lake. Tension seemed to hover around him.

The kids decided on their own to get going on the assignments they'd brought from home. It was amazing, Miranda thought, how interesting they found schoolwork now that they didn't have a TV or computer.

Jacob found a flashlight by the front door. "I think I'll hike over to the main lodge and check messages," he said, heading outside again. Camp Kioga had one phone, they'd been told, and there wasn't a cell-phone signal in a five-mile radius.

"Jacob," said Miranda, following him out. She bit her tongue to keep from saying more.

He clearly knew what she was thinking. "It's our livelihood, Miranda. It would be irresponsible of me to lose an account because I was playing *Last of the Mohicans.*"

"Is that what you think this is?" she asked. "Some drama we're playing? God, Jacob. We haven't done anything as a family in over a year. This has nothing to do with drama or role-playing or fulfilling some kind of fantasy."

He held up both hands, palms out, in a gesture of surrender.

"Okay, sorry. You're right. We need to be here, and from here on out, I'll try to park my worries at the door."

She knew he was sincere as he spoke the words, but she also knew he'd continue to worry about work. He would just do so quietly, not sharing his concerns with her. She sighed. "Is this what the whole week is going to be like?" She picked up an embroidered pillow and tossed it at him. "I miss the way we used to fight."

"Come again?"

"You heard me. Before I got sick, we'd fight like equals instead of you backing down as soon as you see me getting upset."

"I don't—"

"And then we'd get furious with each other, and then the fight would end and we would forgive each other and then we would make love and—"

"Could we maybe just skip the fighting part?" He slipped his arms around her from behind. "Maybe just cut to the chase?"

She laughed and turned to face him. "You can chase me anytime."

He switched off the flashlight and kissed her, and finally, she had the sense that they were making progress.

# CHAPTER
## ⟢ SEVEN ⟣

"**I**'m bored," said Andrew the next day, coming down from the sleeping loft.

Miranda was sitting in a window seat, idly drawing in a sketchbook. She looked over at her son and smiled. "Good morning to you, too. Is your sister still sleeping?"

"Of course. She'll probably sleep the whole time we're here."

"You and I are the early birds of the family," Miranda said. "We always have been." To her surprise, Jacob, too, was still sound asleep. Back home, he was up before the sun every day. In fact, when she'd awakened this morning and seen him lying next to her, she'd been startled. She couldn't remember the last time she'd awakened to a warm, sleeping husband.

"So we've got art supplies, blank journals, board games, decks of cards, sports equipment," she pointed out. "Not to mention that." Her gesture indicated Willow Lake, which looked mystical and gorgeous, with a light mist swirling across the surface and the sun breaking through the trees. "I don't think being bored is an option."

"I can't help it," he said. "I don't feel like doing anything."

"Draw something," she suggested. She turned the sketchbook so he could see. Using colored pencils, she had done a passable sketch of the view from the window. It was no work of art, but when she'd looked out the window at the misty lake and the fall color, she'd been possessed by a desire to draw it.

"That's really good," Andrew said.

"It's really not, but you're nice to say so. I took a lot of art classes when I was in college."

"Why?"

"Because I loved it." The words were out before Miranda had a chance to think about what she was saying. Her degree was in marketing, which she didn't love. She'd chosen that because it was practical. Something that would help her get a job after college. All her adult life, she had made choices based on expedience rather than passion.

She tore the drawing out of the sketchbook and wrote her name with a flourish in the bottom right-hand corner of the page. "I'm going to take this home. It'll remind me of this trip every time I look at it. Here, your turn."

Andrew looked dubious as he took the sketchbook from her. "I don't know what to draw."

"Draw something from your imagination."

"Like what?"

Her son, she reminded herself, was the most concrete thinker she knew. "Draw the first thing you thought of when you woke up this morning."

"Taking a leak?"

"Okay, the second thing."

He looked out the window, his face solemn. "That would be the same thing I think of every time I wake up."

"What's that?"

"Gretel."

Her heart lurched. "Maybe you should draw her, then."

He picked out a brown pencil and stared at the blank page. "That'll just make me sad."

"You look kind of sad now," Miranda pointed out. "Do you think it'll make you sadder?"

He thought about that for a moment. "I don't think I could get any sadder than I already am."

Miranda nodded. "I'm sad about Gretel, too. I miss her so much."

"You do?"

"Of course I do. I adored Gretel. It was sad to see her get old and sick, but when I think about her, I think about what a happy dog she was, and how happy she made us while she was here, and all the happy memories I have of her time with us.

Tell you what. You sit here and draw a picture of anything you want, and I'll fix breakfast for us. Sound good?"

He nodded, and she moved to the kitchen to fix his favorite—cornflakes with a banana, and honey drizzled on top. She glanced at Andrew, who had quickly become absorbed in his drawing. Good, she thought. Creative expression was beneficial in ways that couldn't be measured. She just knew it was true. When she drew or arranged flowers or even hummed a song out of tune, just the act of doing it was soothing.

She took her time making breakfast, wanting to give him plenty of space for drawing. After a while, she brought two bowls of cereal to the table with a bottle of milk.

"Hungry now?" she asked.

"Starving," he said without looking up. He added a few more flourishes to his drawing, then angled the sketchbook to show her. "This," he said with a chuckle, "was kind of fun to draw, but it's really bad."

"How can it be bad if you had fun drawing it?" Miranda looked at the picture. "And how can it be bad if it's Gretel?"

"It doesn't even look like her," he complained.

"Sure it does. It looks like a smiling, cartoon Gretel. Now, come and get your breakfast."

He wrote his name in the bottom right-hand corner of the picture, just as Miranda had. Then he came to the table. "You're having the same thing I am."

"Yep."

"I didn't know you liked cornflakes with banana and honey."

"I didn't used to. I've decided I need to try something new every day, even if it's just something minor, like cereal."

"Why?"

She took a bite of cereal and chewed it thoughtfully before answering. "Trying new things is good. It means you're moving forward."

He shrugged. "I guess."

They finished their cereal and put the dishes in the sink. Glancing at Andrew, she could see the "I'm bored" cloud creeping across his face. "Tell you what," she suggested. "How about we go for a hike?"

"A hike to where?"

Miranda paused. Not too long ago, she got tired just going up the Harbor Steps in Seattle. How would she manage this?

Steeling her will, she indicated the array of trail maps the Bellamys had left for them. "We can just pick something. There's a mountain we could climb—Saddle Mountain. On the way down, we'll pass a waterfall called Meerskill Falls. Sound okay?"

Another shrug. "I guess."

"Don't wet yourself with enthusiasm, kiddo."

They left a note—illustrated with Andrew's silly drawings— and put some bottles of water and PowerBars into a day pack. The trail up Saddle Mountain was well marked, winding through the breathtakingly beautiful forest. Miranda took it all in, the crisp scent of the air, the rustle of fallen leaves on the forest floor, the fecund aroma of plant life. It didn't take long to climb the mountain. The Catskills were old, gentle rises in the earth, and the trail curving up its side an easy walk. Even so, she had to stop and catch her breath; Andrew was heartbreakingly patient.

"I love this," she said as they reached the summit and headed down the other side. "I love being out in the woods. I love it even more because you're with me."

"Uh-huh." Andrew looked pleased. "I guess it's okay."

"Okay." She imitated his tone. "Here you are, playing hooky from school for a week to come to this incredible place, and it's just okay?"

He didn't seem to be listening. He was looking past her at something on the trail. "Whoa," he said.

She heard the rush of the falls below and moved ahead, eager to have a look. It was just beautiful, a small pool formed by the waterfall. The rocks had been smoothed by the water constantly pouring down on them. Miranda felt drawn to the place, mesmerized by the beauty. The water was perfectly clear, its motion throwing rainbows against the backdrop of rock. Thick mosses and ferns fringed the edges, lush from the microclimate created by the ever-present falling water. Taking out her camera, she veered off the path to get some pictures. She hoped the rainbows would show up in the pictures.

"Come check this out," she called to Andrew. He probably couldn't hear her, though, over the sound of the water.

She took some pictures and then put the camera in the backpack, because a fine mist sprayed everything in the immediate area. There was something almost magical about standing here, on this rock, with a cloud of mist rising up around her. She felt strong and hopeful, and the fine spray on her face felt impossibly soft and gentle.

I'm so glad to be alive, she thought. So glad to be standing here in this place.

"...are you?" Andrew's voice, all but drowned by the roar of the falls, stirred her from the moment.

"Over here," she called, heading back toward the main path. "I wanted to get some pictures of—Andrew?"

He was standing alone in the middle of the trail, his eyes wide with panic as he looked around, yelling, "Mom! Where are you!"

"Hey!" she called back, hurrying over to him. "Hey, buddy, I'm right here."

"Mom!" And then he was hugging her hard, burying his face against her shoulder. "Mom, where did you go? I couldn't find you."

He was crying. Andrew almost never cried; he'd left that behind like the toys of his childhood, but he was crying now, hard.

"I'm right here," she said, closing her eyes and holding him.

"You just...disappeared. Why didn't you say something?"

"I'm sorry, Andrew. I thought you were right behind me."

"I wasn't. I left the trail to get some pictures, and then I looked up and you were gone. I thought you'd fallen or that you were lost."

"I'm truly sorry," she repeated. "I'll be more careful from now on. I promise."

He seemed a little embarrassed by his outburst as he stepped back and scrubbed at his face with his sleeves. "Yeah, okay," he said.

"Andrew, I know this whole year has been terrible for you—"

"Mom."

"No, listen. I know you hate talking about this, but that's one of the reason's we came here." This was perfect, she realized. Here they were in the middle of nowhere. He couldn't retreat into his computer world. He had to listen.

"I don't see why we have to talk about anything." His chin jutted out, stoic resentment banishing his tears.

"Because we have lots to talk about," she said. "This family has spent a whole year being worried and scared and I don't know about you, but I'm ready to get over it." She knew the real reason he was so upset had nothing to do with hiking in the woods. "Andrew, I made a mistake just now," she said. "I should have made absolutely certain you saw where I went. I'm sorry."

"Oh, boy. Now you sound like Barbara," he said. Barbara Mills was the medical family therapist they'd been seeing.

"I'm trying to sound like your mom, but I'm out of practice. Anyway," she went on, "here's the deal. I used to wish I could be exactly like the mom in your story game. The mom with the perfect health and the strength of Hercules and the superpowers. The mom who will never die. That's who I wanted to be for you."

She smiled, took out the water bottles. "I don't really want that anymore," she continued. "Not at all. I want to be myself, and I am *so* not perfect. But I am what I am—your mom, warts and all."

"You have warts, too?"

Laughing, she ruffled his hair. "It's just an expression. What I mean is, I'll never be that perfect video mom, and that's actually a good thing. Sometimes I think it's the things that aren't perfect that make a person so easy to love."

"So, like, when I bring home a really bad report card, you'll be okay with that?" There was a teasing note in his voice.

"I'll be okay with you no matter what," she clarified. "That's the point I'm trying to make. I really would like to guarantee that you'll never lose me, ever, but that would be wrong of me. What I can guarantee is that I'll always love you, and I'll never be perfect, but I'll never stop trying. How's that?"

He was quiet for a while. He leaned down, picked up one of the rounded white quartz pebbles that lined the gorge. He put the rock in his pocket. "Sounds good to me."

She studied him for a long moment, seeing a boy who was growing up, a boy who still needed his mother. "I love you, you know," she reminded him.

"Yeah," he said, then flashed her a smile. "Me, too."

They started walking slowly down the trail together.

# CHAPTER
## ～ EIGHT ～

**M**iranda was on the porch swing, intermittently dozing and reading a book, enjoying the warmth of the Indian summer sun. Jacob had taken Andrew fishing, and though she couldn't see them, she could hear the sounds of their laughter carrying across the water. Down by the dock, Valerie was checking the rigging of the catboat, singing along with the tunes coming from her iPod.

It was a moment of supreme contentment for Miranda, something she'd rarely felt this past year, but a feeling that crept up on her frequently here at Willow Lake. She loved the slow, dreamy rhythm of their days, the delicious simplicity of having nothing to do.

It was their fourth day at Camp Kioga, and things were going better than she'd expected. The shock of being deprived of phone, TV and computers had worn off. In fact, they'd amazed themselves with their own inventiveness. None of them could deny the charm of sitting around the fire in the evening, playing Parcheesi or Scrabble. Yesterday, Andrew had found a book of ghost stories, and Jacob had treated them to a spooky reading of a tale by Edgar Allan Poe. With each passing hour, it seemed, they were acclimating to the place and to each other. It was a magical time, remarkably undisturbed.

Miranda wasn't idle, though. Whether she carried it out or not, she had made a plan for herself when she got back to Seattle. She wanted to pursue the partnership with Lucy. The prospect of doing something so risky and entrepreneurial was frightening. But after surviving the past year, she was intimately familiar with risk and fright, and nothing could daunt her anymore. Nothing, she thought, except presenting her idea to Jacob.

"Ready," Valerie called out from the dock. "I think I've got all the rigging done."

Miranda set aside her book and headed down to join her daughter. "I have a confession to make," she said as they pushed the catboat away from the dock. The little wooden sailboat thumped against the pilings and listed in the water while Miranda pushed at the tiller.

"What's that?" Valerie asked. She leaned back to study the single gaff-rigged sail. The boat inched forward, the sail hanging slack.

"I have no idea what I'm doing," Miranda said.

Valerie twisted around to look at her, clumsy in the bulky life jacket. "Now you tell me. You mean you don't know how to sail this thing?"

"In theory, I do. I was on the high-school sailing team, but we used Lasers. This is just a bit different. We'll figure it out, though." Miranda injected a cheerful note into her voice. "There's a nice breeze. It should be enough."

The catboat was beamy, with a shallow draft and center-board. The wind was adequate for a sail this size. How hard could it be?

"Hey, Mom." Valerie swiveled back around. "It's working."

She was right. The wind took the sail, and Miranda showed her how to control it with the main sheet. "You watch the sail," she said. "Stay as close to the wind as possible."

"Does it matter?"

"It does if we want to get anywhere and back before dark."

They were a good team, considering their lack of experi-ence. They got the little boat up into the wind, and Valerie gave a little shriek of delight as they heeled. "Now what?" she cried. "We're going to go over."

"No, we're not," Miranda assured her. "Just sit up on the side, there, to counterbalance the weight."

"Sit where?" Valerie asked.

"Wherever the boat sails best."

She leaned out over the edge, whooping excitedly as the boat scudded along on a gust. It was thrilling to Miranda to see her daughter so carefree for a change. Caught up in the moment, Valerie dropped her surly persona and yelled with delight. "This is awesome," she said. "I had no idea you knew how to do this."

"I know how to do lots of things," Miranda pointed out. "Are your arms getting tired?"

"Totally. I'm about to lose it."

"Hang on, and we'll jibe."

They executed the maneuver and practiced some others, scudding back and forth on the lake. Miranda loved the feel of the wind ruffling through her short hair, the golden warmth of the sun on her face, the sound of her daughter's laughter on the wind. "This," Miranda declared, "is as close to a perfect afternoon as I've ever had." She grinned at Valerie. "I need more days like this, days when I can forget I was ever sick."

"I'm glad, Mom. Really."

"So how about you? How are you liking our vacation?" Miranda asked. It was a daring move, she knew. She was giving Valerie an opening to list a whole litany of complaints.

"It's all right," Valerie said, surprising her. "I had no idea Dad was so cutthroat at horseshoes."

"Or that Andrew knows words like *shirk* and that you can add an *S* to *naked* and get something totally different," Miranda added, referring to last night's game of Scrabble.

"The important thing is, Dad lost," Valerie reminded her. "That means he has to fix dinner tonight, start to finish."

It wasn't such a hardship. This past year, Jacob had done

more than his share of the cooking, and so had the kids. "We should head back," Miranda said. "Give ourselves time to clean up."

It took some maneuvering, but they managed to bring the boat around to the dock. The afternoon had turned hot, a reminder that it was the height of Indian summer. Once they got the boat tied up, Miranda took off her sandals. "You know what I feel like doing?"

"What?"

"Jumping in the water."

"But it's——"

Miranda didn't wait to be talked out of it. She peeled off her life jacket and jumped off the end of the dock into the crystal-clear water. It was so cold, it felt as if her body was going into shock. She bobbed to the surface, her legs working like eggbeaters. Because of the cording in her arm, she couldn't swim, but managed to stay afloat by kicking. "Feels great," she lied.

"You're insane," Valerie said.

"Come on in. You know you want to."

"Insane," Valerie repeated, falling forward into the lake, as if she'd been shot. Seconds later, she came straight up out of the water, her mouth working like a fish's. "Omigod," she gasped. "This is the coldest water I've ever felt."

"Swim around a little," Miranda suggested through chattering teeth. "You'll get used to it."

"Your lips are turning blue," Valerie pointed out after a while.

"Your makeup's all washed off," Miranda said. Without the

thick mascara, blood-colored lipstick and gel-spiked hair, Valerie looked like herself again.

They lasted maybe five more minutes, then raced for shore. Gasping and shivering, they lay side by side on the dock and waited for the sun to warm them up. Miranda looked up at the sky, seeing pictures in the clouds. "This is what I call a gift moment," she told Valerie.

"What's that?"

"A really great moment you don't go looking for but it happens anyway. I just like being here with you, feeling the sun on my face."

Valerie was quiet for a minute. Then she said, "I like it too, Mom."

"Andrew and I had a good talk the other day, when we hiked up to Meerskill Falls," Miranda said. "I thought maybe you and I could do the same."

"We talk all the time, Mom."

"I know, but—"

"Look, you got sick and now you're better and I'm good with that, okay? Do we really need to analyze it to death?"

"That's why we came here."

"Great. Go ahead, then. Analyze me."

Miranda hesitated. "You know what? You're right. We can just enjoy being together."

Valerie gave a soft, knowing laugh. "You want to talk about it. You know you do."

Miranda chuckled. "Busted."

Valerie was quiet for several moments. Finally, she started to speak. "Okay. I never told you this before, but you getting cancer—Mom, I'm sorry, but it made me feel like a freak, okay? And breast cancer. The same thing Grandma died of. God, do you know how many 'helpful' people came up to me to say they're sorry for me, they're praying for me, because my risk for getting the same disease is now, like, ten times higher than normal?"

Miranda turned on her side to look at Valerie. "Who said that?"

"People who called themselves my friends. So I figured, who needs friends, anyway?"

Oh, God. Miranda's heart sank as she pictured Valerie suffering at school, turning her back on her friends and hiding her pain. "Baby, I wish you'd told me—"

"I'm sorry, okay?" Valerie's anger bubbled up quickly. She sat upright, drew her knees to her chest and glowered out at the lake. "I'm sorry I'm not the kind of daughter you want."

"You know the only kind of daughter I want is one who's happy being who she is. And I'm sorry, too. I'm sorry that it's true—you are at a higher risk. But that doesn't mean you have to be miserable, worrying about something that is probably never going to happen. All it means is that you and I both need to take extra care of ourselves. Why do you think I started getting mammograms at thirty-five?"

"It's scary, Mom. I can't be brave like you."

Miranda sat up, propped her hands behind her. "Oh, baby.

You have been so incredibly brave this whole year. So have Andrew and your dad. I wish you'd think about something, Valerie. This girl, the one you've been for the past year—is this who you really are?"

Valerie pushed a hand through her damp, artificially black hair. "I have no idea. All I know is that, after you got sick, it felt stupid to go to pep rallies and football games."

"But having friends isn't stupid. Your friends are the ones you lean on when the going gets tough. Hey, if it wasn't for my friend Sophie, we never would have had the chance to come here." She paused, studying her daughter's profile, so innocent-looking without the makeup. "Don't you miss them, Val?"

Her daughter nodded slowly. "I was horrible to them. To Megan and Lyssa, and especially to Pete. I just didn't want them around. I hated everyone, hated the world, because they were all normal while my life was falling apart."

Miranda winced. "I blame my cancer for a lot of things, and you're allowed to do that, too. Up to a point. Sweetie, it was your first year of high school. I wanted to be there for you so badly. But this happened, and I wasn't there for you, and we both have to forgive ourselves and each other and move on."

"I have moved on."

Miranda brushed a damp lock of hair off Valerie's forehead. "I think you ran away."

Valerie surprised her by nodding in agreement. "I think you're right."

Miranda chuckled. "All right, now I'm speechless. You're agreeing with me?"

Valerie dropped her head down into her folded arms. "I miss them," she said. "I wish we could go back to being friends. But how do I just start over with them?"

Miranda slid her arms around her daughter. "Ah, honey. You'd be amazed to see how forgiving people can be. That part is easy."

"Sure."

"Have you given Pete an answer about the Homecoming dance yet?"

"I, um, I couldn't really figure out how to tell him no."

"Because you didn't really want to tell him no," Miranda said.

Valerie looked over at her, grinned. "You think you're so smart."

# CHAPTER
## ~NINE~

"I can't believe we have to go home tomorrow," Andrew said, following Jacob out onto the sunny front porch of the cottage. "I bet no one would notice if we stayed an extra week."

Miranda and Valerie were sitting on the porch steps, painting a little scene on an oar to commemorate their stay at Willow Lake. It was a long-standing tradition at Camp Kioga to paint an oar, and there was a display of them in the main lodge, some of them dating back to the 1930s. Miranda and Valerie had created a rustic lake scene, depicting themselves in the catboat. Under it, they made a banner that read Thank You from the Sweeney Family.

Miranda put aside her paintbrush. She sensed that the moment had arrived to tell her family what she'd been thinking about. "All week long," she said, "I've been asking myself who I was before I got cancer. And you know, I was okay, because I have a family I adore. But one thing being that sick taught me was the importance of time. I spent every single weekday at a job I didn't like. And you know, the way you spend your day is the way you spend your life. I don't want to do that anymore. Now I wake up each morning, and I tell myself, 'Don't waste this day.' It's really changed my perspective."

"We thought you liked your job, Mom," Valerie pointed out.

"It wasn't like I was being tortured," Miranda said. "I worked with good people. The job was predictable, secure. Then I got cancer and I figured out that you can surround yourself with all the security in the world, and crazy things still happen to you. Like cancer. When we get home, I want to make a change. Because in all the shuffle and planning, I forgot to do something very crucial. I forgot to follow my dream." She looked at Jacob. "I sometimes wonder if you did that, too."

"Nope," he said immediately. "I never think that."

"Come on, I know you. Your dream was never commissioned sales."

"Maybe so, but you asked about my dream. And that's always been you, Miranda. You and the kids. This family. *Us.* And that's why I'm so happy to have our life on any terms. All the rest— the work, the traffic, the bills—it's nothing but details. That's what being at this cottage has reminded me. I'm going back to the same old thing but I'm different. I'm glad I had a chance to remember the things that are important to me."

By the time he finished speaking, Miranda was staring at him with tears of joy running down her face. "I love you, Jacob. When you talk like that, it reminds me just how much."

"Whoa," said Valerie. "Way to go, Dad." They high-fived each other.

"Now, wait a minute." Miranda dabbed at her cheeks. "I hope this isn't your very charming way of saying I should be thankful for what I have and go back to the same old thing. I meant what I said," she insisted. "I want to make a change."

Jacob regarded her with apprehension. "Can you be more specific?"

"I can be very specific." She felt her heart speed up as she told them about Lucy's café and her idea of joining her friend. It was the kind of excitement she'd felt when she was on the verge of realizing a longed-for goal—going to college, marrying Jacob, having her children. This was something she hadn't felt in a very long time. "I know what I'm asking," she said to Jacob. "I know it might not be the best thing for us right now, financially. But—"

"But nothing," he said. "I can't believe you never told us this before."

"I thought you'd tell me it was a terrible idea, financial suicide."

"Maybe you should check with me before you decide what I think."

* * *

Later on, Jacob invited Miranda to come with him on a sunset paddle on the lake in the two-person kayak. The evening promised to be absolutely beautiful. There were only a few high, torn clouds in the sky, and the lowering sun turned the lake to a vast sheet of gold.

The hush of nature surrounded them—a light breeze in the high branches of the maples and willows, the lonely cry of a loon, the quiet dipping of their paddles into the still water. The lake gave all the colors and sounds a special clarity. Nature had its own special healing power, Miranda reflected. Each day they spent here she felt stronger, closer to her family.

"I'm so glad we made this trip," she said over her shoulder to Jacob.

"So am I. It's been good for all of us. I've finally stopped dreaming work dreams at night."

"I didn't know you had work dreams."

"Nightmares. Workmares, I guess you'd call them. Classic stuff—I'm late for a meeting, or I show up without my pants on, or I get lost."

"You never told me that. We used to tell each other all our dreams, good or bad. When did we stop?"

"When mine got boring because they were all about work," he said.

"Maybe we ought to start telling each other again."

They rowed toward the windward side of a small island in

the middle of the lake. According to the hand-drawn map in the cottage, it was called Spruce Island.

"The people who own this camp—the Bellamys—were married on this island more than fifty years ago," Miranda told her husband. "Last summer, they came back to reenact the wedding for their fiftieth anniversary."

"Let's go check it out," he said. They paddled to the shallows and brought the kayak ashore on the sloping beach. Everything on the island was tiny and intriguing, a whole world in miniature. There was a path leading to a garden gazebo, now overgrown with roses and dahlias gone to seed. It was marked with a commemorative plaque that read, Charles Bellamy and Jane Gordon were married here August 26, 1956. Renewed their vows here August 26, 2006.

"They've been married fifty years," Miranda said. "Imagine that." To her surprise, she saw a dark flash of anger in his eyes. "Jacob?"

He made a visible effort to smile. "I just want you to get old, Miranda. That's all I want. I try to be happy for people like the Bellamys, but it's damn hard sometimes."

"I know," she said, slipping her arms around him. "I know."

"I wish I'd been better for you when you were sick," he said, his voice low with emotion.

"Jacob—"

"No, let me finish. I wish we'd spent more days like this. But I was just so scared. The cancer took over our lives, and no matter how hard I tried, I couldn't fight it. So instead, I focused on something simple—my work. I shouldn't have done that. I should have been there for you more, instead of burying myself in work. It's no excuse, but the truth is, I was freaking terrified, Miranda, at the idea of facing life without you, and at how much that would hurt. And so I...I stepped back, bracing for a blow. As if, by pulling away before you were even gone, maybe I wouldn't miss you so much." He shoved a hand through his hair. "I'm a freaking idiot. I should be shot."

Miranda took hold of his hand and brought it to her mouth. "I've got an idea. Let's do this. Instead of worrying about being married for fifty years, let's just work on being married right now."

He held her gently, yet she sensed a desperation in his embrace. "Good plan," he whispered.

They waited for sunset, then paddled back to the dock. Miranda frowned, seeing an unfamiliar car parked in the cottage driveway. "I wasn't expecting anyone," she said to Jacob. "Were you?"

He didn't answer, but his telltale grin gave him away. "Help me tie up the kayak, will you?"

"What's going on?" she asked.

Just then, Sophie and her two kids, Daisy and Max, came out of the cottage. "Surprise," yelled Sophie. "We were just in the neighborhood..."

Miranda laughed with joy and went to give her friend a hug. "It's fantastic here. I can't thank you enough."

"We have a little something planned for your last night at the lake," Sophie said, leading the way into the cottage.

Miranda gasped. The table was set for a candlelit dinner for two, with a linen tablecloth, a bottle of wine and a beautiful meal set out. "I'm taking the kids to the drive-in movie in Coxsackie for the last show of the season. We probably won't be back until late…if that's okay with you."

"We already said it would be okay," Valerie said, coming down from the loft. She looked a lot more like her old self, in cropped jeans and a Camp Kioga sweatshirt.

"Fine by me," Miranda said, feeling a little thrill of anticipation.

They left in a swirl of laughter, and Miranda found herself alone with Jacob. He held out a chair for her. "Dinner is served."

It felt exactly like a date, with a lovely meal, a glass of wine and the knowledge that they would make love afterward. She looked at her husband's face in the glow of the candlelight and felt such an intense wave of love that it brought tears to her eyes.

Though she hadn't said a word, he must have felt something from her. He set down his wineglass, and said, "Let's go to bed."

She took her time getting ready, putting on a spritz of perfume the way she'd done when she was younger, and taking out a nightgown she'd bought just for this trip. It was cream-colored and floor length, gathered softly at the waist.

She stepped out into the bedroom. Jacob was standing by the night table in boxers and a T-shirt. He'd turned down the bed and was flipping through some photographs.

When he saw her, his face lit with a smile. "You look good, Miranda."

"I feel good." She crossed the room to him. "What's that?"

"These are the pictures I took of you the night before the surgery," he said.

Miranda felt as though she'd been punched in the stomach. She remembered that night well. She had wanted him to photograph her, naked and whole for the last time. The pictures had a quality of searing intimacy, the camera somehow revealing more than a mirror ever did. She remembered how they had talked that night, and cried together, and made love with a fierce intensity they'd never recaptured.

"I had no idea you carried these around," she said. "My God, Jacob. No wonder you can't get used to me the way I am now."

"Miranda, no." He grabbed her hands. "You don't understand. These are pictures of my wife, my best friend, my college sweetheart, the love of my life. You were getting ready to face unbelievable pain, and you still had the strength to look at me like that. I don't keep these around to remind me of what you used to look like, Miranda. I keep them to remind me of how brave you are."

It struck her then that they hadn't made love in the daylight since before her surgery. And whenever they did make love, Jacob was careful and considerate, straining to hold her gently— too gently. "Then treat me like I'm that woman, Jacob," she said. "That brave woman. Not like someone who'll break. That's what I've missed this past year. You've been too careful with me."

"I don't want to hurt you, Miranda."

"I swear I won't break." She moved forward and kissed him—

not a good-night kiss but a frank, sexy, openmouthed, how-about-it kiss.

He pulled back and smiled at her. "You sure?" he whispered.

"Of course. I'm ready to quit acting like a patient, you know?"

"I know."

There was something shining in his face, a love so strong that she felt warm all over, as though she were standing in the light of the sun. And she realized something then, something she'd always known but had managed to forget in all the busy chaos of their lives. Their love was a force so strong that it would never end, no matter what happened to her.

"Oh, Jacob," she whispered. "I feel like I've come back from a long trip. And I've missed you so."

He pressed her down on the bed and unbuttoned her nightgown. "Ah, honey. I've missed you, too."

# ∽— EPILOGUE —∾

"**S**mile, just one more time." Miranda knew she was probably trying Valerie's patience, but she couldn't help herself. "You look incredible in that dress. How about right here, on the front porch?"

"Okay, Mom." Valerie seemed happy enough to pose but cast a worried look at her date, Pete. In a crisp, rented tux, his hair newly cut and his shoes polished to a sheen, he appeared both nervous and elated. "Just a few more minutes, okay, Pete?"

"I don't mind." He blushed, looking so boy-next-door cute that Miranda herself wanted to hug him.

"I lied," she confessed. "I don't want just one more picture."

"Miranda," Jacob said. "You've probably got enough."

But she didn't, and in the end, she got her way. She took pictures of every possible combination—Valerie with her date, with her dad, with her brother. And then a shot of Valerie and Andrew and the puppy, Kioga. When they returned home from their week at the cottage, they had adopted the pup from a local shelter. At about twelve weeks old, he looked like a shepherd mix, with one ear up and one flopped down, and he had become the center of Andrew's universe. Andrew was raising the dog, training him, and it was hard work. So hard, in fact, that he almost never had time to get on the computer anymore. And he didn't seem to miss it one bit.

"Good night, Mom and Dad," Valerie said. She gave them each a hug before getting into the car with Pete. As she hugged Miranda, she gave her an extra squeeze. "Thanks, Mom," she whispered.

Jacob stood behind Miranda and put his arms around her as they watched the car drive away. The last of the evening sunshine lingered, painting the front garden with a deep sheen of gold. She leaned against Jacob, grateful for his solid presence, grateful for…everything. This past year, she'd learned not to fear death but to accept its presence—a reminder that you can do anything with this day except waste it.

Dear Reader,

Thank you for spending some time with Miranda and her family. I hope you were as moved as I was by the great work done by Cottage Dreams. Marie S., a cancer survivor who corresponded with me about Cottage Dreams, writes, "Even though I feel a part of my spirit was taken from me during my cancer journey, I can't help but look at the importance of people who continue to reach out to others in trying times."

Now you have an opportunity to reach out. In the fictional story, Sophie took inspiration from Cottage Dreams to offer a haven to a family that desperately needed to heal and reconnect. In reality, this organization is able to carry on its work only through the charitable contributions of caring people. If possible, please open your heart and your purse strings and make a contribution to Cottage Dreams. There is also a need for items to go into "Welcome Baskets" for arriving families. To find out how you can reach out, please visit their Web site at www.cottagedreams.org or send a check to Cottage Dreams, The Heritage Building, 33A Pine Avenue, P.O. Box 1300, Haliburton, ON K0M 1S0.

Thank you for caring,

Susan Wiggs

# P.K. BEVILLE
## ⤴ SECOND WIND DREAMS ⤴

O ne month shy of her 100th birthday, Flossie's dream came true. She got her very first motorcycle ride— in a pink leather jacket.

Flossie's dream ride was made possible through Second Wind Dreams, a nonprofit organization that fulfills the dreams of those living in elder-care communities—improving their lives and changing society's perceptions of aging. Flossie and hundreds like her have shown that our elders can still dream, and dream big, even when society is telling them they're too old.

Paula Kay (P.K.) Beville, Ph.D., began Second Wind Dreams with the goal of bringing seniors to the forefront of our society and making them feel what they are—special. Since 1997, Second Wind Dreams has made dreams come true in over 400 facilities in 41 states, Canada and India.

*One woman's passion*

P.K. is a trailblazer in her passion to bring something positive to nursing homes and develop ways to improve them. For the past twenty-four years P.K. has designed and implemented mental health services that are currently provided to more than 800 nursing homes throughout the United States. She co-authored *SecondWind,* an uplifting, heartwarming look at people in nursing homes, and she worked with seniors in nursing homes as a psychologist for over 20 years.

P.K. was continually struck by how much spirit and excitement residents had, even though they were frail and living in nursing homes. Yet, as a frontline caregiver, P.K. knew too well how these seniors were slipping into insignificance at the very time they should feel important and honored.

The idea for Second Wind Dreams came when P.K. asked some nursing home residents, "If you could have anything in the world, what would it be?" The answers were small and relatively simple requests, such as a new dress to attend a church group. P.K. realized that the hopes and dreams of residents were so simple that she was determined to make these dreams a reality. So P.K. gave up a six-figure salary to begin Second Wind Dreams, working single-handedly for one and a half years from the basement of her Marietta, Georgia, home. Even today as CEO of Second Wind Dreams, P.K. has never received a paycheck.

*A forgotten population*

Second Wind Dreams focuses on fulfilling the dreams of those living in nursing homes and elder-care communities. Nursing homes are where the frailest, weakest and, some say, the most burdensome among us spend their final days. These are the seniors who most need the program's assistance, yet nursing homes occupy the last rung on America's health-care ladder. Only 2% of nonprofit donations go to the elderly. Funding continues to be challenging, but P.K. believes that through programs like Second Wind Dreams, much can be done to improve the lives of those who live in nursing homes as well as those who work with them.

The lack of dreams and goals can have physical and mental consequences. The Dreams program stimulates residents both physically and mentally—fighting the triple threat of pain, boredom and loneliness found in so many of these residences, while giving seniors the special attention they deserve. As P.K. points out, you need only look at the faces of these seniors to see the results.

*Dreams fulfilled*

Second Wind Dreams makes possible about three dreams a day. Need-based dreams—something as simple as a cup holder for a wheelchair or a new pair of bedroom slippers—account for a humbling 22% of the dreams. Others are relationship-based dreams like the one of a resident who was flown across the country to reunite with a brother he hadn't seen in forty years. Many seniors dream of reliving past experiences such as driving a big rig again, or getting back out in the fresh sea air to catch the big one. And for residents like Kay, lifelong dreams are fulfilled. Ninety-two-year-old Kay, who never got the chance to graduate from university, was given full honors, with cap and gown and all the pomp and circumstance.

But as P.K. discovered right from the program's inception, an unbelievable 46% of the dreams are just for fun! The first dream P.K. fulfilled was that of ninety-two-year-old twins who wanted an Elvis impersonator to visit their nursing home. So many seniors are still kids at heart—like Mae, who was wheelchair bound, blind and on dialysis, yet dreamed of riding all seven roller coasters at a Georgia amusement park. In P.K.'s eyes the dreams are equal, big or small—even if the price tags for fulfilling the dreams differ. The dream itself is what it's all about.

*Inspiring staff and the community*

P.K. knows the only way to change society's perception of aging is through community involvement. Second Wind Dreams relies heavily on volunteers—individuals, families, church groups, student groups of all ages and corporations. Participating in a dream often leads to long-lasting partnerships with facilities and special relationships with residents. Those who have been a part of a dream-come-true are never sure who got the most out of it, the volunteer or the dreamer.

Those who work with the elderly are motivated by P.K.'s passion and vision. She pays positive attention to staff, knowing how hard they work and how they are underpaid and often feel unappreciated. P.K. recently completed a study to determine the impact of the Dreams program. The study showed that through Second Wind Dreams, depression among nursing home residents decreased by 56% and staff morale increased by 65%—proof that long after the dream has been fulfilled, the effects linger, giving all involved a sense of renewal and hope.

P.K. believes that the ability to dream is a life-affirming experience that can transform lives. She is so touched by each dream she witnesses that watching is like having her dream fulfilled, as well. P.K.'s dream has *always* been to enhance life in nursing homes and to honor the resilience and vitality of the human spirit in our elders. Because of P.K. Beville's vision and passion, Second Wind Dreams is changing the perception of aging...one dream at a time.

For more information visit www.secondwind.org or write to Second Wind Dreams, 1031 Cambridge Sq., Suite G, Alpharetta, GA 30004.

# SHARON SALA
## ∽ THE YELLOW RIBBON ∽

## ‑SHARON SALA‑

*New York Times* bestselling author Sharon Sala has written more than sixty-nine books. Her novels regularly hit all the bestseller lists. She's a five-time RITA® finalist, five-time winner of the National Reader's Choice Award, five-time winner of the Colorado Romance Writer's Award of Excellence and has won many other industry awards too numerous to mention. During her writing career, she has captured the hearts of countless readers with her award-winning romances written under her own name, Sharon Sala, as well as her pseudonym, Dinah McCall.

She was born and raised in rural Oklahoma and still calls the state her home. Being with her family is ultimate joy, although her life has changed drastically, from the time she made her first sale to the way it is now. Sharon claims it is her greatest satisfaction to create her stories, then share them with people who love to read.

# CHAPTER
## ∞ ONE ∞

I t was almost 9:00 a.m. and Frances Drummond was late. She was due to be at Just Like Home no later than nine. The residents of the assisted living center where she worked held her to a high standard and she tried never to disappoint them.

But disappoint them she would if she didn't get there in time to help with shampooing. Today was beauty day. Although she wasn't a licensed beautician, she was a perfectly willing shampooer, and was often called in to remove hair curlers so the beauticians could do comb-outs and styles more quickly.

Beauty day was the female residents' favorite day, and Frankie loved to see the women giggling and fussing over different hairstyles and nail polish colors.

A bread delivery truck was leaving the parking lot just as she drove in. The driver turned and stared as Frankie jumped out of her car. Self-consciously, she pulled up the neck of her pink cotton sweater, wishing she'd worn a turtleneck, and tried not to stumble as she hurried across the lot.

She entered the lobby of the home, breathless and limping more than normal from moving too fast. The girls, as she called them, waved at her from outside the little beauty shop, which was in a corner of the lobby. It was open only two days a week—one for the women, the second for the men—so no one wanted to miss out.

Haircuts and dye jobs were regular requests, both for men and women, along with the occasional permanent. The residents ranged in age from sixty-seven to ninety-eight. For Frankie, whose parents had died when she was twenty, these senior citizens had become the family she no longer had, and they took it upon themselves to give her advice, whether she asked for it or not.

Frankie had been in college when she and her parents were in the automobile accident that had killed her parents and left her with thick, puckered burn scars on her neck and arm and a painful limp. When she was tired, the limp was more noticeable. The scars and the handicap were usually enough to put most men off giving her a second look.

After years of disappointment, she'd given up hoping she'd ever find a decent man who could look past her imperfections to the woman beneath, and had created a satisfying life by helping others with much larger problems. This attitude was what had led her to the job she had now, working as the recreation director in a home for the aged. She loved her work and she loved the people. They had way more wrinkles than she had scars, and they all dragged their feet a bit when they walked.

The residents of Just Like Home were also funny, wise and to Frankie's unending surprise, often a little bawdy. She'd gotten more sexual advice from the girls than she'd ever be able to use.

Once she'd crossed the lobby, Frankie stepped into the site manager's office long enough to lock up her purse and hang up her coat.

"Good morning, Mrs. Tulia," Frankie said. "Sorry I'm late."

Mavis Tulia was on the phone, but she wiggled her fingers and mouthed a hello.

Frankie hurried back to the lobby, hugging girls on her way into the beauty shop, then waving at the three beauticians already at their chairs. One was in the midst of a cut, one was doing a dye job, and the third was putting curlers in Margie Potts's hair.

"Good morning, Margie," Frankie said.

"Hello to you, too," Margie replied. "I'm thinking of Ravenous Red for my nail color today. What do you think?"

"I think you would look ravenous," Frankie teased.

Margie laughed.

"Hey, Frankie," the beautician said. "Didn't think you were gonna make it."

"Traffic."

Margie rolled her eyes. She'd driven a cab for more than thirty years, and for the past five claimed to be working on a book about her life and her fares.

Frankie doubted the book was a work in progress, but it hardly mattered. It gave Margie an identity. Here in Just Like Home, she was known as the writer, just as she'd been the cabby before.

"What do you want me to do first?" Frankie asked the beautician working on Margie.

The woman pointed out to the lobby and the residents who were sitting there, waiting their turn.

"Louise is next. If you do the shampoo, Lori should be through with her cut and style by then."

"Will do," Frankie said, and stepped outside the little salon. "Louise, you're next, dear. Here's your cane. Let's go to the shampoo station."

And so the morning began. By noon, they were down to two beauticians, one having returned to her regular salon. When Frankie had Doris shampooed and ready for the stylist, she went back into the lobby to get the last resident.

Charlotte Grace was eighty-seven years young and never married. Some of the girls called her the Old Maid, but only in jest. Charlotte never seemed to mind. She'd usually fire back a comment that being single didn't mean being a virgin, which always made the others laugh. Only Frankie saw the sadness in Charlotte that the other girls seemed to miss.

"Charlotte, you're next," Frankie said.

The older woman looked up from the magazine she'd been reading.

"About time," she said. "I was afraid I wouldn't get to show off my new do before they laid me out."

Frankie grinned. When she'd first begun working here, the death and funeral humor had taken her aback. But she'd long since gotten used to it. Only yesterday, Marvin Howard had flagged her down to look at some snapshots. When she realized they were of the new headstone set at his prepaid burial plot, she'd oohed and aahed the same way she might have done if she'd been looking at a picture of his great-grandchildren.

Charlotte's step was spry and her figure trim, her only frailty a slight tremble in her hands. She wore her hair short and fluffy, so the shampoo and styling wouldn't take long.

Frankie settled her into the shampoo chair and began to fasten a clean cape around her neck to protect her clothes. As she did, the Velcro fastener caught on the yellow ribbon that Charlotte always wore around her neck.

"Oh, wait…I've caught your ribbon," Frankie said.

"That's okay," Charlotte assured her. "I need to get a new one anyway. Can't let my locket go begging."

Frankie eyed the small oval locket hanging from the ribbon. She'd never seen Charlotte without it.

"That's really pretty," Frankie said. "Is it an heirloom?"

Charlotte's smile faded.

"I suppose it is now," she said, rubbing it between her thumb and forefinger. "Or at least it will be soon. That's what happens when you get as old as I am."

Frankie frowned. She'd said something wrong, but she wasn't sure what. She laid her hand on the back of Charlotte's neck.

"I'm sorry. I didn't mean to pry."

Charlotte shook her head and managed a teary smile.

"Oh, pooh, you're not prying. I'm just a sentimental old woman. I bought the locket for myself, you know. It wasn't handed down or anything."

"It's beautiful," Frankie said.

Charlotte opened it.

"So was he," she said softly, revealing the photo inside.

Frankie bent over for a closer look and saw a young man with a very sober countenance.

"Who was he…your husband?" Frankie asked.

Charlotte's chin trembled, but she didn't cry.

"I never married," she said at last, then looked up at Frankie. "But he asked. He did ask me to marry him."

Frankie pulled up a stool and sat down beside her.

"What happened?"

"I said no."

Frankie didn't know what to say. She could tell that Charlotte viewed this as a tragedy.

"Father didn't like him," Charlotte explained, then shrugged. "Back then, a father's opinion still held water. But he was wrong… my father…I should have married my sweetheart. His name was Daniel Louis Morrow."

"What happened to him?" Frankie asked.

A tear rolled down Charlotte's cheek. Frankie leaned over and blotted it with the tail of the cape.

"After I refused him, he didn't wait to be drafted," Charlotte told her. "He signed up for the army right after Pearl Harbor was bombed." Her voice shook a little as she added, "He never came home, you know. He was shot by a German sniper near a little town called Positano, in southern Italy. He's buried there."

She shut the locket with a snap, then pulled the cape down over the front of her dress and leaned back. It was obvious she was through talking.

Frankie got up and turned on the water, letting it flow until it ran warm, then began to work shampoo into Charlotte's hair, scrubbing gently until her scalp had a good massage and her hair was thoroughly clean.

She rinsed it twice, then wrapped a clean towel around Charlotte's hair and twisted it into a turban before helping her up and moving her to the stylist's chair.

Charlotte sat down, then took Frankie's hand.

"I always meant to go there…to his grave. All these years and I kept saying I would go. I even got myself a passport and took all my shots a couple of years back, then didn't do it. Now it's too late. Don't do that to yourself, you hear? If there's something you know you should do, don't put it off."

"I won't," Frankie said, and then leaned over and kissed Charlotte's cheek.

Charlotte smiled. "Thank you, dear. I don't know what I would do without you."

Frankie smiled back. "That works both ways," she said, then went to gather up the wet towels and clean up the shampoo area.

When it was time for lunch, Frankie played the piano for the residents as they ate. Quite often they would shout out a request. They rarely asked for any modern tunes, and Frankie was becoming quite competent at playing songs from the big band era of the thirties and forties.

She was in the middle of "Old Buttermilk Sky," a song Hoagie Carmichael had made famous, when she saw Charlotte come into the dining room. Her hair was freshly fluffed and styled, just as she liked it, and her expression pleasant. Frankie watched her nodding and waving at her friends as she took her seat at the table.

Since their earlier conversation, Frankie saw Charlotte in a different light. What she'd viewed as a calm, complacent demeanor was really a quiet sadness. And she knew now that Charlotte's shy personality was actually an expression of regret. The dress Charlotte had on was such a dark purple it looked almost black, and Frankie realized that the older woman never wore bright colors. It seemed to Frankie as if Charlotte were in permanent mourning.

Poor Charlotte Grace.

She'd lived an entire life without joy and it broke Frankie's heart.

Frankie thought about Charlotte all the way home, and even through her solitary dinner and a lingering bubble bath. As she was brushing her teeth, she caught a glimpse of her own reflection and froze. The scars were redder than usual from the heat of the bathwater. She glanced at them, then focused on her face. For a moment, everything looked blurred, and she could almost see her features aging and her hair turning gray.

She shivered, then shook her head to make the image go away. When she looked again, she was her normal self, but she'd gotten the message. If she didn't make some changes in her own life, she was going to wind up just like Charlotte—old and saddened by the things she'd missed.

Her mood was somber as she got into bed. She lay motionless, willing herself to relax, then wound up doing the opposite. She thrashed and turned until she'd messed up her sheets and was more awake than when she'd gotten into bed. Every time she closed her eyes, she imagined a lone tombstone in an empty field with Daniel Morrow's name on it.

Of course, she knew her imagination had exaggerated the facts, but she was certain the young soldier never dreamed his final resting place would be half a world away from his home.

Still wide awake at midnight, Frankie slapped the mattress with both hands, pushed herself up, and rolled out of bed. Within moments, she was heading for the library, where she kept her computer. She booted it up and got online, then typed in the words *Positano, Italy*.

To her surprise, a colorful Web site popped up. One of the more imposing facts about the little fishing village was that it had turned into quite a tourist spot, and the foremost hotel in the village was a former palace that had once been owned by Charles Murat, the brother-in-law of Napoleon Bonaparte. The palace had long since been turned into a hotel called the Hotel Murat, and boasted an aging elegance.

She sat there for a moment with her fingers resting on the keyboard, then impulsively clicked onto a form to e-mail the hotel and began to type.

Dear Sirs,

I am looking for the grave of an American GI who died during World War II. His name was Daniel Louis Morrow, and I was told that he'd been buried in a small cemetery in your area. If there is anyone who can help me verify that, I would greatly appreciate it.

Time is of the essence, since the woman for whom I'm writing is very elderly. Please help me. It matters so much to her that we know for certain the location of his final resting place.

Sincerely,

Frances Drummond

Chicago, Illinois

USA

The moment she hit Send and the e-mail went out, she felt a weight roll off her shoulders. Her efforts might not amount to a thing, but whatever the outcome, she felt better for having made an attempt to verify this for Charlotte.

Frankie went to bed with a light heart, and as soon as she closed her eyes, fell fast asleep.

A half a world away, Giuseppe Longoria, the hotel manager at the Hotel Murat, was checking the hotel's e-mail. He was down to the last message, and when he opened it up, he realized it wasn't a request for reservations but a letter of inquiry instead. Being bilingual, he scanned it quickly, then frowned. This was beyond his expertise and had nothing to do with hotel management. He started to fire back a response that said as much, when one of the maids came into the office to empty the wastebaskets.

Her name was Maria Romano. She didn't read English, but he knew her nephew, Daniel Sciora, did. He also knew that there were several American GIs buried in the little cemetery on the outskirts of Positano where Maria lived. He explained the situation, asking if she would pass this message on to Daniel. When she agreed he printed it out and gave it to Maria.

It was after seven o'clock in the evening before Maria returned home. She had forgotten about the paper until she was changing out of her uniform. She took it from her pocket and laid it on the bed. Once she was dressed in her regular clothing, she headed across the road to her nephew's home.

\* \* \*

Thirty-six-year-old Daniel Sciora was a lonely man, although his family was large, even by Italian standards. His aunt Maria and uncle Paolo lived across the road. Eight cousins and their spouses lived nearby in Positano, twelve cousins and their families lived a couple of hours north in Naples, while most of the others were in Sicily. Once a year, they made it a point to get together, renew family ties and catch up on family news. And every year, the aging grandmothers and aunts gave Daniel grief because he was still an unmarried man.

Daniel knew he was considered a good catch. He was tall and good-looking, and had inherited the vineyard and winery that his great-grandfather had begun. He could have had his pick of a dozen pretty women from the village, but he didn't want to settle for just any match. He wanted "love at first sight." A woman who took his breath away with nothing but a look, and he had yet to find her.

On this particular evening, he was about to serve himself dinner when there was a knock at the door. He dropped the spoon back into the pot and went to answer it. When he saw who it was, he smiled.

"*Zia* Maria! Come in! Come in! The pasta's ready. Have you come to eat dinner with me?"

Maria Romano rolled her eyes.

"Your *zio* Paolo would never get over it if I did," she said.

"Then bring him, too," Daniel offered. "I made plenty."

"You're a good boy," Maria said, and kissed him on both cheeks. "But food is not why I've come."

She handed him the e-mail that the hotel manager had printed out.

"This came to the hotel today, and Giuseppe asked me to bring it to you. He says it's a request for information from a woman in the United States. He thought since you understand English, you might be able to help."

Daniel frowned slightly as he took the paper.

"Sure, *Zia*, I'd be happy to help, but what is it?"

"I don't know. He didn't tell me. You read it. You're so smart, I know you'll understand what it's about. Now I must get back to the house and prepare our evening meal. *Ciao, bello*."

"*Ciao, Zia*."

He closed the door, and began reading the e-mail as he went back to the kitchen. But halfway there, he stopped. His throat tightened and he felt himself struggling for breath.

"*Dio mio!*"

There was little more to be said. A ghost from the past was staring up at him. Someone was asking about the grave of an American GI—a man by the name of Daniel Louis Morrow.

His aunt was right about one thing. He was definitely better equipped to answer this e-mail than the hotel manager. He knew for certain that there was a grave for Daniel Morrow. He knew because he was named for the man—the man who had been his grandfather.

What he had to decide was whether or not to answer the

e-mail. If this woman who was asking was family, she might get more than she'd bargained for. He knew she had no idea about his existence. Not even Daniel Morrow had known he had a daughter—Daniel's mother.

The infantry that Daniel Morrow belonged to had been bivouacked outside Positano for two days when he'd met Angelina Ricci. He'd been taken with the petite, dark-haired, dark-eyed beauty and a romance had ensued. But he'd died before he knew that Angelina was carrying his child—Daniel's mother. Daniel had grown up knowing about the GI who was his grandfather, and was proud of the fact. But it remained to be seen what these two American women would think of the truth.

He took the e-mail with him to the kitchen, reading it again and again as he ate his evening meal.

Even after he'd gone to bed, it was still on his mind. Whoever this Frances woman was, she seemed genuinely concerned about her elderly friend. Just as he was drifting off to sleep, he made a decision. He would tell her of Daniel Morrow's final resting place. The rest he would leave up to fate.

Frankie went through the next day on pins and needles, hoping for an answer to her e-mail. But there was an emergency at Just Like Home that evening. One of the elderly gentlemen who'd been living there for more than ten years sat down in his chair to read the paper and died. Of course, Frankie had stayed to help out, mourning his loss along with the others.

By the time she got home, it was almost midnight. The last thing she thought about was e-mail. She was aching all over and felt shaky and weak. She chalked it up to the trauma of the day, although death was something they dealt with at the home on a regular basis.

The next morning, she woke up with fever and chills. She sat up on the side of the bed for a few minutes, then got so dizzy she had to lie back down. There was nothing to do but call in sick. Even if she'd felt well enough to drive, it was critically important not to expose the residents to any viruses. So she reached for the phone and dialed the home.

"Just Like Home. Mavis Tulia speaking."

"Mrs. Tulia, it's me, Frankie."

"My stars, dear...what's wrong with you? You sound terrible."

"I feel terrible," she said. "I felt weird last night when I got home, but blamed it on Mr. Ellard's death. But this morning I woke up feeling even worse. I have a fever, so I know I'm contagious."

"Well, you must stay home, of course. We can't have anything like this running through the residence if we can prevent it. Take care of yourself, dear, and call if you need me."

"Thank you," Frankie said. "I'm really sorry. I had planned some craft activities today, but since I won't be there to help start them, look in my locker for movies. It's Perry Monroe's turn to choose what the group gets to see. He's partial to World War II movies, which the women hate, but there are three that have love stories in them. Maybe you could offer him a choice between those three and everyone will be happy."

"Don't you worry," Mrs. Tulia said. "I'll make sure he chooses one that everybody can enjoy. I'm just sorry you're so sick. Get better soon. Love you."

"Love you, too," Frankie said, and hung up the phone.

After taking a warm shower and changing into a clean nightgown, Frankie made herself some hot tea and took it to bed. Once she'd finished the tea, she crawled beneath the covers.

Just as she was falling asleep, she remembered Charlotte and the e-mail she'd sent.

"When I wake up," she mumbled. "I'll check it when I wake up."

While Frankie was fighting a flu bug, Daniel Sciora was fighting a battle of his own. He revisited the little cemetery where his grandfather was buried, and as he stood at the grave, it occurred to him that not once had he ever considered what Daniel Morrow's life had been like before he'd come to Italy. All he'd known of Morrow was what his grandmother had told him, and that hadn't been much.

He shoved his hands in his pockets and read the name on the tombstone, as he'd done a thousand times before.

Pfc. Daniel Louis Morrow
Born October 10, 1919
Died May 8, 1943

"So, *Nonno,* you had your own set of secrets, didn't you?" Daniel's eyes narrowed. "I wish you were still here. I need someone to tell me what to do."

But there were no answers for Daniel, and to his growing dismay, no answer from the woman in America, either.

Frankie woke up twice during the day, both times to go to the bathroom. She still had a fever, and her throat was dry and scratchy. When she went back to bed, she couldn't help but wish there was someone special in her life to tuck her in. Most of the time she didn't give much thought to her solitary state, but there were times, like now, when being alone felt like a failure.

The next morning was Saturday, and since she didn't work on the weekend, she was counting on the extra rest to help her feel better. She got up, weak and shaky, but minus the fever, to make some coffee. Once she'd poured herself a cup, she remembered the e-mail and took her coffee with her into the library.

When she checked her in-box, she was elated to see there was a response to the e-mail she'd sent to Italy.

She opened the message and began to read.

Dear Ms. Drummond,
I received the request you sent to the Hotel Murat regarding information on the grave of an American soldier named Daniel Louis Morrow.

There is, indeed, a soldier by that name who is buried in a small cemetery on the outskirts of Positano. If there is anything else I can do for you, please let me know.
Daniel Sciora

The news was all that Frankie hoped for and then some. Not only had Daniel Morrow's final resting place been verified, but the man had offered further help. She wasn't sure just what that might be, but she was definitely excited.

She hit Reply, her fingers pausing momentarily on the keys, and then she began to type.

# CHAPTER
## ～ TWO ～

The American woman had responded. Daniel felt a kick of excitement as he opened her message.

Dear Mr. Sciora,

Thank you so much for answering so promptly. I would have replied sooner, but I've been a bit under the weather. This is the first day I've been out of bed in the last thirty-six hours. It feels good to be up and moving around.

My friend Charlotte is such a dear, but I'm going to have to think about how to tell her what I've learned. Her story is quite a sad one, you see, and I don't want to upset her needlessly. Daniel Morrow was her sweetheart. He asked her to marry him, but for some reason, her father didn't approve and refused his permission. Charlotte told me that she resented her father for his interference and regretted that she had followed his wishes. As a result, she never married.

Life is sometimes very sad, isn't it?

But then, I've never married, either, although not for the same reasons as Charlotte.

I am twenty-seven to Charlotte's eighty-seven and, as yet, unwilling to classify myself as an old maid.

I fear I'm rambling, but it's from joy. I do not yet know how I'm going to use the information you have given me, but I thank you again for taking the time to help me.

With much appreciation,

Frankie Drummond

Daniel was smiling. Her English was sprinkled with idioms he wasn't familiar with. *Under the weather* was a new one for him, but after further reading, he guessed it meant she'd been sick.

The reference to being an "old maid" must have to do with being unmarried, but it still made him laugh. He could almost hear her voice, full of life and laughter, talking about first one subject and then another, with hardly a breath in between.

His mother had been like that. Always laughing and teasing. His father, Antonio, had been a solemn man, but one who had loved his family dearly. It was a tragedy when he had died of a heart attack at forty-one. Daniel's mother had never recovered from the grief and had passed away within five years of his death. Sometimes it seemed to Daniel that he'd been alone most of his life.

This woman who called herself Frankie sounded like someone he would have liked to get to know better. However, distance prevailed. But he could answer her e-mail. It would be the proper thing to do.

Frankie held her news close to her heart all weekend, wondering if telling Charlotte would be wise. What good would it do for Charlotte to know that Daniel's grave was, indeed, in the location where she'd been told? Frankie didn't imagine the older woman had enough money to get there now even if she wanted to.

Still, Charlotte's story was so sad. In the grand scheme of life, her wish to visit Daniel's grave seemed such a small thing.

By Sunday night, Frankie had pronounced herself well and was making plans to return to work the next day. She was out of the shower and preparing to dry her hair when she heard something from the television in the bedroom that caught her attention. She hurried into the room and sat down on the end of the bed to watch. A slender woman with delicate features and a confident, easygoing manner was being interviewed.

"So, the purpose of Second Wind Dreams is to grant dreams to the elderly?" the reporter asked.

"Yes, that's correct," the woman replied.

"Tell me, how does it work?"

"It's pretty straightforward. We all have regrets for something we didn't do. You know…that missed opportunity we turned down. Sometimes it's the reverse…there was something we wanted to do but were never given the chance. Well, it's my belief that age should never be the reason for giving up dreams. That's why I began Second Wind Dreams.

"Usually, the recipients of the dreams are discovered by someone else. Always, the recipients' doctors must pronounce them physically fit for whatever it is they dream of doing. Once that's accomplished, the rest is left up to us at Second Wind Dreams to make the magic happen."

"How can people contact you?"

Frankie's heart was thumping with excitement as she reached for a pen and paper. She took down the information, then ran to finish drying her hair. What if Charlotte qualified for something like this? What if these people could help Charlotte get to Italy to visit Daniel's grave? Frankie could hardly contain her excitement.

By the time she was ready for bed, she had a plan. Tomorrow she would have Second Wind Dreams fax her an information sheet. It might all come to nothing, but she wasn't going to give up on Charlotte's dream until someone told her it was impossible.

It was just past noon the next day when Frankie finished filling out the form that had been faxed to Just Like Home. She hurried into Mavis Tulia's office and sent it back to Second Wind Dreams, then breathed a sigh of relief. She had followed her heart and could only hope for the best. Whatever happened, it was out of her hands.

She worked late that night to get caught up after her time away, and when she got home she was so tired she forgot to check her e-mail. The next morning, to her delight, she discovered a message from Daniel Sciora.

Dear Frankie,

I must say that I like Frankie better than Frances. I like a very happy woman. I think you must also be a selfless woman. Not everyone cares for the older generation. You are to be commended for the life you have chosen to live.

I think your Charlotte is a very lucky woman to have you for a friend. As for being an "old maid," I take it that means an unmarried woman of a certain age. That makes me laugh. Twenty-seven is not old. At least I certainly hope not. I am thirty-six and to the disappointment of my large family, unmarried, as well. We could probably exchange amusing stories about what you Americans call "blind dates."

I wish you the best in giving your Charlotte the news of her sweetheart's final resting place. If it matters, please assure her that the grave site is well cared for and often bears fresh flowers. If you have need to call me for any further details, my phone number is posted in the address of this message.

Ciao,

Daniel

Frankie sighed. Unlike Daniel, she didn't have amusing blind date stories. In fact, since she didn't date, there were no stories at all.

She reread the message, smiling to herself as she pictured him trying to figure out idioms of the English language.

He sounded nice.

She stared at the phone number.

She knew it didn't mean anything that he'd given her his number, but it *was* a generous offer of further contact. She wanted to tell someone about contacting Second Wind Dreams about Charlotte, but if it all came to nothing, then there would have to be explanations about why not. Still, she could call him without mentioning what she'd done.

Before she had time to change her mind, she grabbed the phone and punched in the numbers, hoping that it would already be morning in Italy.

Daniel was on his way out the door when the phone rang. He started to let it go, then changed his mind and ran back inside to answer.

"*Ciao?*"

"Hello, this is Frankie Drummond. Is this Daniel?"

Daniel's heartbeat stopped.

It was her!

The woman from America!

She sounded so young and happy. He shifted mental gears into English and took a deep breath.

"Yes, this is Daniel Sciora. It is a pleasure and a surprise to speak to you. Is everything all right?"

"Yes, yes, everything is fine. I just read your e-mail, and since you were kind enough to give me your phone number... well... I was just curious enough to call."

Daniel laughed. Her honesty was refreshing.

"Then I am happy you were curious. It is, indeed, good to hear your voice, as well. And how is your friend, Charlotte? Have you told her anything yet?"

Frankie sighed, and the sound made Daniel smile.

"No, I haven't. But I'm working on something that might prove to be exciting for her."

"Oh?"

"Yes, but I'm not going to say anything just yet for fear of jinxing it. If it happens, you'll be one of the first to know."

"Jinxing? What is this jinxing?"

Frankie laughed.

"Sorry. Your English is so good I forgot myself. A jinx is like having bad luck."

"Ah...that I understand," he said. "But your call is definitely not bad luck for me. It is good to hear your voice. Now all I need is a picture of you."

There was a moment's hesitation, and Daniel wondered if he'd pushed too far with such a request.

"That I can furnish," she said at last. "I'll scan one into an e-mail to you, but don't expect a glamour girl."

Daniel heard a change in the timbre of her voice, but thought nothing of it.

"I will send one to you, as well. As for glamour girls, that phrase I understand. Just so you know, Frankie Drummond, glamour girls are usually all glitter and no substance."

"I'll look forward to your picture."

"And I will look forward to yours," Daniel echoed.

"Yes, well, goodbye, then," Frankie said.

"Since I don't want to say goodbye, I will just say *ciao*," Daniel told her. "And I hope there will be a next time."

Even after the dial tone was buzzing in her ear, Frankie still listened, hoping for just one more word. Finally, she had no option but to hang up.

"Well," she said, and then grinned. She put her hand over her mouth to stifle a giggle.

She was acting silly and she knew it, but she didn't care. This was the most excitement she'd had in years. So much was happening. Even though she knew Daniel was nothing more than an e-mail pen pal, it made her very dull personal life suddenly interesting. She didn't know what the outcome of her request to Second Wind Dreams would be, but she would never regret the inquiry she'd sent to Positano.

*Eight days later: Just Like Home*

Mavis Tulia stepped outside the office, searching the lobby for Frankie. She saw her in a corner, playing checkers with Al Janey.

Al was their eldest resident and fancied himself quite a checker player, even though he often cheated by claiming he got the colors mixed up. As usual, Frankie was letting him win.

The manager glanced at the clock. It was almost time for lunch, so she didn't mind disturbing their game.

"Frankie! Frankie!" she called.

Frankie looked up, saw her boss waving at her from the office, and breathed a sigh of relief. Al had drifted off to sleep twice since they'd begun their game. Waiting for him to wake up each time was definitely an exercise in patience.

Frankie put her hand on Al's arm so that he would know she was talking. She suspected he'd turned his hearing aid off earlier and had forgotten to turn it back on.

"Al! Al! Mrs. Tulia is calling me. I have to go, okay?"

Al frowned. "I won, right?"

Frankie grinned.

"You sure did. Fair and square."

Al nodded.

"See you later," Frankie said.

Al was already setting up the checkerboard again just in case someone else came by and offered to play.

Frankie hurried over to the office.

"What's up?" she asked.

Mavis smiled. "I think this is yours."

Frankie took the paper and scanned it quickly. Then her heart skipped a beat. She looked up.

"Did you read this?" she asked.

Her boss nodded.

"So, what do you think?" Frankie asked.

"I think Charlotte Grace is lucky to have you for a friend."

Frankie clutched the paper to her chest. She couldn't believe it. Second Wind Dreams would make Charlotte's dream come true. If her doctor pronounced her fit to travel, Charlotte was going to Italy. Frankie wanted to scream—to shout the news from the rooftops—but she couldn't. Not until they knew for sure Charlotte's health was good enough for her to go. And Second Wind Dreams liked to make a big event out of the presentation, so that meant waiting.

During her afternoon break, Frankie called her bank and checked the amount in her savings account, then contacted a travel agent and asked what a first-class ticket to Positano, Italy would cost. The rate was staggering. Well over two thousand dollars. But she had the money, and if she could make it work, she wanted to accompany Charlotte on her trip.

Still, there was one person she could tell about her exciting news, and that was Daniel. She couldn't wait to get home and give him a call.

Yet that evening when she did get home, it occurred to her that he would most likely be asleep. Frustrated, she opted for e-mail, and scanned a snapshot of herself taken at Just Like Home to send along with her message. It wasn't a bad photo. You could see the scars on her neck and arm, but she had a nice smile on her face. It would have to do.

*  *  *

Daniel was on his way home after more than a week on the road, visiting his customers and taking orders for new shipments of wine. He'd been to Rome, then Milan, then back south to Naples. From there, he'd caught a flight to Sicily and made the rounds of his customers there.

As always, he'd been anxious to get home, but never as much as he was this trip. He'd thought of his new American friend several times while he was away and couldn't help but wonder if he'd have another message from her. He was also hopeful that she'd sent a picture. He wanted a face to go with that delightful voice.

He did, however, have reservations about the old woman's feelings. He couldn't help but worry about what might happen when she learned that the man she'd loved had fallen in love with another woman and left a part of himself behind when he died.

Maria was outside working in her garden when Daniel's car came down the road. She straightened up and waved as he passed. Only after he waved back did she return to her weeding.

Seeing his aunt in the garden gave Daniel a sense of homecoming. While many things in his life were in a constant state of flux, it was the things that never seemed to change that provided him with a sense of well-being.

Still, when he unlocked the door and carried his suitcase into the house, he felt a moment of letdown. If only there was someone in his life to come home to.

He glanced at the clock. It was just after noon. There were

countless things he could do, from unpacking dirty clothes to checking mail and phone messages. Instead, he found himself heading for the computer.

It took a while for all the e-mail to download, but when he sorted through it, to his delight, he discovered a message from Frankie.

He opened it first and noticed there was an attachment. When he opened that and saw it was a photo, he leaned back and let himself absorb her image.

"So...hello, Frances Drummond," he said softly.

In the picture, she was standing behind an elderly woman, leaning down, arms around the woman's neck. There was a birthday cake in front of them, and they were both looking at the camera and smiling.

He caught himself smiling back.

Frankie had a pretty face and long, dark hair and he wondered what it would feel like to have her arms around his neck and her breath upon his cheek. He saw what appeared to be scarring on her neck and arm and winced, thinking of the pain she must have endured, then looked back at her face.

He knew what she sounded like. Now he knew what she looked like. For some odd reason, he wanted more.

He sat staring at her for the longest time before he remembered there was a letter that had come with the photo.

He opened the letter, then sat back and relaxed, as he would have if he'd been sitting face-to-face with her.

Dear Daniel,

I have the most marvelous news. There is an organization here in the States called Second Wind Dreams that makes dreams come true for the elderly. In this case, if Charlotte's health is good, they will pay for her trip to Positano so that she can visit her Daniel's grave.

I haven't told her yet, because I don't want to get her hopes up only to have them dashed, but I am so excited I can hardly contain myself. And I have another request of you that I hesitate to ask. However, since it's not for me, but for Charlotte, I will ask it of you, anyway.

If, indeed, she is able to travel that distance, I am going to pay my own way and come with her. So I was wondering, if it wouldn't be too much of an imposition, would you agree to be our guide and translator while we are there? Neither Charlotte nor I know any Italian.

I know it's a lot to ask, but I promise we wouldn't be any trouble. Charlotte is a very quiet, dignified woman and would not be demanding, and I promise not to cause you embarrassment. However, if you feel this is asking too much, I will definitely understand, and hope that we will at least get to meet you while we are there.

Thank you in advance.

Frankie

Daniel's heart skipped a beat. Suddenly, every little fantasy he'd let himself weave about this Frances Drummond had the possibility of becoming true. He didn't know whether to be excited or alarmed. Then he glanced back at her picture and decided that it was definitely excitement he felt.

Before he did anything else, he got a snapshot of himself that had been taken in the vineyards near the winery and scanned it into the body of his message back to her.

It had been days since Frankie had sent her photo to Daniel. Her first inclination was that he'd been disgusted by the scars and ended their long-distance chats. She'd been disappointed and had just gotten to the point of convincing herself it didn't matter, when she opened her e-mail and found a message from him.

"Fine, now you surface," she muttered as she clicked on the message to open it. But as soon as she started to read, her heart skipped a beat.

*Dear Frankie, you are beautiful.*

Frankie shivered. She could almost hear him saying those words, even though she knew he was just being kind.

I am sending a photo of myself. It was taken last year before harvest in front of my winery. As you see, I grow several varieties of grapes and make marvelous wines.

Frankie scrolled down to the bottom of the page, realized there was a photo attachment and quickly opened it.

"Oh, Lord," she muttered. "He's a bona fide hunk. The women in Positano must be absolutely stupid to have let you stay single. If I were there I'd—"

Then she sighed. So much for dreaming. She'd have no more luck with him than she did with the good-looking men here.

"Face it, Frances, you are what you are."

Having given herself a firm dressing-down, she printed out the photo and then returned to the body of the message.

I'm sorry I was so long in answering your message, but I have been traveling. It was business for the winery. Something I must do several times a year. I should hire a salesman, but I've always done it myself, and change is something that rarely agrees with me.

It is wonderful news about your friend Charlotte, and of course, if you are able to come, I will not only be your tour guide, but I would gladly offer myself to play host.

Please let me know how your plans evolve. I anxiously await your next message, and I also see that you have given me your phone number. Alas, it is night where you live now, so I will not give you a fright by calling at this time. However, do not doubt my intent to call you soon. I desire to hear your voice again.

Until later, bella signorina. And just in case you don't know what that means, I'm telling you that you are a beautiful young woman.

Daniel

If Frankie had been a puppy, she would have rolled onto her back and wiggled. As it was, she had to settle for a shriek, followed by a fit of hysterical giggles.

"Oh Lord, oh Lord, I'm too old to be acting like this," she said. Grabbing the photo from the printer, she managed a little two-step as she hurried down the hall.

# CHAPTER
## ∽THREE∾

T wo weeks passed before Frankie heard from Second
Wind Dreams again.

She was busy painting Margie's nails. The color
Margie had chosen was Passionate Pink, to match her mood,
she'd said. Frankie had finished her fingernails and was
working on Margie's toenails when her cell phone rang. She
glanced at the Caller ID and stifled a shout. It was Second
Wind Dreams.

Frankie knew she couldn't let Margie know something was
up. The woman couldn't keep a secret for beans.

"Excuse me a minute, Margie. I need to take this."

"I'm not going anywhere," Margie told her, waving her nails

to let them dry as she leaned back in the lounge chair and closed her eyes.

"Thanks," Frankie said. As soon as she was out of earshot she answered the phone. "Hello, Frances Drummond speaking."

"Frances, this is Jean from Second Wind Dreams. I just thought you might like to know that Charlotte Grace's doctor cleared her for travel, so everything is a go. Does she have a passport?"

"Oh, my gosh!" Frankie squealed. "I am so excited, and Charlotte is going to be stunned. Yes, she told me a while ago that she has a passport. So what now?"

"Well, here's what we want to do. We always like to make a big surprise out of the news. Do you think she's up to it?"

"Oh, she'll cry," Frankie said. "We'll probably all be crying, but that's okay. She will be so happy."

"Then this is the way it will work. Continental Airlines has comped you both first-class, round-trip tickets. The Hotel Murat in Positano has comped your suite for a week. We have arranged for her to have a guide to—"

"Did you say *both* of us were getting complimentary tickets?" Frankie interrupted. "*And* a hotel suite?"

"Yes, I did. Second Wind Dreams always ensures the dream-weaver's costs are covered, too."

"Wow! This just keeps getting better and better. I assumed I'd have to pay my own fare."

"We couldn't do our work without people like you, Frances, so we're happy to arrange your plans, as well. Do you have a passport?"

"Yes." Even though she hadn't traveled since her parents' deaths, Frankie kept her passport up to date. "Oh, and one more thing. I have an e-mail acquaintance who lives just outside Positano. He has offered to be our guide. If you don't mind, I would really like to use him. I can give you his name and phone number. You can check him out. He owns a vineyard and winery in the area."

"I'm sure that won't be a problem, either. I didn't know you knew anyone there."

"Well, I didn't until I began trying to find Daniel Morrow's grave. I contacted the very hotel in which you've made Charlotte's reservations to ask if there was anyone in the area who could help me verify the grave location. They gave my request to this man, and he's been more than helpful in answering my questions and concerns. In fact, I've spoken to him on the phone now a couple of times, as well. He seemed excited to be able to help us."

"Fantastic," Jean said. "So...we'll go from there."

"Oh, I'm so excited for Charlotte," Frankie said.

"So are we," Jean echoed. "Until later."

She was standing in the middle of the office with a silly grin on her face when she remembered Margie's toes and dashed out.

Margie was right where Frankie had left her, feet up on the little plush pillow waiting to be finished.

"Sorry," Frankie said. "I didn't think it would take that long."

Margie smiled.

"No problem. I've been going through chapter eleven in my head and think it needs some punch. I believe I'll add the story about the time I got robbed."

Frankie's eyes widened. "You got robbed when you were driving a cab?"

Margie's eyes danced with delight. "Yeah, and guess what he took?"

"All your money?" Frankie said.

"No. My lunch. He stole my Big Mac and fries. And here's the funny part," Margie added. "He was wearing Armani. It just goes to show that thieves come from every corner of society."

Frankie laughed, then picked up the bottle of fingernail polish and finished what she'd started. When she was through with Margie, she went to look for Charlotte. She wasn't going to tell her anything. She just wanted to be with her—maybe judge her state of mind.

She couldn't help but worry just the tiniest bit that she might have breached Charlotte's privacy. What if Charlotte wouldn't go? What if she decided the trip would be too painful?

Frankie saw her sitting outside in a chaise lounge beneath a trio of ancient magnolias, working on her knitting. She took a deep breath and hurried out to join her.

"Hi, honey," she said, and pulled a chair up beside Charlotte's. "What are you working on?"

Charlotte smiled a hello as she held up a partially finished afghan.

"Charlie Coogan's birthday present. It's in a couple of

months. Do you think he'll like it? The color is burgundy. That's sort of a manly color, don't you think?"

"I think it's great," Frankie said. "Charlie will love it."

Charlotte nodded. "Yes, Charlie gets chilled easily."

Frankie sat for a moment, watching Charlotte's fingers fly as she worked the knitting needles in and around the yarn. Then her gaze went to the bit of yellow ribbon at the neck of Charlotte's dress.

"Charlotte?"

"Yes, dear?" Charlotte said.

"Are you happy?"

Charlotte's fingers stilled. There was an odd little smile on her face as she looked up.

"Why...yes, I suppose I am," she said. "Why do you ask?"

Frankie shrugged.

"I don't know. After what you told me the other day about Daniel..."

Charlotte waved a hand in the air, as if to brush away the subject.

"Oh, my goodness, honey. I didn't mean for you to think I've been traumatized by my lack of spine. And that's what it was, you know. I never did know how to stand up to Father. Everything that happened was my own fault. I was grown. I could have defied him. But I didn't. I put Father's wishes above Daniel's. I have no one to blame but myself."

"I know, but it—"

Charlotte leaned forward and patted Frankie's hand.

"Do I wish my life had been different? Yes. But I have lived a good life, even if it wasn't as full as I might have liked." Then she shrugged. "Besides, you can't go through life wishing for things that will never be. That's why I told you not to live with regrets. If you see something…or someone…that you want, go after it with all you've got. You'll learn as you get older that it's not what you failed that haunts you, but what you never tried."

"I think I see what you mean," Frankie said.

Charlotte smiled.

"Of course you do," she said. "That's because I'm old and wise."

Frankie laughed out loud.

Charlotte smirked, then resumed her knitting.

They sat like that for a long while afterward. Charlotte with her knitting and Frankie with her dreams.

It was the perfect way to while away an afternoon.

Second Wind Dreams was coming to the seniors residence in the morning to make the presentation to Charlotte. They would have the travel itinerary and tickets for the trip, which was scheduled to begin in eleven days. Frankie had also been told that they were bringing a film crew, and she was beside herself with anxiety. She needed to calm down, but there was so much riding on Charlotte's reaction, she couldn't relax.

It was almost 1:00 a.m. and she'd read the same page four times in the last fifteen minutes. She glanced at the clock again and then laid down her book. She wasn't certain, but she thought it would be early morning in Italy. Before she could talk herself out of it, she picked up the phone and punched in Daniel's number.

Because of his marketing trip last week, Daniel had fallen behind on paperwork. He'd let it go until it was in chaos and was now forced to spend a perfectly beautiful morning stuck indoors. His mood was dour and his shoulders were slumped as he slogged through the stack of bills and invoices.

Just as he was about to enter another set of figures into the computer, his phone rang. Grateful for the interruption, he answered on the second ring.

"*Ciao.*"

"Daniel? It's me, Frankie. Am I interrupting anything?"

A wide smile spread across his face.

"Frankie! Yes, you are definitely interrupting, and for that I am truly grateful."

She laughed, and the sound soothed the frustration Daniel had been feeling.

"I have news," she said.

"I hope it's good news."

"Oh, yes! The best! The surprise I told you I was working on for Charlotte is going to happen. Second Wind Dreams has agreed to grant Charlotte's dream to visit Daniel's grave. And we're both coming to Positano! Charlotte is going to get to say her goodbyes to Daniel the way she's wanted to for all these years. Isn't that wonderful!"

Daniel's heart was racing. Frankie was coming here?

"Is this true?" he said. "You are really coming to our village?"

"Yes! I hope you don't mind, but we want to take you up on your kind offer to be our guide and translator."

"Mind? Dear Frances…Frankie…I can think of nothing I would rather do." He bounded up from his chair and began to pace. "This is marvelous. Just marvelous. When are you coming? Are you flying into Milan? If so, you can take a smaller plane to Naples, but you will have to come by car from there. I can pick you up at—"

Frankie laughed as she interrupted him.

"Wait! Daniel! Take a breath!"

"Yes, yes, you are right. But it is such wonderful news. So tell me your plans."

"Second Wind Dreams has already organized everything all the way to Positano, including a reserved suite for Charlotte and me at the Hotel Murat. If we called you once we got there, maybe you could come and—"

"If you tell me when you are coming, I will be there waiting." Then he realized that, for the first time in his life, he would have a chance to ask questions about the man who had been his grandfather. "This is the best news I've had in a long time. I am so happy for you, my dear."

"Anyway," Frankie said, "I just couldn't wait to tell you the news. I will send you an e-mail with our itinerary, and thank you again for being so generous with your time."

"Getting to know you and your Charlotte better is never a waste of time."

Daniel heard Frankie sigh, and imagined someone kissing her neck—or maybe the spot right behind her ear—and eliciting the same response.

"Frankie?"

"Yes?"

"I have never asked, but…do you have someone special in your life?"

"You mean a man?"

"Yes, I am speaking of a man…a boyfriend, as you Americans say."

"Hardly. You've seen my picture, so you must understand."

Daniel frowned.

"Yes, I saw that most beautiful picture, but I don't know what you mean."

Frankie laughed, but there was a bitterness in the sound.

"You're just being kind. You saw the scars. What you didn't see is that there's a limp to go with them. The only men in my life are all over the age of seventy, and one of them cheats at checkers."

Daniel's frown deepened. His voice was calm and quiet as he answered.

"I'm sorry, Francesca, but I think you do yourself an injustice."

"I'm just being honest," she said shortly. "It saves a world of hurt. But I must tell you that I do enjoy hearing the Italian version of my name."

Daniel realized that she wanted to shift gears. And, to be truthful, he didn't know that he'd called her Francesca, although he often thought of her by that name.

"Yes, it is a beautiful name," he said. "And I can't wait to meet you. I feel as if I already know you, but it will be wonderful to see you face-to-face."

"Yes, I know what you mean," she said, then added, "How about you? You must have girlfriends."

"I have many friends, but none of them special in that manner. I guess I've always wanted what my father and mother had."

"What was that?" Frankie asked.

"Love at first sight. That's what my mother told me. I never wanted to settle for less."

"That's good," Frankie said, and Daniel detected the note of longing in her voice.

"What is good?"

"Love at first sight. I don't know if I believe in it or not, but I'd sure like to experience it if it's for real."

"So would I," Daniel said softly. "So would I. Now rest well, little schemer. We shall meet soon."

"Yes, we will," Frankie said. "Until then."

"As you say…until then."

For the past thirty minutes, a news van had been parked in the lot of Just Like Home. Every resident had been to the windows at least a half-dozen times, giving their opinion as to why it was there.

Frankie had had a smile on her face all morning, and there was nothing she could do to hide it. Even Charlotte had made a couple of trips to the windows with her knitting. When it was obvious that nothing was happening, she'd returned to her favorite chair in the lobby to finish Charlie's afghan.

Mavis Tulia bustled about like a warden, fussing with the potted plants and straightening pictures on the walls. The floors had been mopped a day early, and if the residents had taken the time to notice, the manager was wearing her best dress and her favorite perfume.

Another van drove up and two people got out. At that point, the news crew started unloading, as well.

"They're coming in!" someone shouted.

Everyone sitting in the lobby looked up. The residents standing at the window suddenly realized that if there was going to be a show, they wanted the best seats. They turned and made their way toward the empty chairs with surprising speed, and were seated when the visitors came in.

Frankie and Mavis greeted the group, and then the camera crew turned toward the residents. Everyone held their breath.

Charlotte's knitting was forgotten as she, too, was caught up in the excitement. Nothing like this had ever happened at Just Like Home.

Margie had announced to everyone that she had it figured out. She was positive someone had won the Publishers Clearing House Sweepstakes and had stuck to her story until she saw that the visitors weren't carrying balloons.

"They always have balloons," she'd said. "It's not them. It's not them."

Frankie's heart was pounding so fast that she was afraid she might pass out. One moment she wanted to laugh and kick up her heels, the next she felt as if she was going to cry.

"Oh, please God, let this be good," Frankie whispered, and then, as they'd planned, she went to stand beside Charlotte's chair.

To Charlotte's surprise, the cameras stopped where she was sitting. She looked up at Frankie.

"What's going on?" she asked.

Frankie knelt down beside her.

"Honey...we have a surprise for you," she said, and then nodded toward the Second Wind Dreams crew.

One of them stepped forward, then sat down beside Charlotte. "Charlotte Grace?"

"Yes, I'm Charlotte Grace."

The woman put her hand on Charlotte's arm.

"Charlotte, we're from Second Wind Dreams. If you've never heard of us, then all you need to know is that we make it our business to give senior citizens in this country a chance to realize lifelong dreams that they think have escaped them."

Charlotte took a slow breath.

"A little fairy told us that when you were young, you had a sweetheart named Daniel Morrow. She said that even though life carried the two of you in different directions, you still hold him close to your heart. Is that true?"

Charlotte nodded, then clutched at the locket around her neck, unable to speak.

"We also understand that he died during World War II and

is buried in a cemetery outside a small village in southern Italy, and that your one big regret in life is that you never got to visit his final resting place. So we at Second Wind Dreams have made it our business to see that your wish comes true. In eleven days, you will be flying nonstop, first class to Milan, Italy. There you will take a smaller plane to Naples. A car will be waiting at the airport to take you to Positano. Upon your arrival, you will be the guest of the luxurious Hotel Murat, once the palace of the brother-in-law of Napoleon Bonaparte. You will have a translator at your disposal, and can spend as much time at Daniel's grave site as you wish."

Charlotte covered her face with her hands and started to cry. Frankie put her arms around her and cried, too. The camera scanned the lobby, capturing the shocked expressions of the residents, which quickly changed from surprise to delight and then tears.

"So, Charlotte Grace, are you ready to take a trip?"

Charlotte looked at Frankie, her face streaked with tears.

"Is this real?" she asked.

Frankie nodded.

"Yes, honey, it's real. And guess what else? You won't have to go all that way alone. I'm coming with you."

Charlotte threw up her hands and fresh tears flowed, but they were tears of joy.

"What am I going to wear?" she asked.

Everyone laughed. It was the perfect question for a woman to ask, no matter what age.

*Eleven days later*

The flight was almost as exciting to Charlotte as the news of the trip had been. Frankie took pictures constantly, so Charlotte would have a photographic record to show the girls back at the home. There were more perks on the first-class flight than either of them had ever experienced.

Champagne cocktails. Pasta salad with lobster. Chicken Cordon Bleu with steamed asparagus. Cheesecake and ice cream sundaes for dessert.

And all served on fine china and silver.

Frankie was just dozing off in the spacious reclining seat when she felt a tug on her arm. She quickly sat up.

"Charlotte, is anything wrong?"

"No. Were you sleeping?"

Frankie smiled.

"Not now. Can't you sleep?"

"No. I'm too excited, and at the same time a little nervous, you know?"

Frankie took Charlotte's hand.

"Yes, darling. I know…or at least, I can imagine." Then she lowered her voice and leaned closer to Charlotte's ear. "You're not mad at me, are you?"

Charlotte's eyes widened, then filled with tears.

"Oh, no, no. I could never be mad at you. You've given me the world. I thought you understood that."

Frankie relaxed.

"I didn't give you the world, Charlotte. Second Wind Dreams gave you the world. I'm just along for the ride."

# CHAPTER
## ~FOUR~

The driver who was to take them to Positano was waiting in the arrivals area at the Naples airport. It took a good half hour to retrieve their luggage, and another fifteen minutes to make their way through the small, but busy airport.

It wasn't until Frankie had Charlotte safely seated in the car and they were headed south out of Naples that she began to breathe easier. It was exciting to be in such a romantic country, but it was daunting not to know the language. Frankie kept thinking of Daniel waiting for them in Positano and finally allowed herself to relax.

\* \* \*

Daniel glanced at his watch, then ordered another lemonade from the waitstaff at the Hotel Murat. He wasn't thirsty, but it was something to do to pass the time.

Two men he'd grown up with waved at him as they walked by on the street beyond the gates, but they didn't stop to visit. The outdoor patio of the Hotel Murat was for guests, although locals often gathered there in the evening for drinks or dinner. Daniel didn't regret their haste. He was too excited about Frankie and Charlotte's imminent arrival to spend time in idle talk.

Another five minutes passed and the ice in his lemonade began to melt. The scent of flowering vines filled the air, masking the faint, but ever-prevalent scent of fish and salt air coming from the Mediterranean and the beach below.

Finally, he abandoned the lemonade and walked around the patio to where he could better see the view. He knew this village as well as he knew his own face, but wondered how it would appear to the American women.

Tiny houses had been built all up the side of the mountain, linked by winding and narrow cobbled streets. Storefronts lined the spiral pathways in colorful array as owners spread their wares on tables or hung them along the high walls that bordered every pathway. Three-wheeled motorcycles had been modified for use as miniature trucks, complete with a cab and a small wooden bed in which to transport goods. They wheeled up and down the streets, weaving in and out among the locals and the tourists with surprising skill, while down on the beach, cafés and restaurants catered to the weary and hungry.

Small, privately owned fishing boats rocked upon the water, their anchors holding them close to the rocky shore. Farther out was an island that appeared to be floating on top of the sea. Gulls and other seabirds perched on mastheads and roofs, darting in and out among the swimmers braving the waters.

Would Frankie see his village for what it really was? Could she see beyond the tourist trappings to the good people who had endured for generations, living out their simple lives with no excuses or explanations? He hoped so. For reasons he didn't want to admit just yet, he wanted Frances Drummond to love his Italy as much as he did.

As he was gazing upon the pure blue of the sea, he became aware of a small car stopping outside the gates to the hotel.

He turned, and then his heart skipped a beat.

It was them.

Unaware he was holding his breath, he stood motionless, watching as two women stepped out of the tiny vehicle. One was young and slender, with wavy hair the color of dark chocolate. The other was small and fragile. Her silver hair was short and curly, and she leaned on the young woman as they walked. He saw the scars that Frankie was so self-conscious about, and he noticed her limp, as well. But they amounted to nothing to him. It was that near-perfect face that intrigued him, as well as the tenderness of her behavior toward the elderly woman.

He began to move, willing Frankie to look up.

Closer and closer he came until he could hear the younger woman's laughter. He felt himself go weak inside. He'd known it would sound like that.

*Look at me, Francesca. Look at me.*

She kept walking, her head bent to the older woman's ear as she helped her up the steps.

*Francesca…Frankie. Turn around and look at me. I am here.*

Frankie was relieved to have reached their destination. As exhausted as she was by the traveling, her main concern was still for Charlotte's health. Charlotte had slept some on the plane, but not nearly enough to maintain her normal routine. Right now, Frankie's focus was on getting them to their rooms, then making sure Charlotte got some rest.

She was laughing at something that Charlotte said, a half eye on the man who was carrying their bags up to the hotel desk, when the skin suddenly crawled at the back of her neck.

She paused, almost stumbling, then caught herself and steadied Charlotte.

Again, the feeling came, only this time stronger.

"Wait," she said softly.

Charlotte stopped.

Frankie lifted her head, then slowly, slowly, began to turn, scanning the faces of the people around them.

And then she saw him, standing just outside the hotel beside a table with a wide, colorful umbrella. His eyes were dark, his expression fixed, as if he was waiting for a sign.

She took a deep breath, then exhaled on a sigh.

Daniel.

He was here, just as he'd promised.

She lifted a hand in a tentative wave and stifled the urge to run into his arms. Instead, she put a hand over the scar on her neck in a halfhearted gesture to hide it.

*What's wrong with you, Frances? You don't know this man.*

Even as she was dealing with that truth, there was another she still had to face. Something had happened just now that she couldn't explain.

When he started toward them, she didn't realize she was holding her breath.

Closer and closer he walked, until she could see the shadows his lashes cast upon his cheeks. He was wearing light-colored slacks and a white shirt, open at the collar, with the long sleeves rolled up almost to his elbows. His stride was long and graceful, and there was a steadiness in his expression that calmed her.

"Daniel?"

He clasped her hand, then lifted it to his lips and kissed it. She felt his breath, and then the firmness of his lips as they brushed the surface of her skin.

While her greeting had been a question, his was a confirmation.

"Francesca."

She smiled. "Yes, it's me." Then Frankie remembered herself and stepped aside to introduce Charlotte. "Charlotte, this is my friend Daniel. He's going to be our guide and translator. Daniel, this is my friend Charlotte Grace."

Charlotte knew she had stopped breathing. It wasn't until a butterfly flitted past her line of vision that she took a quick breath and shuddered.

A ghost. She hadn't expected to see Daniel's ghost. Was he going to haunt her? Was he still angry after all these years for the way she'd let him down?

*Oh, Lord, why did I come?*

The man before her reached for her hand, as he had Frankie's, and brushed a soft kiss upon the thin, papery skin.

"May I call you Charlotte?" he asked.

Charlotte nodded, but her gaze never left Daniel's face.

"You must be exhausted," he said, and cupped her elbow with one hand, offering Frankie his arm. "Come, ladies, let me help you get settled in your room. You must have traveled all night. Did you get any sleep on the plane?"

Despite his lovely accent, it was the ordinary questions he was asking that settled Charlotte's nerves. She kept glancing at him off and on as they made their way to the suite that was to be their home for the next six days, until her notion of a ghost had passed.

Of course he wasn't Daniel's ghost. Just because they bore the same name didn't mean anything. Yes, he was tall as her

Daniel had been, and he had a way of holding his shoulders as he walked that reminded her of Daniel, as well. But her Daniel's hair had been chestnut, his eyes a bright blue, and he'd had a cleft in his chin. This man's hair was dark and wavy, with eyes so dark they looked black, and a face that could have been carved by Michelangelo himself.

By the time they reached their rooms, she had regained her composure.

"Thank you for all of your help," Charlotte said, as the bellman unlocked their door.

Daniel looked at her and smiled. "You are most welcome… both of you," he said, and his gaze shifted to Frankie.

Frankie was speechless. There was an invisible something in the air between her and Daniel that was almost frightening. She'd never felt so helpless. She was out of her element with this magnificent man.

"Are you hungry?" Daniel asked, as the bellman led them inside.

"Yes," Frankie said, and then gasped as she looked at their suite. "Lord have mercy. Would you look at this."

Charlotte was beaming, but far more practical in her acceptance.

"It used to be a palace, my dear. It's to be expected that some of the grandeur would have survived."

The blue-and-white floor tiles were Italian marble and the ceilings at least twenty or thirty feet high. The furnishings were old, but elegant, and spoke of a time long past. The bedroom was enormous, with floor-to-ceiling windows that opened out onto a small terrace, and there was a closet that ran the length of one wall. The bed was at least twice the size of an American king-size bed, and Frankie had a childish urge to jump on it, just to see how high she would bounce.

When the bellman showed them to the bath, even Charlotte had to gasp. Like everything else, it was massive, lined in amber-colored marble with gold streaks running through it. The sunken tub and shower were so wide and deep that it required six stair steps to get down into it. Had it been full, it would have been over Charlotte's head.

Charlotte actually clapped her hands in delight.

"Frankie, get the camera. Margie is never going to believe this unless she sees it for herself."

Daniel laughed, and the sound echoed within the room, filling Frankie with what could only be pure joy as she got the camera and took pictures for Charlotte.

"It is quite something, is it not?" Daniel said, then he took Frankie by the hand. "May I speak to you alone in the other room for a moment?"

Frankie managed a nod.

"Charlotte, will you excuse us?"

"Don't mind me," Charlotte said, as she dug in her purse for money to tip the bellman.

"Keep your money," Daniel said. "It's all been taken care of by the people who brought you to me."

"Oh! Well! This just gets better and better, doesn't it, dear?"

Charlotte said, and then wandered back into the bedroom and sat down on the side of the bed.

Frankie followed her out and saw the exhaustion on her face.

"Daniel, will you give me a minute? I want to make sure Charlotte is...comfortable."

He understood.

"I'll be in the drawing room," he said, and walked out.

Frankie knelt at Charlotte's feet and began removing her shoes.

"Just lie back, dear. The room is nice and cool, and you can have a good nap. I'll have food for you to snack on when you wake, and we don't have to go anywhere tonight."

"I'm not going anywhere tonight," Charlotte said. "But if that gorgeous young man in there wants to take you somewhere, I'll be very disappointed with you if you don't go."

"Oh, but—"

"But nothing," Charlotte said. "You came as a companion, not a nurse. I'm not sick, just tired. I'm not dead, just old. So go have fun for both of us and tell me all about it when you get back. Right now, I just want to sleep and dream of Daniel, and then tomorrow...tomorrow..." Her voice trailed off and tears came to her eyes. She took a deep breath and made herself finish. "Tomorrow I shall go see him, again."

Frankie hugged her close, then helped her off with her dress, leaving Charlotte in her slip and undies.

"Here, let's pull the covers back," she said. "You might get too cool with the air-conditioning."

"That feels wonderful," Charlotte said, her head sinking into the pillows. "Oh, Lord," she added. "The pillows are filled with down. I haven't slept on a feather pillow since Mama died."

Frankie grinned. "Sweet dreams, dear," she said, and pulled a sheet and blanket up over the older woman's shoulders.

"Go away now," Charlotte ordered.

"Yes, ma'am," Frankie said, and tiptoed out of the room.

Daniel had opened the blinds and was standing at one of the windows overlooking the village below. At the sound of her footsteps, he turned and was again struck by the sight of her face. He could tell she was self-conscious about her limp, and to save her, he didn't wait for her to cross the room. Instead, he went to meet her, and when they were face-to-face, he opened his arms.

Frankie didn't give herself time to think about what she was doing. She just followed her heart and let his arms close around her.

"Welcome to Positano," Daniel said softly. "Welcome to my world."

Frankie shivered.

Daniel leaned back so that he could see her face.

"Are you ill? Do you need to rest, too? I can come back later tonight and—"

"I'm not ill," Frankie said. "As for sleep, I can do that when I go home. For now, I don't want to miss a moment of anything."

Daniel stilled. She'd done it again—said what he'd been feeling before he gathered his wits.

"So, you feel it, too, don't you, *bella?*"

Frankie looked away. She didn't want to get hurt, but she felt this was a chance of a lifetime. If the man was kind enough to pretend he didn't see her flaws, she wanted to make as many memories with him as she could—memories that would last the rest of her life.

She took a deep breath, and then made herself look at him.

"If you're talking about the rapid heartbeat, sweaty palms and loss of good sense, then yes."

Daniel laughed, then kissed her.

It was the litmus test that branded them goners.

The kiss sparked a hunger within Frankie that was so sharp she wanted to cry, especially when he finally tore himself away. The absence of his lips was actually painful.

"Starvation," she muttered.

Daniel cupped her face. "I am sorry. Of course, you are hungry. You already said so once. Come, come. We will go down to the beach. There are some wonderful little cafés. You can eat and I will watch you smile. Then we will both be fed."

*Oh, Lord, it isn't enough that he's unbelievably gorgeous. He has to talk pretty, too.*

"I didn't mean I was starving for food," she said. "But you can feed me just the same."

After she freshened up, Daniel took her by the hand and escorted her from the room, taking care to lock the door behind them, leaving Charlotte to her rest.

Careful not to go too fast, Daniel held tight to her arm as they walked all the way down to the beach. They strolled past a church and bell tower, as white as the clouds above the horizon.

"Oh, my gosh!" Frankie exclaimed with delight. "It looks like something out of *The Godfather*."

"What is this godfather?" Daniel asked.

Frankie grinned.

"Sorry. It's an old, but very famous American movie made about Italian immigrants who came to America and who were part of the Mafia. I was speaking of the church. There is one just like it in the movie."

Daniel nodded. "Yes, I believe I do know of this film. I had just forgotten the name." He glanced at her and smiled. "Americans are very fascinated with the Mafioso, are they not?"

"Yes, I suppose we are," Frankie said, looking all around her. "This village is marvelous. So many different styles of architecture."

Daniel nodded.

"Just about every country in ancient Europe with an army and ships raided these shores. The faces of our people and the architecture of our homes and buildings are evidence of these invaders."

Frankie couldn't quit talking and pointing, and Daniel couldn't quit looking at her. Even as they were seated at a table underneath a colorful awning and sipping cool drinks, he was trying to come to terms with the truth of what had happened to him today.

He'd known the first moment he saw her, head bent to the needs of another, laughter only a whisper away, that he'd found the woman he'd been looking for. His mother had been right. There was such a thing as love at first sight. Daniel knew he'd been smitten, and he had only six days to do something about it.

They ate and they laughed and watched the sun go down behind the mountains. Then Daniel took her by the hand and walked her back up the winding paths. The streetlights cast shadows on her delicate features. He wished he didn't have to say good-night.

All too soon, they were at the hotel. He escorted her through the lobby, then up the staircase until they were standing outside the suite.

Frankie turned to Daniel and put both hands on his chest, feeling his heart beating steadily beneath her palms.

"I don't know how to thank you," she said softly.

"I do," he said, and cupped her face with his hands.

The kiss was tender, yet the depth of emotion behind it was anything but. This bond between them made no sense, and yet there it was.

Frankie's hands slipped up around his neck and suddenly she was kissing him back, but when Daniel slid his hands to the back of her neck, she flinched.

The scars. He'd felt the scars. Surely he would be disgusted. She pulled away from him first, unable to bear the hurt and embarrassment of his rejection.

Daniel knew what had happened, but he wouldn't let her go. He continued to hold her, his fingers locked at the back of her neck and his thumbs rubbing against the curve of her cheeks until she was breathing easy. Only then did he bend down until their foreheads were touching.

"I will dream of you tonight," he said softly, brushing a second kiss upon her brow. "Sleep well. Tomorrow I will take you and Charlotte to see Daniel's grave."

Frankie waited as he opened the door, then handed her the key.

"Lock it after I leave you," he said.

"Yes, I will."

"Until tomorrow."

Frankie sighed. "Until tomorrow."

Inside the room, Frankie listened to the fading sound of his footsteps. She was setting herself up for a great big hurt, but God help her, she didn't care. She wanted whatever he would give her, even if it didn't mean anything to him.

Blissfully tired, Frankie quickly showered and got ready for bed. She checked on Charlotte, who hadn't seemed to have wakened since she'd left, then gratefully crawled into her own bed in the next room and closed her eyes.

Breakfast was a hasty affair. Charlotte had been so distracted that morning she'd put on two different shoes, and it was all Frankie could do to get her to settle down and eat.

"You have to eat something," she argued. "You skipped dinner last night, so you don't have a say in the matter."

"Oh, pooh," Charlotte said as she slathered a soft cheese on some warm bread and took a bite. "Umm, good." She took a piece of melon that Frankie had put on her plate.

Frankie ate without tasting. Her thoughts were filled with Daniel, and she was afraid. She'd let herself become infatuated with a man she hardly knew. She could only imagine what he must be thinking of her. She was a novice when it came to worldly men, but as she'd told herself last night, she wouldn't regret the sadness she might feel later. Even if she did wind up getting hurt, she wasn't going to deny herself the luxury of Daniel's company.

Just as they were finishing up, there was a knock on the door and a bellman was on the stoop, telling them that Daniel was waiting for them below.

They gathered up camera and film and hats for the bright Italian sun, then as soon as Charlotte took her daily meds, they were off.

*"Buon giorno,"* Daniel greeted them in the lobby. "Forgive me for not coming up myself, but I've been on the phone all morning with an unhappy customer."

Frankie frowned. "If there's a problem with you taking time away from your work, I'm sure we can——"

Daniel put a finger on her lips, then shook his head.

"There is no problem. Only the wishes of two beautiful women to grant."

Charlotte smiled and clapped her hands lightly.

"Well said, young man, and you must know how anxious I am to get started."

"Then we are off," he said grandly. "We must walk about the length of one block up this street to a small courtyard where my car is parked. Unfortunately, it is too wide for our narrow streets. Is that all right?"

"Perfect," Charlotte said. "I like to walk. It's good for my constitution."

Daniel slipped his arm through Charlotte's and Frankie did the same on the opposite side, almost carrying the older woman to the car. Daniel helped Charlotte into the backseat and buckled her in, then settled Frankie in the seat beside him. Soon, they were scooting through the streets and out onto the highway.

"It's not far," Daniel said. "Enjoy the sights, and if you have questions, please feel free to ask."

"I have one," Charlotte said. "What are all these trees?"

"Olive trees," Daniel said. "But it's not yet time for harvest."

"I like green olives," Charlotte said.

"Not these, you wouldn't. They are very bitter. It is the process they go through as they are bottled that gives them a milder taste."

"Is your home in this direction, too?" Frankie asked.

Daniel ventured a glance at the woman beside him.

"Yes, it's less than a half kilometer from the cemetery."

He hoped Frankie would come to his home before her visit was over.

Finally they arrived at the cemetery. It was quite large and scattered up and down a hillside, its boundaries marked by a three-foot wall built from the rocky earth on which it stood. There were all manner of gravestones and tombs, some grand, some little more than a cross. Flowers in different degrees of decay decorated the graves, making it obvious which ones had been recently visited.

Daniel parked, and they got out. "I'm sorry, but it is a bit of a walk to where we must go."

All the joy was gone from Charlotte's face, and had been from the moment they'd stopped.

"That's all right," she said. "I've come this far. A few more steps can't matter."

"Then take my hand," Daniel offered.

"And mine," Frankie added.

"I want my camera," Charlotte said.

"I have your camera," Frankie told her. "And a blanket, as well. I thought you might like to stay there awhile."

Charlotte nodded, her soft curls bouncing lightly around her face. But her eyes were already on the tombstones.

Daniel took a bundle from the trunk of the car and led the way. Countless times he had come with his grandmother and mother to place flowers on the grave.

No one spoke as they walked, and when Daniel suddenly stopped, Charlotte stumbled. If he hadn't been holding her, she would have fallen.

"This is it," Daniel said, and pointed down.

The tombstone had been hand-carved out of local stone, the words cut roughly into the surface, and then worn smooth by the passage of time.

Without thinking, Charlotte reached for her locket as she read the words on the stone. Her hands were shaking, her chin trembling as she struggled with her emotions.

Frankie spread out the blanket, then took Charlotte by the hand.

"Sit here, dear," she said. "Stay as long as you like. We'll be on that bench just over there, okay?"

Charlotte nodded without looking, unaware that Frankie had just taken her picture at the grave.

Frankie glanced at Daniel and started to speak, then caught a strange expression on his face. He wasn't looking at Charlotte at all, as she might have expected. Instead, he was staring intently at the tombstone marking Daniel Morrow's final resting place.

To her surprise, he walked over and removed the dead flowers from the vase beside the marker, unwrapped his bundle, and put a fresh bouquet of flowers in their place.

He took Frankie's hand, and as they turned to go, they heard Charlotte say, "Hello, Danny, it's me, Charlotte. I've come to say I'm sorry."

Frankie bit her lip to keep from crying. Her toe caught on the uneven ground, and she stumbled. If it hadn't been for Daniel's quick reflexes, she would have fallen headfirst onto the rough ground. Her face turned bright pink as she righted herself and looked away.

"Sorry," she said. "I'm always so clumsy."

"Sssh," Daniel silenced her. "No explanation is necessary. I am just glad you're not hurt."

Frankie nodded, but was still unable to look at him. When they reached the bench, she was thankful to sit down.

Daniel dumped the paper he'd had around the flowers into

a trash bin beneath the tree, then sat down beside her. For a few minutes, he just held her hand without talking.

Finally, it was the chirping of a bird that started their conversation.

"He sounds happy," Frankie said, pointing to the creature perched high in the tree.

"He should be," Daniel said. "Here he has nothing to complain about."

Frankie sighed.

"Thank you for this."

He nodded while still eyeing the old woman on the blanket a short distance away.

"Is she strong...your Charlotte?"

"You mean healthwise?"

"Yes."

"She seems to be," Frankie said.

"Her heart is strong?"

"To my knowledge." Frankie frowned. "Why do you ask? Is something wrong?"

Daniel didn't answer. He wanted to, but he didn't know what to say. Then he turned to her, staring long and hard into the sweetness of her face.

"This trip for Charlotte...it is filled with sadness and regret, is it not?"

Frankie nodded.

"Life is so short." Daniel lifted his hand to smooth away a stray strand of hair that had blown near her eyes. "Do you remember what I said about love at first sight?"

Frankie felt the blood draining from her face and wondered if she looked as faint as she felt.

"Yes. I remember."

He took her hand, absently threading his fingers through hers.

"I'm going to say this now, because I don't want to be like Charlotte someday. Old and filled with regret for what I should have said or done. I felt it, Frances. Yesterday, when you turned around and looked into my eyes. The breath left my body and then came back like a blow to my belly. I didn't know whether to grab you and run and never look back, or trust fate to promise you would return my feelings in kind."

Frankie panicked. She'd dreamed of hearing something like this from a man one day, but this man was a stranger.

"Oh, Daniel, if—"

He put a finger on her lips.

"Say nothing now. It's enough that you know how I feel."

Frankie was trembling. She didn't know whether to laugh or cry. Like Daniel, she was troubled by what she was feeling. It was too much too soon. Then she reminded herself that it wasn't so soon at all. In fact, she'd been waiting twenty-seven years for this moment to happen. That it was happening in a cemetery in a country foreign to her own seemed immaterial. The miracle was that it had finally come.

She leaned against Daniel's shoulder. He put an arm around her and pulled her close.

The bird continued to sing as Charlotte Grace said her goodbyes.

# CHAPTER
## ❧ FIVE ❧

Three days had come and gone since their initial visit to Daniel Morrow's grave. Each day, Charlotte had asked to be taken there, and each day, Daniel had done so. Because of an emergency at the winery, he'd been unable to spend the rest of the time with them and had given the responsibility of getting them back to the hotel to his uncle Paolo, who spoke no English.

Each visit was shorter than the previous one, until on the fourth day, Charlotte came only to place fresh flowers on the grave. After that, she was ready to go. Neither Daniel nor Frankie knew what had transpired for Charlotte during these visits, but whatever it was, she'd come to terms with her loss.

\* \* \*

Charlotte stepped back from the flowers she'd laid on the grave and glanced up at Daniel. Again, as she had done so many times before, she felt as if she was staring at a ghost. This time, she decided to mention it.

"You know something, Daniel?"

He smiled at her.

"Yes, but probably not your something."

She shook her head in pretend disgust, although her eyes were dancing with delight.

"Such a tease. That's good, though. A man should have a sense of humor."

His grin widened, and a chill ran through Charlotte.

"I don't understand it…maybe it's because we're here in this place and it's the closest I've been to my Daniel in more than sixty-seven years…but there are times when you look like him."

Daniel reeled as if he'd been slapped. He tried to recover his smile, but it just wouldn't come.

"Really," he said.

She nodded, then tugged at the yellow ribbon around her neck until she had pulled the locket out.

"Yes, really. Look. This is a picture of him when he was about twenty."

She opened the locket.

Daniel leaned down.

Charlotte watched his eyes narrow and his nostrils flare.

Again, she was struck by the notion that this man had secrets he wasn't willing to share.

"Do you see it?" she asked.

He straightened, then momentarily looked away. When he turned back to Charlotte, she was still there, waiting for his answer.

He put a hand on her shoulder.

"Yes...I do see it, Charlotte. It's a strange thing to see oneself in another's face."

She wanted him to say more, but it was obvious he would not. There was a moment when she wondered if he knew something about her Daniel that he couldn't tell. She shook off the thought as nothing but an old woman's foolishness. How could he know anything? He was far too young.

Charlotte tucked the locket back into the neckline of her collar and smoothed her hands down the front of her dress as they walked back to the car.

"Thank you so much for being so generous with your time," she said. "I won't be needing to come back again. I've said my goodbyes, you know."

"Have you now?" Daniel asked.

She nodded.

"I hope they were fond goodbyes?"

"They were as they should be," she said, and then changed the subject as they reached the car. "Where's Frankie?"

Daniel frowned slightly as he looked around, but his frown disappeared as he spied her.

"She's over there." He pointed to an outcropping of rock beneath some trees.

"What's she doing?" Charlotte asked.

"I don't know," Daniel said. "But I'll go get her."

Charlotte got into the car as he went to get Frankie. Just as he was walking up, he saw her drop something into her pocket.

"Hey…I thought we'd lost you. What are you doing?" he asked.

"Leaving a piece of myself behind," she said, and pointed at the dead tree trunk.

Daniel's gaze immediately caught on the heart she'd cut into the bark, and the initials she'd carved inside.

*F.D. loves D.S.*

Daniel smiled as he traced the shape and words, then took her in his arms.

"Ah, Francesca…again, you…how do you say…beat me to the drink."

Frankie laughed. "The phrase is, beat me to the punch."

He frowned. "I thought a punch *was* a drink."

She jabbed him lightly on the shoulder with a clenched fist.

"That's the punch referred to in the expression," she said.

"The English language is a puzzle," he mused. "Still, you say what is in your heart, while I seem to fall short of doing the same. So, you carve your feelings in this bark, as you have carved yourself into my soul. I cannot think of life without you. The fact that I've had to be away from you so much these past three days has been a big disappointment. I had planned so much for us to do, and yet life kept interrupting."

"I know it couldn't be helped," Frankie said.

She couldn't think of life without him, either, but wasn't willing to get her heart broken by saying any more. The way she looked at it, what happened to them next was up to Daniel.

"Will you and Charlotte come to my house for dinner tonight?"

The question both surprised and delighted Frankie. "Yes. We'd love to."

"If I ask, would you both stay the night, as well?"

"Yes, so please ask."

Daniel started to smile. "So, Frances Drummond, then I am asking you to stay with me tonight."

"Yes."

He shook his head, then kissed her gently.

"Tonight I have things to say to Charlotte that she might not want to hear, and I need you with me."

Frankie frowned.

"I can't imagine what they could be. She likes you, you know."

"And I like her, as well. Now come. I need to get you back so you can both pack an overnight bag for the visit."

Charlotte fussed over her clothes like a girl going on a first date, then fussed again about what to take to spend the night at Daniel's house.

Frankie packed her bag almost as an afterthought. She knew what she wanted to happen tonight, and if it did, a nightgown was going to be the last thing on her mind. Still, she prepared for a disappointment by packing it anyway.

Daniel picked them up just as the sun was going down. He spoke to the hotel clerk, letting him know that the two American women would be spending the night at his home, and that, when they were ready to come back, he would return them to the hotel personally. With that, they walked the short distance up through the narrow streets to his car.

Daniel alternated between bouts of nervousness and bouts of elation. He knew what he wanted to happen tonight, but after he revealed the truth about his family, he had no idea if either woman would speak to him again.

The drive was brief. They arrived at his home just as the sun disappeared over the mountains, although the vineyards could still be seen, clinging to the mountainside. The winery was a distance from the house, maybe a quarter of a mile, but still visible in the fading light.

Daniel helped both women out of the car.

"Welcome to my home," he said. "Come inside. *Zia* Maria has fixed some special dishes for us tonight and there is much for me to show you."

Frankie could see how anxious Daniel was, and knew that he was working up his nerve to tell them whatever it was he had to say.

"Does your aunt live close by?" Charlotte asked.

Daniel smiled and pointed to the small house just across the road.

"Yes, she and *Zio* Paolo live right over there. Actually, she is the reason we met. She works at the hotel where you are staying. The manager gave her your first e-mail to bring to me."

"Really?" Frankie said. "I wonder why?"

"Because I speak English, and because he knew we both lived near the cemetery where the American GIs were buried."

"Oh." Frankie glanced at the house across the road again. "Will we be eating with them?"

"Not this time," Daniel said. "But maybe another."

"We leave in two days."

Daniel's eyes darkened.

"Don't remind me," he said, and then shook off the dark feelings. "Come, come, we'll go inside now. We'll eat…laugh… make memories."

Charlotte took the arm that he offered.

"I like that phrase…making memories. It's a good thing to do."

When they finished the main meal, Charlotte wandered about the living area while Daniel and Frankie carried dishes into the kitchen, then prepared coffee and dessert on a tray.

Charlotte walked over to a massive fireplace at the end of the room and glanced absently at the framed photos sitting on the mantel.

Reaching up, she took one down and turned it toward the lights to see it better. She was still staring at the photo as Daniel came into the room with a carafe of coffee and three cups on an ornate silver tray.

He set it down and started to speak, then realized what

Charlotte was doing. He glanced at Frankie and took a deep breath. It was time.

"Charlotte."

She looked up. Her eyes were bright with unshed tears, and even though he was at the other end of the room, he could tell her chin was trembling.

"Who is this woman and this child?" she asked.

"Daniel, what's wrong?" Frankie sounded concerned.

He squeezed her hand, then let it go and crossed the room

Charlotte took a deep breath and s—

Daniel took her by the hand and led her to a nearby chair. Frankie followed, aware something momentous was happening.

"Charlotte, I have come to care for you a great deal, and because I do, this is very difficult for me to say. I don't want to hurt you...ever. But if the truth is to be told, I have to risk that. Will you hear me out without judging me?"

She nodded.

"My grandmother was seventeen years old when the war came to Europe. She was barely eighteen when the American GIs liberated Italy."

Charlotte gasped and reached for her locket, clutching it tightly in her hand.

Daniel saw her fingers wrap around it and groaned inwardly.

"She met and fell instantly in love with one of the soldiers."

"Danny," Charlotte said softly.

Daniel nodded. Frankie gasped.

"All my life I've known that Private first class, Daniel Louis Morrow was my grandfather. I have lived with that knowledge with a sense of pride. But you also have to realize that he knew my grandmother less than six weeks. He was killed by a sniper before he learned that she carried his child."

Charlotte moaned and leaned back in her chair, closing her eyes. The picture she'd been holding fell into her lap.

...was only silence, and then they heard Charlotte sigh. To their relief, when she opened her eyes, they were clear and dry.

"I think I've suspected this from the moment I saw you, then when I saw this picture, I could no longer deny the truth. Your mother is the image of Danny." Charlotte looked up at Daniel. "You know what my first impression of you was?"

"What?" he asked.

"I thought I was seeing a ghost."

"Oh, Charlotte, I'm so sorry," Frankie said. "I would never have done all of this had I known."

Charlotte grabbed at Frankie's hand.

"Oh dear...oh, no...you both misunderstand. This was somewhat of a shock, but not in a bad way. You see, I don't view this as any kind of betrayal on Daniel's part. I'm the one who turned him down. I'm the one who sent him away." Then she did start to cry. "This is actually the best news I could have been given."

Daniel was so stunned, he sat down with a thump.

"How so?" Frankie asked.

"All these years, I've pictured Danny brokenhearted, then dying and being buried alone in a foreign land. Knowing that he'd found some happiness again, however brief, lifts a burden of guilt that I've carried for most of my life." She looked at Daniel again. "You have just given me the best gift. Seeing you is like seeing Danny again. He's still alive to me now, because of you."

Daniel couldn't speak. He took both of Charlotte's hands and lifted them to his face, then kissed the palm of each.

Charlotte removed her hands from his and cupped his face, smiling through tears.

"You poor dear. All this time you were afraid you were going to hurt my feelings. Thank God you found the courage to tell me. I wish I could make you understand what a miracle this is for me."

Suddenly she clapped her hands.

"Oh! I just realized! You have family in the States. A lot of family, and most of them still live in the state of Illinois, where we're from. This news is going to send them over the moon."

"Then you're not angry with me," Daniel said.

"Haven't I just been saying that?" Charlotte wiped her eyes and sat up. "I can't wait to get home and give the Morrow family a call."

Daniel hugged her, then turned and hugged Frankie, too.

Smiling, Charlotte pointed to the coffee.

"Weren't we about to have dessert?"

Daniel glanced at the melted gelato. "I'm afraid it's ruined."

"It's just as well," Charlotte said. "I have to watch my girlish figure. And on that note, if you don't mind, I think I'd like to go to bed. This has been a long day and I have a lot to sleep on."

"I'll go with you," Frankie said, then touched Daniel briefly. "Be right back?"

"Of course," he said.

A few minutes later, Frankie returned. Daniel was standing in the open doorway, looking out into the dark. She walked up behind him and touched his shoulder.

As she did, he turned. There was an expression in his eyes that she didn't want to decipher.

"She's smiling," Frankie said. "I haven't seen Charlotte smile like this…well…ever. It's as if she's a young, carefree girl all over again."

Daniel turned and hugged her, then whispered in her ear.

"I want to make love to you."

Frankie's heart almost stopped. She was afraid—so afraid. But not of letting him see her scars. She was afraid that if they did make love, she would die when they had to say goodbye. Still, she wanted him and these memories more than she'd ever wanted anything in her entire life.

"Then do it," she whispered.

A light glittered in Daniel's eyes, and then he swept her off her feet and into his arms.

His bedroom was at the other end of the house, and Frankie had brief glimpses of wide hallways, low ceilings and arched doorways as he carried her there.

The massive four-poster bed was turned back, revealing gold satin sheets beneath a red-and-gold tapestry spread.

"Daniel! This is beautiful," she said.

He laid her on the bed. "No more than you are, Frances Drummond. I have been dreaming of you and this moment all my life," he said softly. "I don't want you to ever forget our first time."

Frankie's heart skipped a beat. First time? Did that mean there would be others?

"Love me, Daniel. Let me love you back."

And so the night passed in passion, until finally they fell asleep in each other's arms. The next morning Daniel was the first to wake. He had been watching her for some time when he saw her eyelids beginning to flutter. She was waking.

Daniel raised himself up on one elbow and looked down at her face.

"Good morning, Francesca."

Frankie smiled lazily, then stretched like a cat that had been sleeping in the sun.

"It's not a good morning, it's a great one," she said.

Daniel smiled and nuzzled the side of her neck, raking his lips across the puckered flesh. Almost immediately, he paused. There was a moment of silence, then she heard him sigh. When he looked up at her, the smile was gone.

Her heart skipped a beat. *This is it. This is the part where he finally admits that those scars he just kissed repulse him.* She braced herself for the pain.

"I can't bear for you to leave me," Daniel said. "I've waited so long for you to come. Please love me back, Frances Drummond. Please say you will marry me and share my world and my life."

Frankie's shattered senses suddenly focused. This was the last thing she'd expected him to say.

"Oh, Daniel, you don't know how long I've dreamed of someone saying those very words to me, and yet we've known each other such a short time. I'm afraid you'll come to regret your offer, and I just couldn't bear to face your rejection."

Frowning, Daniel shook his head and gathered her up in his arms.

"My only regret will be if I lose you," he whispered. "Please, don't make me beg."

Frankie rose up on her elbows and cupped her face with both hands.

"I have things to deal with back home," she said. "I have property and—"

"I'll come with you," Daniel told her. "Please say I can come with you. We'll make it happen faster if we do it together, and…and I can meet my grandfather's family at the same time. After that, I will ask you the same question again, and if you say yes, which I pray you will, then we can get married in your town and have a reception in mine. What do you say?"

Frankie started to cry, but they were wild, happy tears.

"I say yes."

Charlotte smirked when she was told the news.

"I suspected it all along," she said, grinning at both Daniel and Frankie.

"Then, if things work out, will you be my matron of honor?" Frankie asked.

Charlotte's features crumpled.

"Oh, darling, you always seem to know the very best thing to say and do. Being a part of your wedding will be the closest I'll ever come to the ceremony I should have had with my own Daniel. I would be honored."

Daniel put his arms around her and hugged her gently.

"The honor will be ours," he said.

"I want to have it at Just Like Home," Frankie told Charlotte. "That's where my very best friends are, you know. Daniel and I have talked about it." She looked at him. "Once we get to the States, if he still thinks he can't live without me, we'll have the wedding there and then the reception here when we return."

Charlotte's smile slipped.

"Oh. Yes. Of course you'll be coming back here." She forced a smile. "And that's as it should be."

Daniel glanced at Frankie and she nodded. Now it was time to break the rest of their news.

Daniel sat down on the sofa beside Charlotte and took her by the hand.

"I haven't known you nearly as long as Frankie has, but I've known you long enough to realize that it would be a great loss to leave you behind. So, when we marry…"

Frankie interrupted. "No…*if* we marry. I'm serious when I say you have to ask me again in a few weeks. Your feelings may change, and if they do, I will understand."

Charlotte just shook her head. How different young people were today. Still, she'd made a mess of her own life. It seemed that Frankie and Daniel were trying to do the right thing.

Daniel frowned at Frankie and put a finger against her lips to silence her, then turned to Charlotte again.

"As I was saying…before my dear Francesca interrupted to tell me what my true feelings are… We want to ask you to come back to Positano with us. My mother and grandmother have been gone for years, as have Frankie's. You are all she has. Will you come and live here in my home and share her with me?"

Charlotte's mouth dropped open and she unconsciously fingered the locket around her neck. There was a hope in her eyes that nearly broke Frankie's heart.

"Oh…you two won't want an old woman interfering with your new life."

Daniel shook his head.

"On the contrary, dear lady. You forget, this is Italy. We love to have our *nonnas* around. My house is huge. You will bring love to this place. Besides, if you don't come, who's going to teach our little girls how to knit?"

Charlotte beamed as she looked from Daniel to Frankie and back again.

"Are you sure?"

"Positive," they both said at once.

A quiet joy came over her face as she leaned back in her chair. Her gaze moved to the window, and she realized how close she would be to Danny for the rest of her days.

"I accept," she said softly.

Daniel grinned. "I will be the envy of every man in Positano. I will have not one, but two beautiful women in my life."

"Then if you don't change your mind later, it's a deal," Frankie said.

Daniel looked at her and laughed.

"Yes, my love. It is, as you say…a deal."

When the three of them arrived back in the States, they were met at the airport by a contingent from Second Wind Dreams. It seemed that after receiving Frankie's call about a possible wedding at Just Like Home, Mavis Tulia had phoned the director of Second Wind Dreams. The sadness in Charlotte Grace's life had been transformed into joy. The story generated so much news across the country that the charity was the recipient of unusually large and much-needed cash donations to further their good works.

True to his word, Daniel met his grandfather's family, and in doing so, felt as if a part of him had come home. He knew that was how the Morrow family felt. They had part of their Danny back, even if it was in an unexpected way.

And also as he'd vowed, Daniel Sciora had once more proposed to Frankie, but this time with a stern expression on his face. He told her that he was unaccustomed to having his word doubted, and hoped that he wouldn't have to propose to her every year or so, just to reassure her that he couldn't live without her.

Frankie had cried and accepted his offer, and then they married in the small chapel on the grounds of Just Like Home.

She walked herself down the aisle, but when it came to the point where the preacher asked who gave this woman to this man, everybody in the congregation shouted out a loud, "We do."

That brought tears to Frankie's eyes and put a big smile on Daniel's face. He would say later that he'd thought his family was large, but he believed hers was larger.

Charlotte had become the center of attention, which was, for her, a bit disconcerting. She'd lived so many years in the background of life that she wasn't sure how to take all this fuss. But she still managed to find time to knit, and on the day she was to fly back to Italy with Frankie and Daniel, she presented Charlie with the finished afghan.

"It's a little bit early," she said. "On your birthday, eat a piece of cake for me."

Charlie blushed and kissed her on the cheek, then beamed with delight as he and the other residents of the home waved goodbye to two of their own.

Charlotte and Frankie walked out of the door, paused on the step and looked at each other. Then they smiled and walked arm in arm to Daniel, who was waiting with their cab.

Daniel knew it was difficult for them to leave their old friends behind. But he also knew that these two women belonged together, and with his help, he would make sure that they soon had a new family to fuss over them.

"So, my two beautiful women…are you ready to go home?"

"Yes," they said in unison.

Daniel opened the door of the cab, then stepped aside.

"Your chariot awaits."

*Four years later*

Charlotte had been gone a whole year now, and still, from time to time, either Daniel or Frankie would start to ask if she was coming down to dinner, then they would remember and smile through their tears.

Today would have been her ninety-first birthday. They were going to stop by the cemetery on their way to Positano, and Frankie was trying to get dressed and still keep their baby girl out of mischief at the same time.

Frankie was doing up the last button on her blouse when she heard a crash behind her. She flinched and turned just as Daniel came running into the room.

Their eighteen-month-old daughter, Charlotte, had pulled a potted plant down from a stand. The pot had shattered, spilling dirt and broken stems all over the floor.

"Oh, Charlotte...no, no," Frankie cried as she leaned down and picked her up.

The baby howled.

"Is she hurt?" Daniel asked, running practiced hands over her black curly hair, feeling for bumps.

"No. Just scared, I think." Frankie frowned. "I'll have to clean this up before we go."

"The housekeeper is here," Daniel said. "I'll tell her while you dry little Miss Nosey's tears." He placed several tiny kisses along Charlotte's arm, all the way to her cheek, and the baby giggled.

With a wink at Frankie, Daniel hurried out of the room.

Charlotte automatically grabbed at the yellow ribbon at her mother's throat.

"You can't have that, either," Frankie said, gently taking the locket out of Charlotte's hands before it could go in her mouth. "But you will someday, when you're older. I promised. Now, let's go find the flowers we're going to put on Grandmother's grave."

Charlotte Grace had lived long enough to see her namesake born, and had rocked her to sleep many times. Then one night she had gone to bed and simply hadn't woken up.

When they arrived at the cemetery a short time later, Frankie took the flowers from the trunk of the car while Daniel got his daughter out of the backseat.

"Come with Papa, little girl. We will visit your great-grandfather and Grandmother Charlotte while Mama brings the flowers."

It sounded like a fine idea to Charlotte, except for the flowers. She pointed to the bouquet that Frankie was carrying and let out a screech.

"Me do," she said.

Daniel grinned as Frankie chose two of the more sturdy flowers from the bunch and handed them to her baby.

"Here you go," she said gently. "One for Great-grandfather, and one for Grandmother Charlotte."

Clutching the stems tightly, the little girl squirmed to get down. She held her father's hand as they made their way to the graves.

When they got to Daniel Morrow's grave, Charlotte put one of the flowers down on the ground, then patted it goodbye and pointed up the hill.

"Yes, Grandmother Charlotte is up there, isn't she?" Daniel said, and took her hand once more.

Together, the trio started up the hill to the spot where Charlotte Grace was buried. In death, as in life, there was still a distance between Charlotte and the love of her life. But Frankie was comforted by the thought that all their sadness had been left behind.

When they reached Charlotte's grave, Frankie stepped forward and replaced the old flowers in the vase with the new ones she'd brought.

"Look, Charlotte, it's wisteria, your favorite."

The little girl moved closer to her mother. Before either one of them could stop her, she'd placed her flower on the grass and then lay facedown on top of it, arms outstretched.

Frankie picked her up and began brushing her off.

Charlotte pointed to her flower.

"Hug," she said.

Frankie smiled. "Yes, you gave Grandmother Charlotte a big hug. She would have loved that."

"Here, give her to me," Daniel said as he kissed Frankie's cheek. "She's getting too heavy for you to carry this far."

As they were walking away, baby Charlotte turned and looked at where they'd been, then began smiling and waving.

Frankie felt the skin crawl on the back of her neck, just like the first day she'd seen Daniel.

"Wait!" she said softly, and stopped.

Daniel took her arm.

"Are you hurt? Did you turn your ankle?"

She shook her head. Her heart was pounding so fast that she thought she would faint, but she had to look. She had to know.

Slowly, slowly, she began to turn around.

They were barely visible, like the shadow of a cloud on the rock-strewn hill. But they were there, just the same.

A young man and a young woman, standing hand-in-hand on the horizon. When Frankie blinked, they were gone.

Daniel frowned.

"What is it? Are you okay? Did you forget something?"

Frankie shook her head, furiously fighting back tears.

"No, darling. Everything is okay. In fact, it's more than okay. It's perfect."

Daniel smiled.

Dear Reader,

A few years ago I was fortunate enough to participate in the Harlequin More Than Words program. In writing my story, *The Yellow Ribbon*, I learned what giving is really about.

Being able to meet P.K. Beville and watch her accept her award was wonderful. But it was what she does, every day of her life, that I found so special. The entire focus of her charity is about giving senior citizens one last chance at realizing a dream— a chance to do something one more time that they used to enjoy— or a chance to see a dream come true that they believed had passed them by.

One of the wishes P.K. granted so touched my heart that I know I will never look at a woman in a wheelchair again without remembering this story.

Once, many years ago, a very young and very beautiful woman aspired to be a fashion model. With her heart in her throat and her dreams held close, she traveled all the way to New York City, only to be told she wasn't tall enough. She went back home with her hopes dashed and her plan of becoming a fashion model nothing more than a fading memory. Years passed and with time came many crises, until the beautiful young woman had become an old woman, living out what was left of her life in a wheelchair.

Through what can only be construed as a maze of miracles, P.K. Beville made the elderly woman's dreams come true. She brought her back to New York City during the most amazing of times—Fashion Week in NY. Through P.K.'s continuing self-lessness, she contacted a famous designer who was also taken with the story and who created a one-of-a-kind dress for the old woman to wear. Then came the fashion show, and this time the elderly woman did make it on stage, in her beautiful gown, only she wasn't walking down the runway. She was wheeling down in her wheelchair as huge close-ups of her face—that beautiful face of the young woman she'd once been—were being flashed on the wide-screen behind her. She was the sensation of the show and went home with a beautiful dress and memories of a standing ovation.

P.K. Beville still makes dreams for the elderly come true—hot air balloon rides, playing the blues once more on Bourbon Street or earning an honorary degree—and in doing so she reminds us what giving is really about.

I hope you enjoy *The Yellow Ribbon,* and as you read, remember the elderly in your family. The elderly couple you know who spends holidays alone. The old woman who sits alone in the church pew in front of you. The nursing home down the street where dozens and dozens of people who were once our brightest and finest are waiting out the last of their days without joy.

Lift a glass to P.K. Beville and Second Wind Dreams, and if you can't make a dream come true on your own, give to someone who can.

With love to all my readers,

*Sharon Sala*

# JUNE NIELSEN
## ~ QUILTS FROM CARING HANDS ~

J une Nielsen wanted to reach out to children in crisis and wrap them in love, take away their pain and let them know there was someone who cared. That dream turned into a very tangible gift for her community—quilts. Now, as founder of Quilts from Caring Hands, June is wrapping an entire community in her love and compassion. Since its inception in 1990, Quilts from Caring Hands has made and donated over 5000 quilts to more than a dozen social service agencies serving children in crisis in Oregon's Willamette Valley area.

Quilts from Caring Hands all began when June's two children were away in high school. June was part of a small quilting circle at the time. She had always sewn—from projects as a Girl Scout to making her own clothes in school, and came to quilting in 1970 when she and her husband were living in

Wyoming. Pregnant with her son, June decided to try making a quilt, learning the craft through trial and error.

In 1989 June read an article about children born with AIDS and was deeply touched. "I couldn't cure AIDS or be a foster mother to a lot of kids," she realized. "I could, however, share a bit of TLC with them. Give them a quilt and let them know people care about them." Through local community groups and social services, June found there were many children-at-risk who could be helped—pediatric AIDS patients, the homeless, those in foster care, abused or emotionally ill children, infants of teenage moms and the visually impaired.

One of the women in her quilting circle was setting up a quilting shop and offered June space at the back of the store to work on the project. Four women with no money, no fabric— just an idea, and agencies who wanted quilts. "We began with the philosophy that we would make as many quilts as we could with the supplies and willing hands that came our way," June recalls. The fabrics were donated bit by bit, a few yards here, some batting there. They were literally making quilts out of whatever they could find.

Women coming into the quilting store heard all the noise and chatter in the back and, drawn by curiosity, came into the fold. By the end of the first year, the group had grown to fifteen women, and one hundred quilts had been made. Today the group numbers forty-five women, and they've expanded into a larger space in a local church. In the past few years, Quilts from Caring Hands has made and donated an average of three hundred quilts a year.

The women in the group range in age from forty to ninety. June describes the women as "energetic, interesting and vital." Some women who've joined have never sewn a thing, but June sincerely believes everyone has something to offer the group, and she encourages them to go as far as they wish in helping. June has been described as a master at encouraging others to stretch out and try something a bit more challenging than they thought they could.

The quilting circle itself is a very important part of Quilts from Caring Hands. Lots of sharing goes on in that circle—sharing of information about the community and about the craft of quilting…and a deeper level of sharing happens, too. Eyes focused on the work means less eye contact, and that makes it easier for the women to open up and confide in the group. That deep bond of friendship and support reaches out well beyond the regular Wednesday meetings.

The love, time and skill that go into making the quilts translate into love and caring for the recipients. June hears all the time from people in social service groups about how much the quilts mean. Many of these children have nothing at all—and they've never had something brand-new of their very own, something made just for them that will always be theirs. The children of women in crisis seem to find strength in being wrapped in a quilt, and find the courage to talk about what has happened to them. One victim of domestic violence received a purple quilt for her daughter. Purple was her daughter's favorite color—and the mother knew, in that moment, that everything would work out.

June gets so many words of gratitude from social agency

workers, telling her that there's something indescribably comforting in quilts. It makes the stay in these social service facilities more comfortable for children. The quilts are for the children to keep, and become a symbol of their strength, of all they've survived. One front-line worker expressed to June how a child, wrapped in her very own quilt, is wrapped, too, in a work of art that means hope and peace. It's beauty where there has only been pain and loneliness.

June says she's motivated to continue her work by the idea that you never know what one event will turn a child around. Maybe it will be the fact that one person who didn't even know the child *cared*. And she's inspired by the women who bring their time and passion to Quilts from Caring Hands. "I'm just in awe of the women in the group," June says. "How they've immediately caught the spirit of what this is all about." She is overwhelmed at the way the group has grown, how doors have opened and little things have led to where they are today.

And as for her own work with Quilts from Caring Hands, June says, "My life is pretty ordinary. Being so blessed, I feel the need to give back. Volunteering gives me the opportunity to give back to the community…a way to say thanks."

June's life is far from ordinary. Her compassion for others and her heartfelt commitment to Quilts from Caring Hands is extraordinary…and an inspiration.

For more information visit www.quiltsfromcaringhands.com or write to Quilts from Caring Hands, 946 NW Circle Blvd. #238, Corvallis, OR 97330-1410.

# EMILIE RICHARDS

## ⟡ Hanging by a Thread ⟡

## ‒ EMILIE RICHARDS ‒

*USA TODAY* bestselling author Emilie Richards earned a B.A. in American studies from Florida State University, and her master's in family development from Virginia Tech. She subsequently served as a therapist in a mental health center, as a parent services coordinator for Head Start families and in several pastoral counseling centers before she began writing full-time. Richards says that in every social service position she has held, she gained more than she gave. "I set out to help people and ended up learning so much more about myself."

Richards has drawn on those experiences while writing more than fifty novels. Although in recent years she has broadened the scope of her writing to women's fiction, she was awarded the prestigious RITA® Award for her earlier work in the genre. *Romantic Times BOOKreviews* magazine has presented her with numerous awards, including one for career achievement.

No doubt Richards's background as a relationship counselor is partly responsible for the award-winning nature of her novels. This background enables her to consistently deliver richly textured family dramas that explore the human condition.

Richards has been married for thirty-eight years to her college sweetheart, a Unitarian Universalist minister. They have three grown sons and a daughter. Born in Bethesda, Maryland, and raised in St. Petersburg, Florida, Richards has lived with her family not only in Virginia but also in Louisiana, California, Arkansas, Ohio and Pennsylvania. They also spent two four-month sabbaticals in Australia.

When not writing or quilting, Richards enjoys traveling and turning her suburban yard into a country garden. She is currently plotting *Sister's Choice,* the fifth book in her Shenandoah Album series, which will be published in 2008.

# CHAPTER
## ❧ ONE ❧

Tracy Wagner pretended not to notice the baby girl in the pink striped coverall who was crawling determinedly in her direction. Little Liza Thaeler seemed to think that "Aunt" Tracy was the top pick in any room, the woman most likely to bounce a baby on her knee or play interminable games of peekaboo.

Tracy could only hope that as Liza grew, her instincts about people improved.

Janet Thaeler intercepted her daughter before she could reach Tracy, then immediately held her away. "Phew! Give me a break!"

"Don't look at me," Tracy said, although Janet never would

have. She knew Tracy was not a baby person. Janet understood Tracy better than almost anyone in the world, except, of course, Graham, Tracy's husband. And even that was up for grabs sometimes.

"When was the last time you changed a diaper?" Janet checked to be sure her olfactory senses were working correctly. She screwed up her face at the evidence.

"Let me think." Tracy rested one sensibly manicured finger against her cheek. "I think it was the day I left home for college. By the time I went back the next summer, Mom had finally declared a childbearing moratorium, and my youngest sister was wearing ruffled training pants."

"Sometimes I'm surprised you even speak to me. I'm recreating your childhood." Janet abandoned the room with a giggling Liza tucked under one arm.

While she waited for her friend to return, Tracy gazed around. Janet was right. Tracy had grown up in a house like this one, if a shade more rustic. Toys piled in every corner. Building blocks and stuffed animals strewn across the floor. Strollers in the hallway, high chairs pushed against the dining-room table, shouts and squeals and demands rending the air.

Janet had four children and another—the last, she swore—due next spring. She claimed she was so used to being pregnant that morning sickness felt normal, and a visible belly button seemed grossly obscene.

Tracy was the oldest girl in a family of eight. She had grown up in Washington's Wenatchee Valley, the daughter of hard-working apple growers. Even now if she looked in the mirror, a farmer's daughter smiled back at her. A healthy round face with pink cheeks and clear blue eyes. Glossy dark hair that was bluntly cut to her collar. A little too plump, a lot too ordinary and much too busy to be worried about any of it.

Her role in the family had been clear as soon as she was old enough to hold a bottle. Tracy was in charge of the babies when her mother was called on to do other things, which was much of the time.

The family was a happy one, and her parents had been as fair as time allowed. But Tracy had gotten her fill of babies by the time she escaped to Oregon State. She loved her brothers and sisters, particularly now that they were more or less grown. But if she never opened a jar of baby food, washed a load of receiving blankets, or walked the floor with a feverish infant, it would be too soon.

Janet returned with a giggling, sweet-smelling Liza. "Thank heaven for Molly." She plunked Liza in the corner with a stack of blocks. "If she weren't here, we wouldn't be able to finish a sentence."

Tracy wasn't sure how many they'd finished anyway. "Molly Baker? The girl across the way?"

"I started paying her to come over every afternoon to play with the kids and keep them out of my hair for a while. They're wreaking havoc in the playroom right now. She's so good with them. She's a gem."

Janet's expression didn't match her enthusiastic words. An

ebullient blonde, pixieish, freckled, Janet was almost always smiling. She wasn't smiling now.

"Some problem?" Tracy probed. "Don't tell me you're feeling guilty because you need a little help."

"Good grief, no." Janet frowned at her, as if Tracy had lost her mind. "I'm an earth mother, not a martyr. No, it's Molly I'm worried about. You know she's a foster child?"

Tracy knew that Molly had lived with the people across the street for most of a year. She was a quiet, self-contained teenager or preteen, Tracy wasn't quite sure which. She was a pretty girl, brown-haired, dark-eyed and slender, and showed the promise of greater beauty to come. During their few conversations, Tracy had been impressed with her manners and a little worried about the caution in her eyes. Molly seemed to weigh every word, as if she needed to be certain Tracy got exactly the right impression.

"What's the problem?" Tracy asked. "Some issue with the courts?"

"No. The Hansens are moving to Europe for a year, possibly longer. He's taking over his company office in Paris—or something like that." Janet lowered her voice. "They can't take Molly, or they won't. But I do know she's free for adoption, and for whatever reason, they've decided not to pursue it. So in three weeks, she'll have to move. And there aren't any foster homes available in this school district. At least not at the moment, and not one for a fourteen-year-old girl. And she's been at the same middle school since sixth grade."

Tracy tried to make sense of this. "So what happens to her?"

"The social worker's talking about placing her in a group home. In a different school district. From what I can tell, the other kids are there because they've had problems in traditional care. Molly's never caused anyone a problem."

"The foster parents told you all this?" Tracy was pretty sure that Molly hadn't confided these details. It was contrary to everything Tracy knew about her.

Janet inspected a fleck of lint. "A neighbor told me the family was moving without Molly. I called social services and talked to her social worker."

Tracy was surprised the agency would have confided so much in a phone call. Then her eyes narrowed. "You didn't call for information, did you? You called to volunteer to *take* Molly."

Her friend looked faintly chagrined. "She's such a great kid, Trace. And here we are, right down the street from her school."

"And?"

"The social worker visited. We have too many kids, and too few bedrooms. And with the new baby coming in the spring..." She shook her head. "I'm afraid she's right, as much as I hate to say it. At Molly's age, she shouldn't be sharing a bedroom with pre-schoolers, or competing for our attention with so many little children."

Tracy fell silent, mulling over this sad turn of events.

Molly chose that moment to appear in the doorway. She had a blond Thaeler girl on one hip and an even blonder boy in the crook of her arm. She was wearing faded jeans and a gold sweatshirt that was at least three sizes too large.

"We finished our third game of Chutes and Ladders," she told Janet. "Alex is still building a city out of Lego in the playroom. I have to get going. I have to practice saying the prologue to the Canterbury Tales in Middle English for extra credit."

"Still?" Tracy was surprised. "They still make you do that?"

Molly didn't exactly smile, but her expression lightened a little. "I chose it. We'll study it next year, and I kind of like it. It sounds so pretty."

"Whan that Aprill with his shoures soote, the droghte of March hath perced to the roote..." Tracy quoted.

"You remember that?" Molly sounded surprised.

"That's about it. And, hey, I'm not *that* old. I remember liking it, too. Maybe you can recite it for me once you have it all learned."

The girl tossed back a lock of her shoulder-length hair and looked appropriately embarrassed. "I'd better go."

The Thaeler kids began to chatter at the same time. Janet got up and took the girl in Molly's arms, soothed the boy, who was trying to tell her how he'd beaten Molly at their game, and simultaneously handed Molly some cash from her pocket.

"Can you come tomorrow?" she asked when there was a lull.

"Yes, but, Mrs. Thaeler, I won't be coming much longer. I'm going to be moving."

"I heard," Janet said, trying to shush her son for a moment. "I'm so sorry, Molly. We'll miss you very much. I hope you'll be close enough that we can still see you once in a while."

Molly didn't respond.

The children waved goodbye, and Molly did, too. Then she was gone.

Tracy thought back to her own middle-school years with a pang. The sense of never really belonging, the fear of being different, the spats with friends and the painful sputtering romances that never ended happily. She remembered a girl who had moved to her school, and the pleasure some of the other kids had taken in making her feel even more like an outsider.

Most of all she remembered that her own parents had guided her through the worst of times with wisdom and love. Who would guide Molly?

"Moving is going to be one huge disaster for her," Tracy said. The children had taken that one moment to fall silent, and her words, though softly spoken, rang in the narrow room.

"I'm afraid you're right," Janet said. "I hate it, but there's not a darned thing I can do about it."


Tracy and Graham's penthouse condominium in northwest Corvallis had walls of windows that overlooked the Cascades and Three Sisters, polished oak floors with expensive Oriental carpets, granite countertops and the chic, uncluttered appearance of a model home. When Tracy let herself in after her visit with Janet, the silence was both blessed and disturbing. Blessed because there were no shrieking children here. Disturbing because there was no one at all to greet her.

Graham wasn't home from his job as the vice president of a financial planning firm. He was often out in the evenings, visiting clients whose days were as busy as his. Tracy was often gone in the evenings, too. She was an interior designer who worked exclusively with a popular local developer. She consulted on the basics of his designs and dealt directly with his clients, helping them choose fixtures and draperies, floors and floor coverings. Tonight, the only reason she was home before six was that both her late-afternoon and early-evening appointments had canceled, giving her time to stop by Janet's.

She didn't kick off her shoes or throw her suit jacket on the back of the sofa. She was tempted, though. The condo would look more lived in if she did, and this evening the pristine beauty of the rooms was oddly unappealing.

She had spent a lot of time decorating their home. She had chosen just the right pieces for display, sculptures and pottery from local Oregon craftspeople, handwoven wall hangings and Indian ceremonial masks, carved candlesticks with hand-dipped candles.

Of course, Graham had provided the most important touches. He was an extraordinary woodworker. He had designed and crafted their dining-room table and chairs of natural cherry. The coffee table was bird's-eye maple, and the end tables beside their sofa—dotted with needlepoint pillows she had discovered on a shopping trip in Portland—were constructed from portions of a mahogany staircase he had salvaged with the help of a local wrecking crew.

Most of the furniture had been finished before they met, when he had dreams of opening his own custom cabinetry and furniture shop. They were display pieces, meant to entice new clients. After their marriage, Graham's dream had gently drifted away, and reality had intruded. Tracy, too, had stopped imagining new and fresher possibilities and settled for maintaining a comfortable lifestyle.

Neither of them despised their jobs. Both of them liked the financial rewards. When they could eke out the time, they had the money to travel anywhere they wanted to go. They drank excellent wines, ate at the best restaurants, gave each other extravagant gifts.

They were lucky. Tracy knew that. Nevertheless, tonight she wasn't feeling lucky. She was feeling lonely, out-of-sorts, unhappy with a world that would take a nice kid like Molly and throw her to the four winds. And there was nobody here to share that with. By the time Graham got home, she would probably be asleep.

She thought about calling her mother, but she didn't want to upset her with the vision of a homeless child. She considered calling one of her sisters, but wasn't sure which one would understand. None of them would ever meet Molly or have a stake in what happened to her.

She wandered into the master bedroom, which was dominated by a king-size bed with no headboard. For the ten years of their marriage, Graham had promised to build one from leftover mahogany but never found the time. She had solved the decorating dilemma by hanging a contemporary quilt of red, black and silver strips behind it and piling the bed with pillows of coordinating fabrics. The room seemed stark and empty anyhow, so she tossed her clothes on the bed as she undressed, just to liven it up.

As she was pulling on sweats, she heard the front door open. She slipped into sneakers and went to check. Graham was hanging up his all-weather coat in the hall closet.

"You're home so early."

He whirled, surprised. "Jeez, Tracy. You startled me. What are you doing here?"

"I live here. Remember?"

He laughed and walked over to her for a hug. "Well, I thought you did. At least I've seen your name on the mailbox and mortgage."

She sank into his welcoming arms. He smelled like the crisp fall air and she laid her head against his shoulder.

Sometimes she was overwhelmed by the knowledge that this man was hers. Graham Wagner had come into her life during her final year at Oregon State. He was broad-shouldered and lithe, with light brown hair and smoky green eyes. His smile could warm the coldest winter night; his generous heart was even warmer.

Sometimes she still wondered why a man with his background had fallen in love with a simple farmer's daughter. His parents were professors, his family as historic as the Oregon Trail. He had grown up a quiet only child in a household devoted to study and debate. The antics of her large, raucous family were as foreign to Graham as picking apples.

She stepped out of his arms after a moment. "Are you home for good? Or did you just stop by on the way to an appointment?"

"I had an appointment. I canceled."

Immediately she was worried. "You're sick. It's that virus that's going around."

"Nope." He loosened his tie, a conservative gray with a thin green stripe that went with the image, if not precisely the man. "I was just tired of being gone every evening. I need a night here with my feet up." He paused. "You're a huge bonus, you know that? And from the way you're dressed, you're not going back out. Right?"

"Right." She rested fingertips on his shoulders. "You're sure you're okay?"

He paused a moment. "Just tired. Really."

She sensed something else but knew better than to push. "Let's see what we have for dinner."

"I could take you out," he offered, although he didn't look enthused.

"No. You need to stay home. Besides, it sounds better. Let's see what we have."

He joined her in the kitchen after he'd changed into khakis and a polo shirt. Together they prepared a meal of jarred marinara sauce over linguine and canned green beans. She set slices of frozen cheesecake on the counter to thaw.

They sat in the cozy breakfast nook, and Graham poured wine from a newly opened bottle. "To being together for a change," he said as a toast.

Tracy tried to remember exactly how long it had been since they had eaten a meal together at home. She rarely needed to shop. She kept emergency supplies on hand, like those they were eating, but she couldn't remember the last time they'd had anything fresh to prepare or any reason to prepare it.

"Two weeks?" she said out loud. "Since we ate together here?"

"Something like that."

"We'd better be careful. Dining in could get to be a habit, although I'd like some mushrooms or peppers to put in the sauce."

"That would be a commitment." He smiled.

"I might be up to a mushroom commitment." She smiled, too, and asked him about his day.

His recital was short, and when it was her turn, she considered whether to tell him about her visit to Janet's. But Graham was too perceptive not to notice her hesitation.

"What's going on, Trace?" He sat back, most of his linguine untouched. She could hardly blame him.

She pushed a few green beans around her plate with a fork. "I went to Janet's today."

"And now you have a migraine."

She laughed a little. "That would be more likely than a sudden yearning to have a litter of tiny Wagners."

"Noisy and chaotic, huh?" He picked up his wineglass. At least the wine had flavor.

The two of them had agreed early in their marriage to delay the question of having children. Graham had had no experience with babies, and she'd had too much. Over the years he had shown no more desire to add one to their lives than she had. The issue had been sidelined indefinitely.

"Absolutely chaotic." She told him about Molly, finishing with a little grimace. "I'm not sure why it's bothering me so much, but it is. I know there are a lot of children out there who get shoved from pillar to post through no fault of their own. I just haven't seen it up close before. The way she looks at me when I talk to her, Graham... It's like she's trying to read what I want her to say. She must have picked that up along the way."

"Maybe that's how she survived the system. She figures out what people need, then she gives it to them. And in return they don't make her life any worse than it already is."

"I can't figure out why her foster parents don't want to adopt her. They could take her to France if they did."

He shrugged. "Maybe they just don't think it matters that much."

"Of course it matters!"

He stared at her.

"I'm sorry." She chased some more green beans with her fork. Her stomach was too knotted to eat them.

Graham sounded as if he were struggling to be patient. "I didn't say it *didn't* matter. I said maybe that's the way the foster parents think."

"It's just pretty screwed up, wouldn't you say? What chance will this kid have now? They're leaving her behind. She has to move to a group home and live with kids who can't get along in regular foster care. She has to change schools. And the social worker won't even let Janet take her."

"Does Janet really want her?"

Tracy considered, then shook her head. "No. She's overwhelmed. She wants to help Molly, but I suspect it was a relief when the agency said no."

"The social worker probably sensed her ambivalence and factored it in."

"I'm sorry," Tracy said. "This isn't your problem. It's not our problem. I shouldn't have brought it up."

He swirled the wine in his glass. "Why not?"

"Because this is our first night home together in ages."

"And the first time in a long time we've talked about anything really important."

She set her fork down. "You sound unhappy."

He reached over and took her hand. "I think I miss you. We're so busy all the time. It's just nice to be here talking to you, hearing you talk about something that matters. Feeling like it matters to me, too."

"Does it matter to you?"

"I like kids. I used to be one. I remember what it was like."

"I wish we could do something."

He waited. When she didn't say more, he cocked his head. "Trace?"

"Well, I'm not sure, but I think we're in the same school district as Janet. She's only a mile away."

"And?"

"Well, all they need is a *temporary* place for Molly to live until a real foster home opens up. I don't really need a study. I could move my desk into the bedroom. We could move in a dresser from our room, buy a twin bed. A daybed would be nice in there, anyway, even when it goes back to being my study. It wouldn't take much work to fix it up a little so she'd feel at home."

"We're never here. You want this girl to take care of herself?"

Tracy thought about that. "I could limit my evening appointments to two nights a week. Maybe even one. You could cover one night, couldn't you? You say you're tired. It would guarantee you a night at home. Maybe your clients could come here if you had to see them."

Graham was silent a moment. She watched his thoughts parade across his face. She was more than surprised he hadn't just said no outright, that it was impractical, not like her at all, a complete intrusion on two lives that were too busy already.

Then he squeezed her hand and dropped it. "Call the social worker. See what she says. We'll talk some more when you find out."

Panic filled her. It had only been an idea. "You're serious?"

"It would be nice to do something for this kid." He stood. "I'll clean off the table."

No matter what she learned from the social worker, she was suddenly, powerfully certain that she had married the best—not to mention the most attractive—man in the world.

"There's not much to clean." She stood, too. "But our room's a different story. I threw my stuff all over the bed when I got home. Did you notice?"

"I did. I think we need to go and clean it off. We can't have a mess in our house."

"It will definitely take two." She leaned against him and kissed him, tasting marinara sauce and wine. "It's a very *big* mess. A skirt, a blouse, a slip. It's possible there could be more soon."

"I'm glad I still have some strength left."

"Oh, so am I," she said with a little smile. "So am I."

# CHAPTER
## ~ TWO ~

M olly had learned a long time ago not to give in to panic when she woke up in a strange house. Through the years she'd taught herself that strange houses were normal, that if she lay in bed without moving and let the early-morning cobwebs drift away, she would eventually remember where she was, why she was there, and if she wanted to make the effort to stay a while.

This morning she remembered quickly. She was living with the Wagners now, Tracy and Graham, who didn't expect to be called Aunt Tracy and Uncle Graham, or worse— much, much worse—Mom and Dad. They were just Mr. and Mrs. Wagner, and this room that Mrs. Wagner had fixed up for her was really a study and would go back to being a study soon enough.

She had lived here three weeks. This was just one more stop until she made it to eighteen and said goodbye once and for all to life as an outsider. When she was eighteen she would get an apartment and she would never leave it. She didn't care how crummy or small it was, it would be her home forever.

She heard noises in the hallway, slippers scuffing their way toward the kitchen. Mrs. Wagner got up every morning to make Molly a hot breakfast before school. Molly figured that would stop soon enough. The woman was playing house, and once she got tired of making the effort, Molly would be rooting in the cupboards to find something to eat.

She'd been there before.

She got up and carefully made her bed, tucking the sheet in the way one foster mother had taught her. Mrs. Grey, two foster homes ago, hadn't been mean, exactly, but she had demanded that every chore be done exactly to her standards. She had stood over Molly, tugging the sheet out over and over again if there was a wrinkle or a sag. Molly had finally met the test just before moving on to a different home.

She showered quickly. She'd gotten in trouble with the last foster family because she used too much hot water. She wasn't sure if that had anything to do with their ditching her before they went to Paris, but she figured she'd better not take a chance. All she had to do here was stay out of the way, follow the rules, until real foster parents turned up to take her, people who needed the county's money and would have something to lose if Molly was moved again.

She knew she was skating on thin ice here. The Wagners didn't need the county's money. All Molly had to do was look around the condo to know that. She was just a good deed, something to do so they could feel proud of themselves, and Molly knew if she tried their patience even a little, she'd be packing her suitcase.

She dressed as quickly as she'd showered and made sure the room was tidy before she grabbed her book bag and headed for the kitchen to choke down eggs and bacon. She was a vegetarian, waiting for the moment when she could choose her own menu. Four years. Just four more years...

Pausing in her doorway, she went back to the bed and lifted the pillow. Her quilt was tucked carefully beneath. She fingered it a moment for good luck, closed her eyes and made a quick wish that she could keep the Wagners happy for a while, then tucked it back in and headed for the door.

Tracy was still surprised how easy it had been to become Molly's foster mother. She and Graham had received emergency training so the placement could be made without delay. Molly's social worker had been so thrilled to keep Molly in the school district that she had cooperated in every way.

Tracy was also surprised how easy it had been to change her schedule, and Graham's, too, so that Molly had the required supervision. Molly went to Janet's every afternoon to help with

Janet's kids, and Tracy or Graham picked her up on the way home from work.

Not that the girl seemed to need adults. Tracy couldn't imagine a child with fewer needs than this one. She suspected that if Molly could learn not to breathe their air, she would permanently hold her nose. She asked for nothing and seemed worried about everything Tracy and Graham did for her.

This absolutely infuriated Tracy. Life had taught the girl this was what she had to do to survive. Some nights Tracy didn't sleep much just thinking about it and wondering how to help.

This afternoon Tracy got off early and went home alone. Molly wouldn't be finished at Janet's for another hour, and Tracy wanted to start a pot roast. The recipe was her mother's favorite, but it had been years since Tracy had used it. Neither she nor Graham really liked beef, but with a teenage girl in the house, a growing girl who needed iron, they were eating more of it.

When she unlocked the front door and stepped inside, she was greeted with silence. The condo seemed as empty as it had before Molly's arrival. As uncluttered, as perfect, as cold.

She resisted the impulse to drop her coat on the floor and went to change into jeans and a cotton sweater before she started the roast. On the way back toward the kitchen she stopped at the door to Molly's room and peeked inside. On one level she was pleased at what she saw. She and Graham had moved Tracy's desk to *his* study and replaced it with a dresser from their bedroom. Tracy had hung flowered curtains at the window and covered the daybed with a matching comforter and pastel throw pillows. She hadn't known what to put on the walls, so she'd left them blank. She hoped maybe she and Molly could buy a few posters, but Molly had resisted every invitation to shop. Still, at least the room was inviting and feminine. She hoped Molly approved.

Despite the cheery floral motif, the room seemed empty. Both Tracy and Graham had been astonished at how little Molly had brought with her. The most basic toiletries, one suitcase of clothing, a few books. Now Tracy stepped inside and looked around. The room was painfully neat, with absolutely nothing out of place. Except...

A colorful scrap of fabric peeked out from under the pillow on the bed. Tracy knew she was snooping, and that snooping was a major offense to a girl Molly's age. Still, she felt justified. She wanted to know more about Molly. She needed to. Leaning over, she tugged. Out came a small quilt, larger than those made for infants, but still too small for a twin bed. The quilt was ragged, tattered at the edges, definitely not as clean as it should be. It looked as if it had been dragged around by a much younger child and nearly loved to death.

Tracy held the quilt at arm's length to examine it closer. It was made of two different types of blocks. Half the blocks were made of three equal fabric strips of different patterns and shades of lilac, sewn into about a six-inch square. The remaining blocks were made of yellow and white patches, four in each square. The pattern was simple, but charming. Or it would have been charming if the quilt weren't so ragged. The blocks in the middle were still in pretty good shape, but the rest of the quilt was hanging by a thread.

Tracy tried a deep breath and found that breathing was harder than she'd expected, because now there was a lump in her throat. The quilt said so much about her young charge. That there was still a little girl inside the self-possessed fourteen-year-old. That Molly had *something* left from her past to treasure. That Molly needed comfort, even if she didn't show it.

When she flipped the quilt to the other side, Tracy saw that the back was a flowered lavender and yellow calico, broken only by the knots of embroidery floss scattered over the surface to hold the quilt together. She almost missed the label in one corner. She was turning the quilt back over when a logo caught her eye—a hand with a heart on the palm.

"Quilts from Caring Hands, Corvallis, Oregon," Tracy read out loud. "This quilt belongs to Molly Baker."

Who had given Molly the quilt and why? Exactly what did it mean to the girl?

She folded it carefully again, lifted Molly's pillow and slipped it back underneath. She couldn't tell Molly she had seen the quilt, since clearly the girl had hidden it. But she was determined to find out more. This was a key, even if only a small one, to her foster daughter's heart.

Molly seemed to like the potatoes and carrots well enough, but her thin slice of meat had gone down quickly and largely unchewed, as if she was swallowing medicine. Graham's slice was every bit as thin, and now he chased it around his plate as if he were designing a still life: *American Pot Roast Supper.* Tracy half expected him to bring out an easel and canvas after dinner.

"Okay," she said, putting down her fork. "The pot roast was not a good idea."

"It's fine," Graham said. "Great. But I had a big lunch."

"Oh, I'll have some more," Molly said. "It's very good. I'm sorry."

Tracy covered the girl's hand as she reached for the serving fork. "You don't have to eat another bite, Molly. If you don't like something here, you never have to eat it."

"But I didn't say I didn't like it." For a moment panic flickered in her pretty blue eyes.

"Honey, everybody likes to eat different things. It's perfectly natural. Tell me what you do like."

Molly's eyes widened. "Oh, pretty much everything."

"Well, I don't really like pot roast," Graham said. "Or steak. Or black-eyed peas, or turtle soup. Or sweet potatoes with marshmallows on top. I particularly despise marshmallows unless they're covering a graham cracker and a square of chocolate."

"Turtle soup?" Tracy said. "Have I ever served you turtle soup?"

"And I don't like kale," he continued. "I *really* don't like mushy peas."

Tracy got into the spirit. "Okay, I don't like lima beans. We used to have them three nights a week when I was a little girl, and nobody wasted food in our house. And succotash. Who ever thought calling vegetables succotash would make *anybody* want to eat them?"

"I'm not that crazy about pork chops, either," Graham said. "I grew up reading *Charlotte's Web*. I practically memorized it."

"I really hate chicken nuggets," Tracy said. "Who are those fast-food people kidding? Like there's any real chicken in one of those things?"

Graham made a face. "You think chicken nuggets are a joke? Read the label on a pack of hot dogs."

"I don't like any kind of chicken," Molly said. Immediately she looked embarrassed and, worse, fearful that she'd just made an error.

"How about turkey?" Tracy asked, keeping her voice even, the question light. "Thanksgiving's coming up, you know."

"I eat turkey." She gave Graham the quickest of glances. "But mostly I eat the sweet potatoes with little marshmallows on them—if somebody makes them. They're my favorite."

He reached over and ruffled her hair. "You and I are a team, Moll. I'll eat your turkey, you eat my sweet potatoes. This is a match made in heaven."

Molly smiled, but she looked more relieved than happy. She hadn't made anyone mad. No one was going to criticize her for speaking her mind or having preferences.

She was safe.

They finished what was left of the meal in silence. When Molly got up to clear the table, Tracy stood, too. "Mr. Wagner and I'll take care of that tonight. Tomorrow's Friday. Don't you have a quiz in history?"

Molly looked surprised. "How did you know?"

"Well, you've had a history quiz every Friday since you came to live with us. I just assumed…"

"Oh." The girl looked flustered. "It's just that… Well, I do. It's just that…"

It was just that she was surprised that anyone had noticed. Tracy saw this as clearly as she saw that the new discovery worried Molly. She understood the girl's train of thought. People here paid attention. Attention meant expectations. Expectations were impossible to meet.

"It's nice to have a teacher you can count on, isn't it?" Tracy said. "I always hated the kind who popped quizzes any old time."

"I never count on anything," Molly said. "Just in case."

She was gone before Tracy could comment. She heard the door to Molly's room close quietly.

Graham's hands were a welcome weight on her shoulders. For a moment she couldn't speak.

"She needs more from us than we're giving her," he said at last.

"But she's only been here a few weeks. It takes time to develop trust." Tracy faced him, her expression pleading.

"Hey, did you think I meant we should pass her on to somebody else?" He smoothed Tracy's hair back from one cheek. "Don't you know me better than that?"

"Then what did you mean?"

"That we have to spend more time with her. Get to know her. Let her know she can speak her mind around here and not get in trouble. How about this weekend? What's on your calendar?"

Tracy's calendar was filled with new homeowners who couldn't see her any other time. Just this once she decided she didn't care. "I can cancel my appointments with the stroke of a pen, except for a couple. And I can finish those by noon Saturday."

"Me, too. Let's go out to Alsea and spend Saturday night. We can show Molly the sights, take her to Alsea Falls. The colors will be at their peak. Besides, now that the renters have moved out, we need to check the old place."

"The old place" was a run-down farmhouse in the picturesque Coast Range mountains that Graham's parents had used as a getaway during the years he was growing up. When his father took a position as a biology professor at the University of Miami, the senior Wagners turned over the house to Graham and Tracy. Graham was waiting for the right moment to sell it, when interest rates and property prices converged and he could make the biggest profit for his parents.

At first he and Tracy had hoped to use the house on weekends, as his parents had, but almost immediately it had become clear there was little point in keeping the house for themselves when they were both so busy. So they had rented it out, instead. Now that the latest renters had moved, it was time to either sell or rent again.

"Do you think she'd *want* to come?" Tracy asked. "She might have something planned with her friends."

"She hasn't had anything planned since she came to live here. If she has friends, she doesn't spend time with them on weekends."

"It's a good idea. A great idea." She rose on tiptoe and kissed him. "You're thinking like a father."

"As long as I don't have to give her a bottle or let her teethe on my finger."

She grinned and kissed him again.

# CHAPTER
## ∽THREE∽

Molly couldn't believe that most of the time nobody lived in the old house in Alsea. The whole area was amazing, like something out of a picture book, with evergreens marching so high up the hill behind the house that they seemed to pierce the sky. She could almost touch the blue-green mountains. There was a creek not far away, and a stone path leading down to it. The kitchen was huge, with a table so large you could seat a dozen people around it without anyone tapping elbows. There were so many bedrooms on the second floor, she had been allowed to choose whichever one she wanted for the weekend.

Sure, the house wasn't up-to-date, like the Wagner condo.

The porch sagged and the wood had weathered to the color of tarnished silver. She knew about tarnished silver. There'd been a lot of it in one of her foster homes, and Molly had volunteered to polish it. The foster mother hadn't let her. Molly figured that was because she didn't want to take it out of the locked cabinet. That family had watched her like she was a thief in training because her real mother had been arrested once and sent to jail.

The Wagners didn't watch her at all. They knew where she was, of course, but nobody paid attention to the little stuff. Their condo was filled with beautiful things, but nobody seemed to care if she looked at them or picked them up. On Thursday morning Mrs. Wagner had caught her looking at a pottery vase with the coolest metallic swirls all over it, and when Molly came home from the Thaelers's that afternoon, the vase was on the dresser in her room, filled with flowers.

Molly wasn't sure what this meant. The Wagners were just playing at being parents. Molly knew Mrs. Wagner wasn't all that fond of babies. Mrs. Thaeler made jokes about it. So maybe this was just their way of showing everybody they didn't *hate* children even if they didn't want any. Not that Molly was really a child anymore.

It was Sunday morning and late. For most of her life she'd been routed out of bed on Sundays to attend some church where nobody knew her. She'd watched foster parents tell pastors the sad story of her life, seen the pity in everybody's eyes, or worse, the distrust. The Wagners seemed too busy to go to church. She'd never seen busier people in her life. Even when they were home they were always working. She wasn't sure why they'd gotten married, since they never seemed to spend time together.

There was a lot to think about here. She was lying in the old double bed in the room at the end of the hall, her quilt against her cheek, sorting it all out, when someone tapped on the door. Before she could respond, Tracy opened the door and peeked inside. "You're awake?"

Molly didn't know what to say. She was always careful to put her quilt away where nobody could see it. It was in sad shape, and one foster mom had tried to throw it away. Molly had learned to keep it under her pillow or in a drawer covered with neatly folded clothing. She bolted up, thrusting the quilt behind her.

"Do you need me to do something?" she asked.

"Nope. Not a thing. I just wondered if you were ready for breakfast. Mr. Wagner's making his famous pancakes and I need reinforcements at the table." She lowered her voice. "They're as heavy as lead, and if I have to eat them all by myself, I'll sink right through the floor."

Molly giggled before she could stop herself. Tracy was pretending to sink right where she stood. "What are they made out of?"

"Some mix with every whole grain known to man. I think he adds ground-up rocks for flavor."

Molly made a face. "What do they taste like?"

Tracy smiled warmly. "Come and see. And after breakfast we're going over to Alsea Falls. You'll like it there. There's a great place to swim at the bottom, but it's probably too cold by now. Besides after these pancakes, you'd sink like a stone."

"I heard that!"

Tracy grimaced, as if someone had caught her doing something she wasn't supposed to. Hands appeared on her shoulders, then one masculine arm came round her neck in a pretend choke-hold.

"Just for that you'll have to do the dishes, woman. And I'm going to get every bowl in the place dirty, just to show you."

"There's, like, one bowl in the cupboards," Molly said.

"Well, there's a measuring cup and a spatula, and a frying pan."

Tracy rolled her eyes. Then she winked at Molly. "You'll be up in a little while?"

"Oh, I'll get up right now. No problem."

"Good. Sounds like I'll need help with *all* those dishes."

The Wagners left, arms around each other's waists. Molly watched them go. For just a moment she wished it was a threesome walking down that hallway, arms entwined. But wishes were pointless, and even worse, dangerous. She tucked her quilt out of sight under her pillow and made the bed before she headed for the kitchen.

By Sunday afternoon Tracy was feeling more relaxed than she had in months. She and Graham had decided—with Molly's input—to stay another night and drive back to Corvallis early enough in the morning to get Molly to school. Graham had gone to buy fresh salmon and vegetables to grill on the old stone fireplace in the backyard.

"Do you like fish?" Tracy asked Molly, who had just come inside from a walk to the creek. "How about salmon?"

"I like almost all fish," Molly said.

Tracy was getting good at interpreting the girl's responses. This one was said with some enthusiasm. "So you're an aquatarian," Tracy said.

"What's that?"

"A vegetarian who also eats seafood? Or maybe that's a vegequarian."

"I'm not a vegetarian."

"Maybe not, but only because you don't cook for yourself. Right?"

Molly smiled a little, but she still looked as if she wasn't sure she should.

"I could be a vegetarian easily. Mr. Wagner, too. Except for fish. I don't think I could give up salmon." Tracy waited, making a point of her silence.

"I don't really like meat that much, I guess," Molly said carefully. "But I'll eat it if you want me to."

"But why should you? We can fix other things. If you're all right with fish, we'll have that a couple of times a week. But we love pasta and vegetables."

"Except lima beans," Molly said.

Tracy felt her smile widening. "You have a great memory."

"I can cook. I learned how a couple of years ago. I like it okay."

"What do you like to make?"

"Cakes. Pies."

"Oh, good. A pastry chef. This is incredible news."

"You don't have any cookbooks."

Tracy was delighted that Molly had been doing some snooping. "I guess they're packed away. I don't do much cooking. I think I have one at home on the bookcase in our bedroom in case I can't remember how to boil water."

"There aren't any here. I was looking around——" Molly stopped and looked embarrassed.

"Had a sweet-tooth attack, huh? We should have told Mr. Wagner to get a cake mix or some ice cream for dessert."

"I like to make cookies."

Tracy tried to remember what was left in the pantry. The last renters hadn't bothered to pack any of their staples since they were moving across the country. And she'd bought essentials like eggs and butter for the weekend. "If we had a cookbook, we could probably put something together." She had a sudden inspiration. "The attic. Mr. Wagner's mother left a bunch of stuff up there for us to sort through. I've never really gotten around to it. But there were boxes of books, and I'm sure some were cookbooks."

She changed her tone to conspiratorial. "Mr. Wagner's mom is a chemist. Whenever we visit, she gives me lectures on proteins and carbohydrates. Every meal we eat is like a science experiment. But the food's pretty good anyway."

Molly looked interested. "Did Mr. Wagner ever really, you know, live here?"

"Just for summers and weekends. But I think this felt like his real home. His parents are pretty formal, but they relaxed more when they were here. He got to run around and be a kid."

"Was your life like that, too?"

"Mine?" Tracy laughed. "Good grief, no. My house was crawling with kids. Still is. There are grandkids now. I'm the only one who doesn't live nearby. I want you to meet everybody. They'll like you."

Molly looked wary.

"Not right away," Tracy assured her. Then she stopped. If she didn't take Molly to Washington right away, maybe Molly would be living somewhere else by the time she and Graham went to visit her family.

She changed the subject abruptly, not wanting to examine that thought too closely. "Let's go see what's in the attic, shall we?" She put her arm around Molly's shoulder. "Let's just hope there aren't any mice."

The fish was a success. The vegetables, although a little on the blackened side, were consumed with enthusiasm, and Molly's oatmeal cookies were a major hit. She went to bed on a sugar high, and high on praise, as well.

Tracy and Graham sat outside by the fireplace after Molly went inside, sharing the last of a bottle of wine they had brought from home.

"The more I get to know her, the less I understand all this," Tracy said. "She's a great kid. Maybe I could see passing her around the system if she was setting fire to mattresses or sticking pins in Barbie dolls. But she's just a normal teenage girl. Too worried about pleasing people. Too quiet and self-contained. But a great kid."

Graham swished the wine in his glass. "You spent a lot of time up in the attic with her. Did you learn anything new?"

Tracy thought about their conversation as she and Molly searched through boxes for cookbooks.

"We found your baby book, Graham. Apparently you were precocious even then. Walked at nine months, spoke in sentences by eighteen months. I'm impressed. Did you know the book was here?"

"I'm not surprised. Mom probably thought I should have it. She knew we'd go through all that stuff eventually."

"Molly was absolutely fascinated. She forgot to be a grown-up and turned into a kid again. I don't know if she's ever seen a baby book before."

"She certainly never had one of her own."

The two of them fell silent. They had learned the basics of Molly's past during their foster care training. Her mother was only sixteen when Molly was born. Molly's father was unknown. At first the mother tried, in her own limited way, to care for the infant, but she was a child herself, with little education and no support from her family.

Molly was removed from the home several times before she was two. When she was three, her mother was arrested, then briefly imprisoned for forging checks. Once released, she was investigated again for child neglect. By the time Molly was four, she went into foster care and never came back out.

The story might have ended happily if Molly's mother had been willing to relinquish her rights so that Molly could be put up for adoption. But even though she'd never made another serious attempt to get Molly back, she refused to give up her legal claim. By the time the courts terminated the woman's rights, Molly was so old she was considered a special needs adoption. And though there was always hope the right family would step forward to take her, so far no one appropriate had materialized.

"My mother was always too busy for baby books," Tracy said. "But she kept shoe boxes for each of us. Locks of hair, hospital bracelets, photographs, notes about the first time we walked, sat up, said 'Mama.' You know. Stuff that proves she was paying attention to all my milestones, even if it wasn't exactly organized."

"I'm guessing nobody cared enough about Molly to make notes."

"She told me about the first foster home she remembers. It was an older woman with a couple of other foster children—kind of a surrogate grandmother from what I can tell. She was good to Molly. I think she's probably the person who set her on the right path and taught her what it was like to be in a family. Molly was there until she was almost nine."

"What happened?"

"The woman died suddenly. The children all went to separate

homes. Molly never saw any of them again." Tracy paused. "At least she had some good years when they really mattered."

"That was a lot of information for her to share."

"It came out in little tiny pieces. She'd say something, then she'd wait for me to respond. If I didn't jump on her or say something stupid, she'd tell me a little more. It was like walking through a minefield."

"And that's why nobody's adopted her," Graham said. "Maybe she's not sticking pins in Barbie or Ken, but she holds back so much that nobody can get to know her."

"So what do these idiots expect? A perfectly normal teenager after all these years in the system? Heck, do they even want a perfectly normal teenager? I mean, I remember what I was like at fourteen. Molly's easier to love than I was."

The words drifted heavenward with the smoke from their fire. Both of them waited for words and smoke to dissipate. But they were left with the residue.

"Be careful," Graham said at last.

"I know. This is temporary. She knows it. We know it. And it won't pay to get too close. Then she'll have trouble leaving us when a real family comes along." Tracy faced him. "This is a lot harder than I thought it would be. And I *thought* it would be hard. I know kids. I know it's never easy."

"You're doing a great job." Graham put his arm around her and drew her closer. "I like watching you with her. It's a side of you I don't get to see unless you're with your brothers and sisters."

She punched him in the arm. "Well, you're pretty squishy

with her yourself, you know. Feeding her pancakes, taking her out back to see your old woodworking shop, teaching her how to skip rocks at the creek."

"She's a good kid. I like being with her. I like showing her things. It's nice to see her in this house. I had some good times here at her age. Being here brings them back, and I like sharing them."

Tracy was unexpectedly attracted to this side of Graham. She had always known he was a warmhearted, caring guy. So why was his concern for Molly such a surprise?

She tried to feel her way. "You were right that night we started talking about taking Molly. Suddenly we're talking about things that really matter again. Not just what we did at work or where we want to grab a quick bite for supper before we both go home and start working some more."

He didn't say anything for a while. When he spoke, it was clear he'd been thinking. "Trace, are you happy? With our lives? With who we've become?"

The fire was dying down, and she shivered. "I'm happy with *you*."

Graham squeezed her shoulder and drew her closer. "And I'm happy with you. But do you remember the dreams we used to have? Did they involve working so hard at jobs we don't love?"

"When did you start thinking about this?"

"When I started spending time doing other things again. Like coming home at a decent hour. Having family dinners with you and Molly."

"Working on your paperwork every night after dinner until midnight?"

"My job is never going to be nine to five."

"Mine, either."

"Which is one reason we haven't really gotten around to having children."

"One reason," she agreed. "But not the only one."

"I've missed you, Trace."

She sighed and turned her face up to his. The fire sputtered and died and the night grew colder. It didn't really matter. They went inside, and for the rest of the night they kept each other warm.

# CHAPTER
## ◦—FOUR—◦

Tracy was so busy for the next three weeks that the dinner hour was the only time in her day when she wasn't working. She looked forward to preparing the meal and spending time with Molly and Graham at the table catching up.

Molly still kept to herself too much, but she did answer when they asked questions about school. The picture of a girl with no close friends was emerging. She seemed to get along well enough, but she resisted any suggestions to have friends over to study with her or just to hang out on the weekends. And if *she* was invited anywhere, she was certainly turning down all the invitations.

On Friday night three weeks after their weekend away, Tracy

knocked on Molly's door. She opened it when it was clear Molly couldn't hear her over the sounds of a voice wailing "I'm not a girl, not yet a woman" from the new portable CD player Graham had installed in her room.

"Molly?"

Molly looked up from the bed where she was reading, her quilt tucked under one arm.

"Dinner's almost ready. We're trying some new veggie burgers." Tracy spied the CD cover beside the player. "Hey, don't tell me that's Britney Spears?"

"Somebody at school loaned it to me. Is it too loud?"

"Not for me. I like the noise. But maybe not the way she dresses." She watched Molly stuff the quilt back under her pillow.

"You know, you can leave that out," Tracy said. "My younger brother took the few shreds that were left of his security blanket off to college. I understand. Nobody here's going to toss it, no matter what shape it's in."

Molly looked embarrassed, and for a moment Tracy was sorry she had spoken. But not speaking wasn't working any miracles. Molly was still too much like a shadow in the house.

She went to sit on Molly's bed. "Tell me about it. Are those your favorite colors?"

"They're all right."

"You've had that a long time, haven't you?"

"Uh-huh."

"May I see?"

Reluctantly Molly handed her the quilt. Tracy examined it, turning it over. "Quilts from Caring Hands."

"It's these ladies who make quilts for kids who have, you know…"

"Kids in foster care?"

"Kids who have messed up lives. All kinds of kids."

Tracy nodded, at a loss for words.

"It's falling apart," Molly said.

Sort of like the girl's future, Tracy acknowledged silently. No telling what the coming year was going to bring the girl or this well-loved scrap of fabric.

"I tried to fix it once," Molly went on, "but I don't sew."

"I sew, but I don't know a thing about quilts," Tracy said. "You know, though, if these people are still making quilts, I bet they could tell us what to do to fix it."

Molly's eyes brightened. "You think? I mean, I know it's silly—"

"It isn't silly. Molly, you haven't had an easy time of it, honey. It would be *silly* of us to pretend you had. And I think this quilt has helped you through the rough spots. It would be an honor to help you fix it up and preserve it. Will you let me?"

"You don't have much time."

Truer words had never been spoken. And wasn't that sad. That something as simple as repairing this quilt seemed impossible with her crowded schedule.

"The quilt's a priority," Tracy said. "Top of my list. Now come and try the veggie burgers and tell me what you think."

"You really won't, you know, decide it's no good and trash it?"

"There is no chance of it. None whatsoever."

Molly smiled for the first time since Tracy had opened the door.

Darla Chinn, Molly's Hawaiian-born social worker, had bone-straight black hair and blue eyes in a classic oval face. Her beauty was clearly noteworthy, but her strength and intelligence were even more so. She and Tracy were becoming friends, and formalized meetings between foster mother and social worker had turned into lunch dates.

On Wednesday they met at a restaurant near the university to munch their way down the salad bar.

"These women get together every Wednesday," Tracy told Darla once they had piled their plates and were back at the table. As they'd loaded up, she had started filling Darla in on her trip that morning to the Lifespring Foursquare Church to see the quilters of Quilts from Caring Hands in action. "And they've made literally thousands of quilts. But you probably know all that."

"We've given away a lot of their quilts," Darla said. "And I can tell you, they make a real difference to the children. The quilt's something to hold on to when there's not much else."

"They make quilts for a lot of different agencies. They even make tactile toys and quilts for blind children." Tracy was still impressed with everything she had seen that morning.

The church where the quilters met—she'd counted at least thirty—had once housed the YMCA. Their regular room was cheery with shelves nearly spilling over with fabric. Tables and ironing boards and sewing machines were set up everywhere. There was so much equipment, the church allowed them to put tables in the sanctuary, too, and the atmosphere in both rooms was charged with excitement and high spirits.

"Sounds like you had a good visit with them."

"It was great. One of the women took me around and showed me everything they were doing. Then she sat down with me and looked at Molly's quilt. Pretty soon a crowd gathered. Everyone oohed and aahed and gave me advice. They handled the quilt with the care I'd give a medieval tapestry."

"Women whose priorities are straight." Darla added sugar to her iced tea.

Tracy envied her thin friend that second packet of sugar and stirred artificial sweetener into her own tea. "The prognosis isn't good. The quilt's in pretty sad shape. The binding at the edges can't be salvaged. The border is threadbare. But most of the blocks in the middle are in good enough condition to save."

She set down her spoon. "The woman who gave me the tour suggested that Molly and I take it apart carefully, then remake it using the good blocks. We can add more—they're really simple, and we can probably find similar fabrics—then sew some borders around it to make it big enough for a twin bed. She said we could have somebody else quilt it if we want, or do that ourselves, too."

Darla stirred her tea. "It sounds like a big project, and one that will take some time."

"Uh-huh." Tracy knew just where Darla was going with that. "Having any luck finding a real foster home for her?"

"At this point it's you or the group home. Things are still going okay?"

Sometimes Tracy wondered if Darla was really looking for another home for Molly. "She's easy to have around."

"Until she starts testing you."

"I don't think that'll happen."

"And if she does?"

Although she wasn't a child psychologist or a real foster mother with a bag of tricks up her sleeve, Tracy wasn't without experience, either. Her brothers and sisters had been teenagers, and not that long ago. "We'll cope if that happens."

Darla reached for a second muffin. Tracy was still trying to rationalize a first. "I say go ahead with the quilt. It'll be a good memory for Molly once she gets another placement."

Tracy couldn't imagine herself as simply a good memory. The image was definitely unsettling. She wondered if Darla had known it would be.

Her cell phone rang. She apologized before she left to go outside and take the call.

Back at their table she scooped up her coat. "Remember that question you asked? The one about Molly testing us?"

Darla lifted one sculpted eyebrow in question.

"That was the school. They've scheduled a meeting in an

hour with Molly's English teacher. Molly was caught cheating on a test."

"Why would Molly cheat? She's smart as a whip and her grades have always been excellent."

Tracy slung her purse over her shoulder. "That's what I'm about to find out."

Tracy had not spent much time in guidance counselors' offices. Her family had expected her to work as hard at school as she did at home. She had been an A student.

But then, until today, so had Molly.

Graham joined her in the reception area outside the door. She hadn't expected him to drop everything and come, but here he was. He took her hand and squeezed it in greeting.

There was another couple waiting, as well. The man, dark-haired and athletic, was dressed in a cashmere sweater and perfectly creased khakis. The blond woman looked as if she had just come from the spa, and although Tracy's suits and dresses were of excellent quality, she and this woman did not frequent the same department stores. For that matter, Tracy was fairly sure this woman did her shopping in San Francisco or Seattle. Or Paris.

The guidance counselor ushered the four of them inside her office. Molly and another girl were sitting on one side of a narrow table with an older woman. Molly was looking down at the table and didn't acknowledge them.

Once they'd all seated themselves around the table, the counselor introduced the other woman as Mrs. Oakley. Then she introduced the expensive-looking couple as Mr. and Mrs. Carvelli, the parents of Jennifer Carvelli, the curvy blond student sitting next to Molly.

Mrs. Oakley was middle-aged with a ruddy complexion and salt-and-pepper hair. The table didn't hide her expansive waist-line. "I'll come right to the point," she said, twisting her hands as she spoke. "I graded my third-period test papers this morning. There were a number of multiple-choice questions, about twenty blanks to fill in, and a short essay at the end. The test counts for one quarter of this term's grade. I graded Jennifer's and Molly's papers back-to-back. Maybe if I hadn't, I wouldn't have noticed the problem."

"What problem?" Mrs. Carvelli said. Her voice was low and husky, but she bit off her words, clearly annoyed.

"Jennifer and Molly sit next to each other, and their papers are identical. Except for the essays, that is, and even those are remarkably similar, with key phrases repeated in both. Unusual phrases. There's no way that these two tests could be so much alike unless one of the girls was cheating."

She handed sheets of paper to both sets of adults. Tracy saw that the papers were copies of the girls' tests. She set them side by side on the table, glancing at Molly as she did. Molly looked miserable. Their eyes met for a moment, then Molly looked away. Jennifer, on the other hand, was examining her nails, which seemed to be decorated with perfect little flowers. Her hair was professionally streaked, and her clothes looked like a hybrid of *Seventeen* magazine and *Playboy*.

Her expression said she had nothing to worry about.

As Mrs. Oakley had concluded, the tests were too much alike to be anything but cheating. Tracy noted that one answer was misspelled on both papers and the essays were phrased a little differently, but the information was identical. There were even a couple of multiple-choice questions where both girls had erased or scratched out one answer and chosen the other.

She looked at Graham. He shrugged.

"What do the girls say?" she asked the teacher after the Carvellis had finished examining the tests.

"Jennifer says that Molly must have copied her paper."

"Then it's clear who cheated," Mrs. Carvelli said.

Tracy wasn't sure which Carvelli female she disliked more at the moment. "I'm sorry, but just because your daughter says Molly cheated doesn't mean it's the truth. Molly?"

Molly looked as if she wanted to shrink and disappear forever. "What?"

"Did you copy Jennifer's paper?"

Jennifer spoke before Molly could answer. "She said she did. Right, Mrs. Oakley?"

"My wife asked *Molly,*" Graham said pointedly.

"You don't want my help..." Jennifer shrugged. "Means nothing to me."

"Molly?" Tracy repeated.

Molly didn't answer.

After a tense silence, Mrs. Oakley said. "Molly did indicate she was the culprit. But frankly, I'm not sure she's telling the truth. Molly is a superior student and doesn't need to copy from anybody. Jennifer..." Her voice trailed off.

"That girl tells you she cheated, and you still want to blame my daughter?" Mrs. Carvelli demanded.

"I know your daughter's work, and she hasn't turned in a test paper anywhere near this perfect in all the weeks she's been in my class."

"Well, I—"

The teacher ignored her and went on. "I took the girls one by one out into the hallway and asked them questions on the material I had tested them on. Molly knew all the answers and Jennifer didn't. Then I asked Jennifer to repeat the written test after school today, and she refused."

"Why would Molly confess if she didn't do it?" Graham asked. He looked at the girl directly. "Why would you, Moll?"

Tracy noted that Jennifer was glaring at Molly now, and Molly was all too aware of it.

"I told the truth," she mumbled. "I...I copied Jennifer's paper. She's the one with the good test, not me."

Tracy was one-hundred percent sure Molly was lying, and she was ninety-nine percent sure why. Jennifer, from the looks of her, was probably one of the more popular students. Molly, judging from her lack of friends, was not. Jennifer had copied Molly's test paper, but Molly didn't want to turn her in. Tracy could only imagine how miserable a girl like Jennifer could make Molly's life.

"I don't know why you had to call us in here," Mrs. Carvelli said. "We're busy people. You have the cheater. She admitted it."

"I still believe Jennifer is the one who cheated," Mrs. Oakley said. "But since Molly is going along with it, I really don't have any choice here. Molly will receive the zero, but *both* girls will have to do a five-page essay on a subject connected with the test material. If either of them chooses not to turn it in, that will be another zero in my book."

"You have no right to punish Jennifer. I have close friends on the school board," Mr. Carvelli said. "I'll be talking to them."

Mrs. Oakley didn't dignify the threat with a reply. "Parents, I hope you'll talk to your daughters and try to get to the bottom of this."

"They're not my parents," Molly said.

Jennifer giggled. Tracy just wanted to cry.

Molly was staring out the window when Tracy walked into her room that night after a very quiet dinner. The girl didn't look at her when Tracy sat down on the bed.

"I have a bedtime story for you," Tracy said.

At her words, Molly turned. Her eyes were shining with tears, but her mouth was drawn in a determined line. The tears wouldn't be allowed to fall. "I'm not a little kid."

"I know you aren't. But I'm about to make up for some of the stories you didn't get to hear when you were."

Molly looked away.

"When I was fourteen, just coincidentally the same age you are, I had my first boyfriend. His name was Al, and I thought he was really hot. I thought I was really hot because he liked me, too."

"Hot?" Molly grimaced.

"I know. I'm trying to be fourteen again. Just temporarily. Play along."

Molly didn't answer.

"Anyway, let's just say that by my standards today, Al was a complete loser. But at the time, I thought he was everything good under the sun wrapped into one gorgeous fifteen-year-old body. One day Al and I were at this little shopping mall where our parents had dropped us off to see a movie. Afterward we went into a department store to look around, and Al saw a belt he liked. So he stuffed it under his coat. I couldn't believe it. I'd never seen anybody shoplift before. I told him he was crazy, but he just walked back into the mall, like he hadn't done anything. I went after him, trying to get him to take the belt back..."

Tracy waited. Molly turned around. "What happened?"

"A security guard at the store had seen him take the belt, so he came after us. When Al realized who the guy was and what he wanted, he shoved the belt at me and took off running."

"But the guard saw him steal it, right?"

"Right. The man knew it wasn't me. But when he finally caught up with old Al and dragged him back to the store, Al kept repeating it was my fault, that I'd taken it. And when that didn't work, he changed his story and said that I'd *made* him do it."

Tracy fell silent. She waited for Molly to speak, but the teenager said nothing.

"I didn't take the blame for him," Tracy said. "Because I knew, even then, that any boy who wanted me to take the blame for something he'd done wasn't worth much." She paused. "Which is not to say I wasn't devastated for days after we broke up."

"Why are you telling me this?"

"Because you took the blame for Jennifer today when you shouldn't have. And she's not worth it."

"You don't know anything about it."

"I know I care about you, Molly. And even worse than that zero is knowing that you're trying to protect somebody at the expense of your own integrity."

"Maybe it runs in my family."

Tracy's heart beat a dozen times before she trusted herself to speak. "I know about your mom. I know she was young, scared, confused and probably not very mature when she went to prison. But I hope if you blame her for the mistakes you make, you also give her credit for all the wonderful things about you. It's not fair to do one without the other." She took a deep breath. "Even more, I hope you don't blame *anybody* for your mistakes except yourself. But don't blame yourself too hard. You're a wonderful young woman."

"I'm going to sleep now."

Tracy wasn't sure what to do. So she did what seemed perfectly natural, perfectly right. She leaned over and kissed the top of Molly's head, then she ruffled her hair. "Sleep tight, honey."

She turned off the light and closed the door quietly behind her.

Graham was waiting in the living room. They had talked

about which of them should speak to Molly tonight, and Tracy had volunteered. But she knew that he had been waiting for her, hoping it went well.

"Did she admit she lied?" he asked.

"She's not going to do that. She'll stick with that story until it comes up at Christmas dinner when she's twenty-eight or thirty-eight. Then she'll laugh about it and tell the whole thing the way it really happened."

"And we won't be there to hear it."

Tracy plopped down on the sofa beside him. Graham put his arm around her shoulder, and she nestled against him. "It's not *what* she said, it's whether she heard what *I* said," Tracy told him.

"Did she?"

"I don't know. I feel so bad for her. I remember how badly I wanted to be liked by the popular kids. We all did. Except you, of course. You were undoubtedly one of the popular kids, or one of the kids who was too mature to care."

"Maybe, but I was never as slick as Mr. Carvelli. Did you get a load of that sweater of his? And he was wearing $800 shoes. I wonder why Jennifer's not in private school?"

"She probably cheated her way out of a couple, which is why she's being educated with the huddled masses now," Tracy said with venom.

"Meow."

She punched him lightly. "What are we going to do?"

"You mean punish the kid even more? I'm against it."

"No, the school's taken care of that. I meant, what are we

going to do to make her feel better about herself so she doesn't have to lie to make friends?"

"Short of vaulting her through time until she's twenty-one?"

"Short of that."

"Spend more time with her. We had so much fun that weekend in Alsea. I think about it a lot. We came home and went right back to being too busy. We sit down at dinner together, but that's about it. She's not getting much from us."

Tracy felt a little thrill of excitement. Graham sounded as lonely, as isolated, as she felt. They had begun making concessions in their schedule for Molly. Now suddenly those concessions weren't enough. She wanted more of Graham and less of her job. She wanted more of Molly, too. She loved having a career—that was never going to change—but she wanted more than work from her life.

"If we go to your folks' house for Thanksgiving, we'll hardly even see Molly," Graham said. "She'll be swallowed up by the thundering herd. Let's go back to Alsea. Just the three of us. We'll see your family at Christmas, instead. If my folks come to visit, we'll just take them along. Tell your mother why and she'll understand."

Tracy realized she hadn't been looking forward to the trip to Washington next week. She adored her family, but Graham and now Molly were her priorities. This felt new, even though she and Graham had been married for a decade. They were finding their way back to each other after drifting apart an inch at a time.

"Who's going to cook?" she asked.

Obviously realizing the answer to that question determined his future, Graham held up one hand as if swearing an oath. "All of us."

"Then I'm in," Tracy said. "But only if you agree not to take any work along. Just the three of us relaxing for four full days. Deal?"

He sealed the bargain with a kiss.

# CHAPTER
## ❧ FIVE ❧

The day before Thanksgiving, Janet brought Molly home from an afternoon of baby-sitting. Janet had promised to drive her if Tracy would let Molly stay longer than usual while she made preparations for the next day's dinner. Janet was entertaining all relatives west of the Rockies, and she was in panic mode.

Molly said hello to Tracy, then scooted through the house to her room. The door shut and seconds later the music went on. Tracy smiled at her friend. "You need a cup of tea. Sit. I'll get it for you."

Janet did just that, perching on a stool at the kitchen island as Tracy put the kettle on. She looked absolutely exhausted. "I don't know what I would have done without Molly today. I got the pies baked and the casseroles made."

"I hope other people are bringing things tomorrow. If they aren't, there's a problem in your planning."

"Everyone's bringing something, and my sister's bringing the turkey. I just wanted to finish all my cooking so I could spend tomorrow morning setting up. That'll take three times as long as it should since all the children will be helping."

Tracy made a face. "Sounds like fun."

"You're sure you don't want to come?"

"I appreciate the invitation, but we're looking forward to going out to the country, just the three of us. Graham's going to smoke a turkey. Molly's going to make a pumpkin cake—she doesn't like pumpkin pie. I'm making my mother's sausage and apple stuffing, minus the sausage, and lots of sweet potatoes with marshmallows. We had a family vote on the menu." Belatedly, Tracy realized what she'd said.

Janet noticed it, too. "Molly's starting to feel like family, isn't she?"

"That's a loaded question."

As if to fill in the resulting blank space in the conversation, the volume from Molly's bedroom went up an audible notch.

"How do you stand that?" Janet asked, putting her hands over her ears.

Tracy checked the hot water. "I like it. The house was pretty quiet before she got here. And you'd better get used to it, kiddo.

With five kids it will be twice as noisy once they're teenagers. Dueling stereos."

Taking pity on her friend, Tracy went down the hall to ask Molly to turn the volume down a notch. When she returned, Janet was leaning on the island, head in hands.

"Hey, you really need that cup of tea, don't you?" Tracy gave Janet's back a brief rub as she passed.

"I'm just having one of those moments of self-doubt," Janet said. "Ever have them?"

"At least ten times a day. What gives?"

"I'm trying to remember why I wanted five kids."

"Bad day with the tribe?"

"No. I love them to death. I love every little thing they do."

"So?" Tracy poured the boiling water into a sleek black teapot and pulled two matching cups from the cupboard.

"I don't think I'm going to like them as much when they're teenagers." Janet lifted her head. "Convince me."

"Teenagers are great."

"That's all you have to say?"

"Janet, you don't want kids who cling to you the rest of your life. Teenagers are fun to talk to. They finally have interesting things to say. They experiment with clothes and hair, and it's great to watch. You're the original earth mother. You'll love it."

"You're nuts. I'm not going to love it. I'm going to wake up every morning and wish I had my babies again. You're the exception to the rule."

"Me?"

"You. Look, I've been watching you with Molly. She's fine with me, but she treats you worse every time I see you together. She's surly and prickly—and listen to that music! And you don't seem to care one bit."

"Don't you get it?" Tracy said. "Every time she's a little gruff with me, that means she trusts me more. She knows I won't overreact. Of course, she also knows she can only go so far or I'll crack down on her. But it's a balancing act and she feels comfortable enough to experiment."

"You make it sound easy. I don't think you get it. You don't understand—teenagers aren't easy for everybody. I'm just glad you'll be around to hold my hand when mine are that age."

Tracy poured the tea and they talked of other things, but even after Janet was gone, her words lingered behind. Tracy thought about them well into the evening.

Molly was so glad to be back in the country. The house was creaky and old, and it took a few minutes for the hot water to reach the shower. But Molly's room had two windows side by side that looked out to the mountains and a big soft bed that sank around her at night and kept her warm.

And on the Friday after Thanksgiving, her room also had a sewing machine.

"Okay, here it is. What do you think?" Tracy came through the door lugging an old black machine with spidery gold lettering. "I told you I'd find it. I just had to look behind every blasted box and trunk in the attic."

Molly had been busy clearing a space on a small table that had held a clock with huge glow-in-the-dark numbers and a collection of silly ceramic dogs.

"Oh, good, you got rid of the dogs." Tracy plunked the old machine where the dogs had stood. "I hope you pitched them out the window."

"I just put them in a drawer. They're pretty dumb, but I kind of like them. I like dogs."

"I like real dogs. I don't know who left those. One of the renters."

"I think the house gets lonely without people living in it. Maybe the dogs keep it company." The moment she uttered the words, Molly was sure this was probably the dumbest thing she'd ever said.

Tracy just smiled. "I like that idea. It makes me feel better. I don't like to see the place standing empty."

"How come, like, you know, it's not rented now?"

"Graham...Mr. Wagner's looking into the local real estate market. This might be the right time to sell it."

"Sell it?" Molly couldn't imagine such a thing. The house was perfect. Old, but perfect. If it was her house, she'd live here all the time and never, never leave.

"I know exactly what you mean. I like it, too. But it seems unfair just to let it sit here and wait for us to visit when there are people who could live here year-round. It needs fixing up. I used to think..." Tracy's voice drifted off.

Molly normally didn't prod people to talk. Most of the time

she preferred not to hear what they had to say, since the news was rarely good. But this time she couldn't help herself. "What did you think?"

"Well, I thought it might make a nice craft gallery."

"What's that?"

"A shop where people come to buy local handiwork. There are a lot of wonderful artists and craftspeople in this area. Potters, sculptors, weavers. There's a stained-glass artist just down the road who makes the most gorgeous windows. I try to get my clients to buy local pieces for their homes, but it's tough because people are busy and there aren't enough galleries for them to make selections without tramping from studio to studio. I'd love to start one."

"Here?"

"Here or somewhere else outside the city. This seems like a good bet. People come here to relax, and they want relaxing things to do. They want to buy things to take back home to remind them of their vacations. We're not far from the main road. It's a nice detour."

"Then why don't you do it? You're a grown-up. You get to do whatever you want."

Tracy laughed a little. "Do you think so? If you're counting on that, I'd better warn you now. There are always things that get in the way."

"Like what?"

"For one thing, it would cost a lot of money. And take a lot of work."

"You have a lot of money. And you work all the time anyway." This made perfectly good sense to Molly, so she was sorry when it was clear her words had hurt Tracy.

"Hey, I don't work all the time. We're here today, aren't we? And yesterday and the rest of the weekend?"

"I'm sorry."

Tracy ruffled her hair. "Don't be. I do work too much, and so does Mr. Wagner. Before you came, we'd almost forgotten how much fun it is to take some time off."

Molly figured she'd have to think about that. She wasn't sure this was a good thing. She wasn't really used to good things happening just because she was living with somebody.

"Anyway," Tracy said, "this is the big moment, kiddo. Are we going to take your quilt apart and make it bigger with the new fabric we bought last weekend? Or are we just going to try to fix it a little so it won't fall apart as fast?"

Molly had been thinking about what to do ever since Tracy had proposed the idea of expanding her quilt. A new quilt would be great, but it would never be the same. It wouldn't feel the same, look the same. On the other hand, it would last a lot longer, maybe her whole life if she took good care of it.

And the new fabric, more lavender and yellow prints, was awfully pretty.

"I think we ought to do it," Molly said, not without reservations.

"Then let's get this antique threaded and see if it really works."

\* \* \*

That night after Molly went to bed, Tracy went in search of Graham. They had dined early on Thanksgiving leftovers, then he had disappeared. She and Molly had hardly noticed since they'd gone right back to work.

The machine had worked surprisingly well, the quilt had come apart with only a little help, and they had been pleasantly surprised to find that most of the original blocks could be used again if they restitched some of the seams. They had made more blocks, following the instructions Tracy had received from the gracious quilters she had consulted. Now, tomorrow, they could sew the blocks back together and begin to add borders.

Meantime, Graham had disappeared.

Tracy thought she knew where she would find her husband, and she was right. He was off in the old woodworking shop where his father, an excellent woodworker himself, had taught his son the basics and beyond.

The shop was compact but well-organized. Graham hadn't used it in a long time, and he kept his tools locked away in the condo's spacious storage area.

This weekend, though, he had brought a few with him, and now they were neatly lined up on a freshly dusted worktable. A space heater warmed the room, and moonlight and two shop lights illuminated it. From the looks of things, there was a project in the offing.

"Don't tell me," Tracy said from the doorway, feigning a

heart attack by slapping her hand over her chest. "You're going to make that headboard at last?"

He turned and grinned. "Nope."

"A woman can dream."

"Maybe that'll be the next project."

She joined him at the table and sniffed the air. "Cedar, right?"

"A couple of good-size trees up on the hill keeled over in a storm a few years ago, so I had them sawed into boards. They've been curing in the garage ever since. I almost forgot they were there."

"What are you making?"

"Well, I thought if you and Molly get into quilting, there might be more quilts down the road a piece. She'll need a place to store them. So I'm making her a cedar chest. I thought I'd give it to her for Christmas."

Tracy was so surprised she blurted out the first thought she had. "What if she's not with us at Christmas? What if she's been moved by then?"

She hadn't wanted to squelch Graham's enthusiasm, but Tracy realized by the way his expression hardened that she had. "And how is she going to take it to her new home?"

"I thought of that." His next comment had a pronounced edge. "Or does that surprise you?"

"I'm sorry. I just hate... Well, you're going to so much trouble, and she's going to be so disappointed if she has to leave it behind...."

"If she's not allowed to bring the chest with her, we'll keep it for her. She'll know that she can have it the moment she has a place of her own. We're not going to just let her vanish from our lives, are we? We're going to stay in touch. She'll be able to visit, I'm sure."

"I'm not. Social services will probably want us to back off and let her get adjusted to the new family. We've only had her a couple of months. We won't have much in the way of rights."

He faced her, arms folded over his chest. "So what would you like me to do?"

She wished they had never started this conversation, but clearly it had been hanging at the edges of their lives, waiting for this moment. This wasn't about a cedar chest. Nor was it only about Molly. A lot of it was about the two of them.

"Our lives have changed since Molly came," Tracy said. "And I think we've been good for her. She's been good for us, too. We've started taking a little time off, working fewer evenings and weekends. We talk more..."

"Right now I wish that part wasn't true."

She winced at his tone. "I didn't mean to rain on your parade. The cedar chest is a thoughtful gift. You're right. We'll find a way to make sure Molly can keep it. But this is about more than the cedar chest. It's about asking Darla if we can go from being emergency foster parents to long-term ones. Isn't it?"

He didn't nod. His shrug was almost undetectable.

"There's a lot more to that decision than meets the eye," she pointed out. "Has the extra time you've taken off made your job as difficult as it's made mine? Are you working twice as fast every day to try to make up for it? Have you thought about summer vacation and how we'll manage when Molly's home full-time?"

"Kids get jobs. They go to camp or summer school."

"Why keep her if our solution is to find ways to dump her somewhere else as often as possible?"

"You know that's not how I meant it."

"But that would be the upshot. My job speeds up in the summer, and I work even harder. You can't afford to take up my slack. Doesn't she deserve a family with parents who are home more? Who don't have to rearrange schedules and juggle clients just to take the whole Thanksgiving holiday off? Who have nine-to-five jobs they can let go of when the day ends?"

"Don't you think half the families in this country have those kinds of problems? They manage."

"And what about the day Darla comes to us and says she's found a family that wants to adopt Molly? We put our careers in second gear, rearrange our priorities and suddenly she's gone anyway? And we're left with a hole in our lives and our hearts?"

Graham was silent. Outside the workshop, the country night was still except for an owl hooting somewhere on the hillside.

"So that's what this is about," he said at last.

"I never lied to you. I told you I wasn't sure I'd ever want kids."

"Trace, it's not about wanting a kid, it's about letting a kid go. You're afraid you're going to fall in love with her."

She gestured to the cedar planks. "And what is that about?"

He didn't answer. She took a deep breath. "I'm trying to be

levelheaded. I'm looking at our lives and what we *don't* have to offer Molly. I'm looking at the very distinct possibility that someone else will have more, and we'll have to say goodbye. I'm warning you not to get too attached."

Graham waited a moment before he spoke. Tracy wasn't sure he was going to say anything at all, but at last he did.

"You know what?" This shrug was obvious. "I'm willing to take my chances. I'd rather give Molly a piece of my heart when she leaves than keep my heart sealed away for no good reason. That's the chance you take when you care about somebody."

He turned back to his project, leaving her to wonder what chances she was willing to take.

# CHAPTER
## ~SIX~

**M**olly didn't really like Jennifer Carvelli. Jennifer was sooo positive there wasn't anybody else in the world as wonderful as she was. But through the years Molly had learned to be practical. In her short life she'd been stuck with a lot of people she had to get along with, whether she liked them or not. Compared with the girl in one of her foster homes who had cut up all Molly's clothes with their foster father's hedge trimmer, Jennifer wore a halo.

Jennifer had been pretty cool after the cheating episode. Everybody knew Jennifer cheated, lied and cut classes. She couldn't be bothered studying when there were so many better things to do. But she was very grateful when other people took the blame for her indiscretions. After Molly lied to save her, Jennifer made sure Molly was welcome at the lunch table where the most popular kids sat. No one talked to her much, but it was better than sitting alone, which had happened too often in the past.

Even now, on the first day after the Christmas break, Jennifer's group still made room for her. And Jennifer asked if she could go home with Molly after school to work on an English report. Molly knew what that meant. She would write most of Jennifer's report while Jennifer tied up the Wagners's phone or watched HBO, but Molly's cooperation would buy her more days at the lunch table.

Molly didn't feel good about this, but she was no dummy. She would feel much worse in the long run if she refused. Jennifer would make sure of that.

She felt especially bad calling Mrs. Thaeler on Jennifer's cell phone to tell her she couldn't baby-sit that afternoon. Even though Mrs. Thaeler said it was fine, Molly still felt bad. But now that she and Jennifer were at the Wagners's condo after a high-school friend of Jennifer's dropped them at the door, the guilt was disappearing.

"Hey, this is tight!" Jennifer threw her books on the sofa and didn't pick them up when two fell to the floor. "How'd you end up in a place like this?"

Molly examined the question and figured that what Jennifer really meant was how did a complete reject like Molly end up somewhere other than an institution straight out of *Oliver Twist*.

"I don't know," Molly said with a carefully nonchalant shrug. "The Wagners are okay."

"What's it like being a foster kid? Who buys your clothes? Do they give you money and stuff?" Jennifer picked up a pottery statue of a Mayan god sitting on an end table and turned it over, as if looking for a price tag.

"It's not too bad," Molly said carefully. "I get to be on my own when I turn eighteen."

Jennifer set the statue down too hard and Molly winced at the thud.

"What happened to your real parents?" Jennifer asked. "They die or something?"

Molly could just imagine how much mileage Jennifer would get from the truth. "Uh-huh."

"Sometimes I wish mine would die. Honestly. They treat me like a baby."

"Do you have brothers and sisters?"

"You're kidding, right? My mom says that one kid was too many. Every time I do something she doesn't like, she fixes herself a martini. She'd be sprawled out on the street somewhere if she'd had another kid on top of me."

It was hard for Molly to imagine the sophisticated Mrs. Carvelli facedown in the gutter. "Maybe we ought to get to that paper. I'm not sure the Wagners want me to have friends over while they're gone."

"Do they lock up the liquor?"

"I don't know. I never checked."

"Find out. This could be a great place to party."

Molly could just picture how fast she'd get booted out if that happened. "What's the subject for your report? I've got a computer in my room. We can check out the Internet just to get some ideas."

"Just don't try to copy one. Mrs. Oakley checks Google to see what's out there. Somebody I know got busted. It's got to be *o-rig-i-nal!* She's a fat cow, isn't she?"

Molly liked their English teacher. She wished she could tell Mrs. Oakley the truth about that test, but she knew the woman would not understand. "My paper's on Wordsworth," she prompted.

"Mine's supposed to be on Colgate or Coldhearted or something like that."

"Coleridge. Samuel Taylor Coleridge."

"Why do you pay attention to that stuff? Do you like it?"

"Yeah," Molly said without thinking. "I'd like to be a writer someday. I figure with everything I've seen, I'd have something to say."

Jennifer looked up. She'd been busily draping one of the handwoven afghans on the sofa around her. "You probably would. You're smart that way."

Molly was warmed by the other girl's reaction. She felt a little better about "helping" Jennifer with her report. "You want to get started?"

"I guess. I got a book on poetry from the library. That might help."

Slightly encouraged, Molly wondered if the afternoon might not be as bad as she'd feared. Jennifer left the afghan in a heap on the coffee table and Molly led the way to her room.

"Not bad." Jennifer glanced around. "But mine's a lot bigger and I have my own bathroom." She wandered to the window and looked out at the incomparable view. "Wow, you can see all the way to Alaska...or wherever."

Molly was beginning to relax. She watched Jennifer examine everything. She seemed to approve. Molly was sure she would not have approved of most of the places she had lived. Jennifer would most certainly not approve of the farmhouse in Alsea. Molly tried to imagine Jennifer in a house without central heating, with limited hot water and the nighttime rustling of mice or bats in the walls and ceilings.

Flopping down on the bed, Jennifer drew Molly's new quilt around her. Molly loved the quilt, even if it would not, even now, win a prize at the State Fair. She and Tracy had laboriously sewn the top, adding strips of fabric in pleasing designs, then Tracy had taken it somewhere to have it quilted on a machine as a Christmas present. Now the entire quilt was covered with little hearts in bright yellow thread. Molly wasn't sure which gift she'd liked better, the finished quilt or the beautiful cedar chest Graham had made for her.

Nor was she sure what either gift had meant.

"What's this?" Jennifer tapped the toe of her leather boot against the chest.

"It's a cedar chest," Molly said, pulling herself back to the present. "To keep blankets and stuff in."

Jennifer stuck her toe under the lid and tried to raise it. "Nice..."

Molly didn't want Jennifer's foot on her chest. She watched Jennifer lift the lid halfway, then drop it. The resounding thunk made her uneasy. "Do you want me to get on the Internet so you can look up Coleridge?"

"I don't care." Jennifer lifted the lid again. Higher this time. This thunk was louder.

"Okay. That's what I'll do." Molly knew enough about human nature to realize if she asked Jennifer not to play with the chest, she would either make fun of her or keep doing it anyway. She hoped to distract her.

At the desk, Molly could hear Jennifer dropping the lid, over and over. She prayed for the computer to boot up quickly and for the Internet connection to be instantaneous.

"Okay, here we go," Molly said. She turned, just in time to see Jennifer give the lid one particularly hard kick. The little chest, with nothing inside to weight it, tilted backward and fell over. Molly heard a crack as the lid hit first, then folded back with a snap as the chest turned over. She was afraid to look.

"Whoops," Jennifer said.

Reluctantly Molly got up and went over to the bed. The top of the chest had come free of one of the brass hinges and lay at an angle. She stared at the gift that had been made with loving hands, just for her, then she stared at Jennifer.

To her credit, Jennifer looked apologetic. "Sorry."

"Sorry?" Molly shook her head. "Mr. Wagner made that for me."

"Then it's no big deal. He can probably fix it."

"It's no big deal to you!" Molly hadn't known she could get so angry, but suddenly a white-hot rage filled her. She wanted to tear out every strand of Jennifer's carefully highlighted hair. "You have everything! You don't know what it's like *not* to be you. You don't care, either. Do you think it's anything except luck that you're not me? Can you even *try* to imagine what it's like not to have everything you want?"

Jennifer stared at her. "It's no big deal. What's wrong with you?"

"Get out." Molly pointed to the door. "Write your own stupid paper."

Jennifer's eyes narrowed. "You think you can talk to me like that?"

"I just did. But don't worry, I don't ever want to talk to you again. We're finished talking."

"Where do you think you'll be eating lunch tomorrow?"

"Maybe I'll be eating it in Mrs. Oakley's classroom, while I tell her what a miserable cheat you are!"

Jennifer gave a short laugh. "You wish." She stood, and Molly's quilt slid to the floor. "I can make your life hell."

"You'll have to stand in line," Molly said.

Tracy's day had been awful. She had risen early to get into the office for two crack-of-dawn appointments. Neither set of clients had liked any of her ideas. The first couple insisted the bathroom tile they had chosen two months before was unacceptable and had to be replaced with something other than the vast array of samples Tracy had on hand. The next couple could not agree on a shade of paint between vanilla and linen. They had left after threatening to find a designer with a better eye for subtleties.

The drapes she had ordered for a new home were five inches too short. The wallpaper mural of mountains her developer had asked for in his office turned out to be a city skyline instead. Six clients called to demand after-hours appointments that week, and three more called to cancel orders already in progress.

By the time she got home, she was ready for a glass of wine, painkillers, a back rub and half an hour of soothing music. In any order.

The house seemed oddly still when she opened the front door. "Molly?" she called as she hung up her coat.

Normally she picked up Molly from Janet's, but this month Janet's oldest son was in a late-afternoon gymnastics class, and Janet had begun dropping Molly off on her way to the gym. Tracy wondered if there had been a change of plans today.

"Molly?" When there was no response, she muttered to herself and went in search.

She stopped at Molly's door and stared. The chest that Graham had so carefully crafted for the girl was lying on its back on the floor, the lid at an odd angle. The closet door was wide-open, and there were no longer any clothes hanging inside.

The quilt had been stripped from Molly's bed. But nothing else appeared to be missing.

"Molly?" she said softly.

The front door slammed and she whirled and ran out into the hall. "Molly?"

Graham appeared, loosening his tie as he moved toward her. "Hey, Trace." When he saw her expression, he frowned. "What's going on?"

"I…I'm not sure. I think Molly's run away."

"What?" He looked as if she'd lost her mind. "What do you mean?"

She stood aside and gestured toward the door of Molly's room. "See for yourself."

He walked over and glanced inside. Then he turned. "Tell me everything you know."

There was so little, she covered it in one run-on sentence. His mouth drew into a grim line.

"Did she say anything to you this morning when you dropped her off at school?" Tracy demanded. "Maybe it's some activity there? A class sleep-over?" She knew she was grasping at straws. All Molly's clothes were gone, not just an extra pair of jeans and pajamas. And the chest, obviously damaged, was still lying on the floor, as if Molly had knocked it over in a fury.

"She told me Janet would bring her home," Graham said.

"Janet." Tracy felt a rush of relief. "I'll call Janet. Maybe she knows something. Molly was there." She hesitated. "She was *supposed* to be there."

He joined her in the kitchen after wandering the living room like a detective looking for clues. Tracy wedged the phone between her ear and shoulder and scrambled for a notepad and pen, although she had no reason to think she might need them.

The phone rang six times, and finally Janet's answering machine picked up.

"I don't believe it!" Tracy told Graham what was happening, then when the beep sounded, she left Janet a message to call her right away.

"I'd go out looking for her, but I don't have any idea where to go," Graham said. "She's either here or she's at school or Janet's. Do you know any of her friends? Is there anybody you can call?"

Tracy had made attempts to get Molly to invite friends to the house, but she hadn't pushed very hard. She knew little about the girl's life outside their walls. With a sinking heart she realized how little she did know. Molly had been with them for four months, and for the most part she was still a stranger.

Graham correctly read her expression. "Don't beat yourself up."

"Why not? I don't have the phone number of even one friend I can call. She's a teenager. They live in packs. What kind of parent am I?"

"For all we know, she doesn't have any friends. She's the lone wolf."

"Yeah, for all we know. And what do we know? Have we made any real attempt to figure that out? We've just been playing at being parents."

"There's Jennifer Carvelli. Molly stuck up for her."

"Yeah, when she shouldn't have." Tracy knew what a long shot Jennifer was. She was not the kind of girl to hang out with anybody who couldn't add to her own social status. But at least it was a start. Maybe Jennifer could give them phone numbers.

"I'll try their house. It's not a common name. How many Carvellis will there be?" Graham dug through a bottom drawer for the phone book.

He straightened, found the right page and dialed, tapping his foot while he waited for someone to answer. Tracy motioned to the receiver and he tilted it to share it with her as the phone rang and rang.

Finally a girl's voice answered. "Yeah?"

"Is this Jennifer Carvelli?" he asked.

"Uh-huh. Who wants to know?"

Tracy pantomimed strangling somebody.

"This is Graham Wagner, Molly's foster dad. I'm looking for Molly. Have you seen her this afternoon?"

There was a long pause. For a moment Tracy wondered if the girl had fallen asleep out of spite. Then Jennifer said, "Yeah, I was over there. Sorry about the chest. I didn't mean to break anything."

Graham snatched the receiver to his ear, as if he knew that Tracy was about to give the girl a piece of her mind. "Never mind the chest, Jennifer. We just want to know where Molly is."

"I don't know. She kicked me out. She was really angry, you know? I had to walk about a mile to a phone so I could get a ride home."

"I hope it did you some good." Graham handed the receiver to Tracy so she could hang up.

The phone rang the moment she put it back on the hook. Tracy snatched it up. "Hello!"

Janet was on the line. "Tracy, good grief. It's just me."

"Janet, do you know where Molly is?"

There was a pause, followed by a sigh. "She's here. We were just finishing a heart-to-heart when you phoned."

Tracy went limp. "Oh. I was so afraid something had happened. Her room's all cleaned out, and her chest is broken and——" She lowered her voice. "Why is she *there*? She didn't baby-sit for you today, did she? She was here earlier. She had a friend over."

"No, she didn't sit for me today. And she must have walked over here while I was running Alex to gymnastics. There's no easy way to tell you this. She claims she wants to stay with us until she can move into the group home. She doesn't want to go back to your house. I've tried to get the story out of her, but she just says she doesn't like living with you anymore. She wants to leave. She's going to call the social worker."

"Darla?" Tracy was too confused to think of anything else to say. "She's calling Darla?"

"I asked her not to just yet, to give this a little more thought. But she's determined."

"And she didn't say why? Janet, she's been happy here. We've gotten along, I know we have. There was no sign of trouble…"

Janet lowered her voice even more. "You can figure this out if you try hard enough."

"What's that supposed to mean!"

"I mean, you just answered your own question. She's happy there. Maybe that frightens her."

"No, I think it's got something to do with Jennifer and the chest and——"

"I've got to go. I'll stall her as long as I can." The phone clicked and the line went dead.

"What'd she say?" Graham demanded.

"She's there. She wants to stay with Janet until she can move into the group home. She wants to call Darla and tell her."

"And Janet doesn't know why?"

"She says maybe being happy here scared her." Tracy felt tears welling, and in a moment they were sliding down her cheeks.

Graham didn't reach for her. "What do you think?"

"I think it has something to do with Jennifer breaking the chest."

"So do I."

She looked up. "How?"

"For somebody who understands teenagers as well as you do, you've got a real blind spot about this one."

Graham didn't sound angry, but she heard the challenge in his voice.

"Then enlighten me," she said.

"She loves that chest, Trace. She loves her quilt. Don't you see? She's starting to love us. Jennifer damages the chest, and from experience, Molly is sure we'll kick her out. So she leaves on her own. That way she won't be abandoned by people she cares about. It's easier and safer to abandon us."

It was so simple and yet so complex. But Tracy knew that what Graham said was true.

"We've been playing at this." She wiped her cheeks with her fingertips. "I was right before. We've been doing our good deed for the year by letting her stay with us. We've made a few accommodations to her schedule, taken a little more time off, given her things, but we haven't given any real thought to what's going on inside her."

"And now she's left us."

*Maybe it's better this way* seemed like the appropriate response, yet it was so far from what Tracy wanted to say, the words wouldn't form. "I don't want her to go," she said softly.

"If she agrees to come back, it'll be even harder next time she leaves. Darla will find her another family eventually, or Molly will run away again the next time she panics. Maybe it's better this way."

She didn't like his tone. He sounded like the financial adviser he was, cool and logical. "No, it's not!"

"You're not thinking straight."

"Who cares! I don't want her to go. I come home in the afternoons now and I look forward to her being here. On the good days, when she shares a little, I feel like somebody's given me a million dollars. And when the three of us are together, we feel like a family. Not just two people pursuing careers they don't really care about, but a *family*. People who are trying to find their way to something better. Don't tell me you don't feel the same way."

He relaxed visibly. She hadn't realized until then how tense his posture had been. "Then I won't," he said.

"Why didn't you say something before?"

"Trace, you're the one who's resisted falling in love with Molly. You've refused to recognize it. I wasn't sure you could see it."

She thought about the Friday night after Thanksgiving. She'd stood in his workshop and cautioned him against getting too attached to Molly. And all the time her attachment had been growing and strengthening, until now she felt as if her beloved daughter had been torn from her arms.

"I didn't want to be a mother," she said, her voice cracking.

"Trace, you've been one for months, and you've loved every minute of it. Taking Molly was your idea, remember?"

"We can't go on the way we have been."

He wrapped his arms around her and pulled her against his chest. He kissed her hair.

"I'm getting your shirt wet," she said in a muffled voice.

"Don't worry. I won't be needing white shirts much longer."

She pulled away just a little to see his face. "Why not?"

"Honey, come on. Don't you see where this is going?"

She sighed and relaxed, hugging him tighter. Because sometimes, when life was taking a one hundred and eighty degree turn, all a person could do was let it happen.

Tracy decided to enjoy the ride.

# CHAPTER
## ~∘~ SEVEN ~∘~

**M**olly hoped that the Wagners would not show up at the Thaeler house, either to yell at her for the broken cedar chest or to talk her into going back home with them. Their home, of course. Never hers, although a few times she'd thought about it that way.

Those thoughts should have been a clue. Little by little she had slipped into feeling like she was part of something there. But she knew better. She was the Wagners's charity project, the poor orphan girl who needed a place to live. She'd seen *Annie* on television. She knew all about Daddy Warbucks.

Of course, Daddy Warbucks had never crafted a cedar chest for Annie. And there'd been no Mommy Warbucks in the movie who helped her make a new quilt, or took her shopping for better jeans, or understood why she had lied about cheating on a stupid English test.

She felt sick about the cedar chest, sick that she had let Jennifer break it. Because Molly knew she was the one who'd really screwed up. She'd been so worried that Jennifer would make her life miserable that she had allowed her to kick the chest again and again.

She didn't *want* to see the Wagners...but she wondered a little why they hadn't tried harder to find out what was wrong.

"Molly?"

Mrs. Thaeler was standing in the bedroom doorway. Molly had agreed to sleep in the nursery with Liza on a fold-out bed in the corner. Liza had gone to sleep hours ago, giggling until her eyes finally closed for good, but Molly hadn't been able to sleep a wink.

"What?" Molly whispered.

"I need you in the living room."

Molly didn't know what to say. Was she being kicked out in the middle of the night? Had Darla come to get her tonight instead of waiting until morning, like she'd said when Molly called her?

"Molly?" Mrs. Thaeler asked in that pleasant tone of voice that still meant Molly had better move quickly.

"I'll put on my jeans."

Once she was alone with Liza again, Molly got dressed. She supposed this wasn't the end of the world, even if it felt like it.

Maybe the group home would be okay after all. At least she wouldn't have to be perfect all the time, no matter how she felt. Where else could they send her after that?

She touched her quilt, then picked it up and smoothed one corner along her cheek. It was old and new, past and present. She wondered if it would be safe at the group home. Sighing, she dropped it back on the bed and walked down the hall.

After too many hours had passed, she'd convinced herself that the Wagners weren't coming to see her. When she saw them sitting on the Thaelers's sofa, she nearly fled.

Mrs. Wagner looked like she wanted to cry. Something clenched inside her. Was Mrs. Wagner upset because of her? That made her uneasy. That made her feel a little sick. She really liked Mrs. Wagner as much as she'd tried not to. She hated to think she could make her cry.

"Hi, Molly." Mr. Wagner stood, like she was a grown-up and he wanted to do the polite thing. It seemed so odd, so formal that she wasn't sure what to do. He didn't look comfortable, either.

She wondered what they were going to say to her. She thought of the chest that he'd worked on so hard, just for her, and she felt even sicker. She looked away.

"I'm sorry about the cedar chest," she mumbled, eyes focused on a plastic dump truck in the corner. "It was an accident. Sort of."

"Jennifer Carvelli already apologized."

That surprised her. She glanced up briefly, then turned back to the truck. She heard a noise behind her and realized that Mrs. Thaeler had brushed past on her way out of the room. Molly was alone with the Wagners.

"I shouldn't have let her come over," Molly said.

"Probably not," Graham agreed. "But that's not why we're here."

She knew better, but she glanced up because now she was curious.

"Molly, come here." Tracy patted the sofa. Graham sat down again, but he left a place between the two of them.

She didn't like this. Emotions churned through her, and she didn't even know what they were. She did not want to sit between them like the filling in a sandwich.

"Please?" Tracy asked.

Molly heard the wobble in her voice and knew that she had to go, whether she wanted to or not. She walked the last mile to the sofa and sat between them, perching forward so she could jump up the moment it became necessary.

"We brought you something," Graham said. "Will you open it?" He lifted a rectangular package off the table, wrapped in flowered lavender paper. The paper reminded her of her quilt. She was suspicious immediately, but still, regretfully, intrigued.

"Go ahead," Tracy said.

"It's not my birthday. Christmas is over."

"I know when your birthday is," Tracy said. "August 18. I'm looking forward to it. But sometimes when people care about each other, they give gifts for no good reason."

Molly considered bolting. Cared about each other? But the

present was too mysterious. If she didn't open it, she was afraid she'd wonder the rest of her life what it was.

"I can cut the ribbons," Graham said.

"Just like a man," Tracy said. "He's in a hurry, Molly. Can you untie it quickly?"

Molly relaxed just an ounce at the glimmer of humor in Tracy's voice. She began to pick at the ribbons. It took her a moment, but at last both ribbons and paper fell away to reveal a white box. She lifted the top to see a scrapbook with a photo of her with the Wagners on the front cover.

She frowned. "What's this?"

"It's your baby book," Tracy said. "Or, I guess we have to say it's your teenage book."

Molly continued to frown. "What's inside?"

"Look and see," Graham said.

Molly was suspicious, but it was hard to say no. The scrapbook was covered in some sort of shiny blue fabric that changed colors, like the water at Alsea Falls. She liked the photo, too. Mr. Wagner had taken it. He always took these crazy timed photos everywhere they went. He put the camera on a rock or a tree limb and ran back to stand with them before the camera clicked. He'd taken this one on the front porch of the farmhouse with the camera on the railing. They were all making faces.

She looked happy.

She had *been* happy.

She took a deep breath and turned the page.

"What's this?" She leaned closer.

"The prologue to the *Canterbury Tales*—in Middle English," Tracy said. "Remember? You were learning it the day I found out you needed a new family."

Molly thought that was a little weird, but nice. She was surprised Mrs. Wagner had remembered something so silly.

She turned the page and stared. "What's this?"

"A menu from the first restaurant we took you to. Remember? You ordered the Portobello mushroom sandwich?" Tracy pointed. "There it is."

"How can you remember what I ordered?"

"I paid attention," Tracy said simply.

Molly looked at the next page. "A shoe?"

"I traced around yours. That's from the first new shoes we bought you. You left them behind."

Before she'd left that day, Molly had carefully put everything the Wagners had bought her in the bottom drawer of her dresser. She was surprised they'd found out so quickly.

"There's a pocket from those old ratty jeans you used to love, too. I discovered them in the trash a couple of weeks ago." She made a little choking noise, then recovered. "I have to confess, I've been saving stuff of yours ever since you came to live with us. I have a shoebox in my closet. I've been filling it with your stuff. My mother did that. I guess I inherited more from her than I thought."

Molly thought that was getting weirder by the moment, but she didn't feel weird. She felt warm and softer inside, and she thought she might start crying if this got any stranger.

"What's this?" But the question was stupid. The next six pages were packed with photographs Mr. Wagner had taken of her. Thanksgiving photos, photos at the falls, photos on the hill behind the farmhouse, photos from their Christmas trip to meet Mrs. Wagner's family.

Mrs. Wagner's family had treated her like she belonged. The memory gave her a brand-new pang.

"Darla—Miss Chinn—says she'll call every foster parent you've had and see if they have any photos they can copy," Graham said. "We'll add them later."

Molly was skimming now. There was a page with her progress reports from school, photos of the Thaeler children, a copy of a speech about World War II that she'd gotten an A on in history, ticket stubs from a movie they'd gone to, the tag for the new coat she'd gotten at Christmas. It had been in the cedar chest with the quilt.

And how had they known how badly she wanted that coat?

She stopped on the next to the last filled page, although there were many blank pages beyond it. This was a drawing. No, it was a blueprint, or sort of. House plans.

She pulled the scrapbook a little closer. "What's this?"

"Those are my plans for remodeling the farmhouse," Graham said. "If we're going to live there, we need to modernize the upstairs a little. A new bathroom, a bigger master bedroom—see, we can knock out walls here, add some built-ins in your bedroom. Until we can afford to build a new house on the hillside."

She looked up, then hazarded a glance at him. "The farmhouse?"

Tracy answered. "We're moving there, Molly. We're selling the condo and moving to Alsea. Mr. Wagner's going to build cabinets and furniture, and I'm going to turn the downstairs into a craft gallery. At the very latest we'll have the new house built by the time you're in high school, or maybe we'll build a gallery instead and stay in the farmhouse. You can help us decide. Meantime, you can decorate the room any way you want."

Tracy pointed to the fabric and paint samples on the final page. "We can start with these, but you can do anything you like. Black walls, cardboard furniture—I don't care. It's yours." She sounded enthused. But underneath it all she sounded scared, as if she was afraid Molly might refuse.

Molly took all this in. She hardly knew what to say. Finally she blurted out, "But I'm just your foster kid."

Tracy put her arm around Molly's shoulders. "Not for long."

There was no way Molly could misunderstand. She thought about life with the Wagners. A real life. Pets and barbecues and vacations. Fights and misunderstandings, love and laughter, a place to come home to once she was a grown-up herself, relatives and holidays and knowing secrets about each other.

A family of her own.

"I'm not as perfect as you think I am," she said doubtfully. "You might not like me as much as you think you do."

"Are you trying to give us a way out?" Graham asked.

She realized his arm was around her, too. She nodded, and despite all efforts, tears filled her eyes.

"We'll take you just the way you are," Tracy said. "If you'll take us the same way?"

What else could she do? What else could she possibly want? She was trapped by what she was very afraid might be love.

Molly nodded, too.

Dear Reader,

Several years ago when I was asked to write a story highlight-
ing the work of Quilts from Caring Hands, I was delighted. As
a quilter myself and one who had made and contributed quilts
to different organizations that needed them, I thought I might
understand what drove the Caring Hands quilters and how they
felt about what they were doing.

That, of course, was before I really knew them. Before I
learned that in the years they've been together they have donated
more than 5000 unique quilts—about 400 a year—to children,
usually those at risk. Before I met these wonderful women
face-to-face, almost sixty of them now, who not only give so
unselfishly, but also take such extraordinary care of each other.
I came home from Corvallis and told my husband we were
moving to Oregon. We didn't, but not for lack of trying.

Kelly Sauls of Trillium Family Services, one of the many
organizations that receives these wonderful quilts, says, "I have
seen a child's eyes, swollen and red from crying, light up as a
counselor wraps a warm quilt around him. These quilts say
'you're safe, you're loved, nothing can hurt you now.' For some
of our kids, this quilt is the first object they have ever owned."

You can see that, like Molly in this story, the real life kids
who receive these quilts are deeply affected by this gift.

As if they weren't busy enough, Quilts from Caring Hands
also makes aprons, tactile quilts and toys for the visually impaired.

and continually looks for new ways to use their talents. As an organization, creativity is their colorful pieced quilt top, compassion their batting, love the stitches that bind each quilt together.

For more information, please visit:

www.quiltsfromcaringhands.com.

Learn how you can help support their work. Or find a similar organization in your own community. If you don't know how to quilt, they'll soon teach you. You, too, can bestow comfort and hope to children who need it.

Thank you for all you do,

*Emilie Richards*

A heartfelt story of home,
healing and redemption from
*New York Times* bestselling author

# SUSAN WIGGS

International lawyer Sophie Bellamy has dedicated her life
to helping people in war-torn countries. But when she
survives a hostage situation, she remembers what matters
most—the children she loves back home. Haunted by
regrets, she returns to the idyllic Catskills village of Avalon
on the shores of Willow Lake, determined to repair the
bonds with her family.

There, Sophie discovers the surprising rewards of
small-town life—including an unexpected passion for
Noah Shepherd, the local veterinarian. Noah has a healing
touch for anything with four legs, but he's never had any
luck with women—until Sophie.

*Snowfall*
at Willow Lake

"Susan Wiggs' novels are beautiful, tender and wise."
—Luanne Rice

**Available the first week of February 2008
wherever paperbacks are sold!**

**MIRA®**

### New York Times Bestselling Author
# SHARON SALA

#### He killed her once...

Throat slashed and left for dead next to her murdered father,
a thirteen-year-old girl vows to hunt down the man who did
this to them—Solomon Tutuola. Now grown, bounty hunter
Cat Dupree lets nothing—or no one—stand in the way of
that deadly promise. Not even her lover, Wilson McKay.

Suspecting that Tutuola is still alive, despite witnessing
the horrific explosion that should have killed him, Cat
follows a dangerous money trail to Mexico, swearing not to
return until she's certain Tutuola is dead—even if it means
destroying her very soul....

# CUT THROAT

"The perfect entertainment for those looking for a suspense
novel with emotional intensity."
—*Publishers Weekly* on *Out of the Dark*

*Available the first week of November 2007
wherever paperbacks are sold!*

**MIRA®**

**www.MIRABooks.com**

MSS2507

The newest
Shenandoah Album novel
by *USA TODAY*
bestselling author

# EMILIE RICHARDS

After narrowly escaping death,
newspaper journalist Kendra
Taylor retreats to a cabin nestled in
Virginia's Shenandoah Valley to heal
and sort out her feelings about her
troubled marriage. And that's where
she finds an heirloom lover's knot
quilt, which is yet another piece of
Isaac's unexplored past.

As a passionate story of strength, loss
and desperation unfolds, the secrets
of two quilts are revealed, and the
threads of an unraveling marriage
are secured. In the rich, evocative
prose that earned high praise for
*Wedding Ring* and *Endless Chain*,
Emilie Richards crafts the third tale
in the Shenandoah Album series,
resonant with the power of love
and family ties.

*Lover's Knot*

"[A] heartwarming,
richly layered story."
—*Library Journal* starred review
of *Endless Chain*

*Available the first week of June 2007
wherever paperbacks are sold!*

**MIRA®**